# L.A. Dreams

# L.A. Dreams

## A Novel

### A.M. Morrell

Salty Shamrock Press

For Elan

Thank you for your encouragement. Without you I'd still be hiding my stories.

# L.A. DREAMS
## BY: A.M. MORRELL

MARCH 1993
Dallas, Texas

The smell of lilies filled the air and "Moonlight Sonata" played over the sound system. I followed the notes in my head so that I didn't have to think about anything else. It seemed lately that thinking only made me angry, so I'd been doing my best to avoid doing too much of it. The others had already left. I should have gone as well and been at his family's house consoling them, the way a good friend would. But I couldn't face them.

My best friend, Edward Allan Cooper, was dead, and I was responsible. We had been friends for over twenty years. And now he was gone. Now there would be nothing left for Jennifer and me to fight about. Except that Eddie might still be alive if it weren't for us.

Eddie would have done anything in the world for me, but I knew now I couldn't say the same. Had he ever let me down? I wanted to remember a time, probably to ease my conscience, but could recall nothing. He'd always had my back. It seemed to come easy to him.

"You must be Corbett Scott," said a soft, deep voice from behind me.

I turned to find a guy about my age, mid to late twenties, wearing torn jeans and a navy tee shirt. He said nothing else for what felt like an eternity. Though his eyes begged for something, fear of losing my composure left me unable to speak. What did this person want from me? I closed my eyes, heaved a sigh, and rubbed my hand over the warmth traveling up the back of my neck. I had not come to terms with my goodbye yet and had stayed long after the others had gone because I wanted to be left alone. And now I had to deal with this guy.

"Jesse Donovan," he finally said and held out his hand. "I thought everyone would be gone by now. I didn't mean to scare you."

I ran the back of my hand across my eyes to wipe away the dampness, then shook his hand and said as firmly as I could muster, "You didn't scare me."

"God, I hate open caskets," he said, looking past me. "It's so degrading."

"Yeah," I agreed. I'd always hated them too. I didn't want people gawking at my dead body, and I was pretty sure Eddie would have felt the same. "He wouldn't want us to remember him like this," I said, looking at the shiny mahogany box and the cream-colored satin that lined it. I ran my hand across the glossy wood and the soft cloth and wondered why Jesse called it a casket rather than a coffin. Was there a difference? Or did it just sound nicer...not as damn depressing? And how much did something like that even cost? It had to be expensive. That fucking funeral home probably guilted Eddie's parents into it. I knew for sure, at that moment, I wanted to be cremated.

I looked at my friend's face. Eddie's wounds had not had time to heal and had forced their way through the makeup like a scar. It ran from his forehead down across his nose and onto his cheek. I shut my eyes again. This time tightly, fighting to suppress the pressure in my chest as I imagined his fear and pain in his final moments. I could almost see everything, as if I was right there with him when the cars collided. Trying to shake the image, I forced my focus back to the present. His light-brown hair looked darker shaved close, and he wore a dark-blue suit. It was only the second time I had seen him in a suit. It might have even been the same one he wore at our high school graduation.

"So, close it," Jesse said.

"What?" I had forgotten for a second that he was even there.

"I said, so close it."

"Well, I don't think—" But before I could finish, he stepped past me and pulled the lid shut. I shot him a look then looked around to ensure no other mourners or staff remained.

"There's nobody here," he said.

I bit my lip and took a beat to calm myself. Not only did I not like the way he took charge, but it also completely pissed me off. Eddie was my best friend, not his. But was I really mad at Jesse? Or was I taking my frustration with Eddie out on him? Why couldn't Eddie have just taken no for an answer? My eyes were heavy and sore from a long day of crying. "Well, I guess that's it," I said.

"Yeah," Jesse said. "I guess so."

After another long uncomfortable silence, I said, "I guess I better go. I have to pick up my girlfriend." I corrected myself. "I mean fiancée." Jesse didn't respond, so I took the opportunity to get the hell out of there and headed towards the door.

"Yeah. Okay," he said, louder than necessary.

I stopped. I wasn't sure why because I desperately wanted out of that funeral home. I didn't know Jesse, and his presence was an intrusion. But he was Eddie's friend too. So, I stopped.

Eddie wasn't like me. He was always smiling, friendly with everybody. I was his best friend, but everybody liked him, and he liked most in return. In his letters and phone calls, he always said good things about Jesse. In fact, he talked about him so much that I felt like I actually did know him. Like maybe the three of us were friends. And now just the two of us. I took a long, deep breath attempting to will the anger away and turned back to Jesse. "You have someplace to be?" I put little effort into hiding my impatience. Everything seemed to take way more energy than I had.

He looked over his shoulder at me. His steel-blue eyes were red and held back tears. The blue iris and redness from crying made me think of Spiderman. "No," he said. "Just back to my hotel."

I nodded, not knowing what to do or say. I didn't know whether to walk away or wait for him and found that suddenly I felt worse for him than for myself. I had my family and, theoretically, Jennifer to feel bad for me. I worried that he might be going back to an empty hotel room after our friend's funeral. "You want to stay at my place?" I finally asked him. I meant for it to sound sincere and caring but knew it didn't. Keeping my voice steady was all that kept me from falling apart.

"No, it's okay. I'm fine at the hotel."

I nodded again. That should have been that, but something kept me from going. Though I wasn't sure what. I could walk away and never see this person again, but there I stood. "Come on," I said. "I can't let you do that. Eddie would be royally pissed at me if I did."

Jesse forced a smile and hesitated before he finally said, "All right. I guess so. Thanks," and followed me out.

We walked to my Jeep in silence and drove away from the last time I would ever see Eddie Cooper. I wiped the lingering wetness from my eyes and said a silent, final goodbye to my oldest and, really, only friend.

"You care if I stop for a six-pack?" I asked. Jennifer had been a total bitch to me about the funeral and now I was bringing home one of Eddie's bandmates. I would need some beer.

"Make it a twelve-pack. Or better yet, a case," Jesse answered, rubbing his eyes with the palm of his hands.

I pulled into a 7-Eleven. Jesse reached for his wallet, but I jumped out and went inside before he had time to get his money. When I returned, he was leaning against the Jeep smoking a cigarette. With the cigarette dangling from his mouth, he took the case of beer from me and removed two. He tossed me one and put the rest in the back seat. He opened his and gulped down at least half of it while I just watched.

"What?" he asked, as he wiped his mouth and shrugged.

"You trying to get arrested?" I was being dramatic but was in no mood to be harassed by law enforcement. Standing around drinking in a 7-Eleven parking lot almost guaranteed it.

He downed the rest, crushed the thin aluminum can, and threw it into the back seat. He grabbed another and took a final puff of his cigarette before he dropped it and rubbed it out with his heavy, black Doc Martens.

"You ready?" I asked, unsuccessful at hiding my annoyance. I didn't intend to sound short with him, but today every little thing bothered me.

"Yep," he said, as he jumped into the Jeep and opened his second beer. I worried a little bit about open container laws but didn't say anything. He was probably a little uncomfortable coming back to the apartment and needed it. Especially if Eddie had told him much about Jennifer.

When we pulled up to her office building, she was waiting outside, talking to a guy she worked with named Michael. She was probably going to be irritated that I invited Jesse to stay with us. Hopefully, she wouldn't say anything in front of him.

As soon as the Jeep came to a stop, Jesse jumped out of the passenger seat and climbed into the back. Michael walked up to my window while Jenny went around to get in. "We've been waiting out here for over an hour," she said as she climbed in. "Have you called to check on my car? I hate riding in this thing."

"I told her I could give her a ride," Michael said through my open window.

She'd rather complain, I almost said aloud. I was still angry with her for not coming with me to the funeral and couldn't shake my irritability. The scowling was giving me a headache.

"Thanks," I said to Michael and gave a quick wave as I drove off. I looked in my rearview mirror to see that he was still standing there when I turned the corner a few blocks away.

"Hey," Jesse said, poking his head between the seats. "You must be Jennifer. I'm Jesse."

I could feel her glaring at me, but I said nothing. She turned to him and said, "Nice to meet you. Are you, I mean, were you a friend of Eddie's?"

"Yeah," he said. "I was. We were in the band together."

Mentioning the band was just going to set her off. I tried to buffer the situation. "Eddie always told me about him—" I started.

"Eddie said a lot of things," Jennifer snapped. "And I see you stopped and got yourself some beer but neglected to get me my Dr. Pepper." I clenched my jaw and could feel my face burn red. She didn't like Eddie, so chances were pretty good she would not like Jesse, but why did she have to be such a bitch in front of him? She didn't like Eddie simply because she was jealous of my relationship with him. Jennifer didn't like anything that took my attention from her. Plus, she hated that he was always trying to get us to L.A. She refused to even discuss California. Her life was in Dallas.

"I didn't realize you were out," I said as calmly as I could. "I'll stop—"

"Never mind. Let's just get home. I'm tired." She fell back into her seat and closed her eyes. It was humid out, and as the sun went down, it started to mist and grow cold. She crossed her arms and rubbed them, so I turned the heat on low. Her face was a little shiny from the humidity and the curl had all but left her long blonde hair, but she was still a beauty. I tried to remember when she lost her kindness. We had been together since high school and now she was having my baby.

I thought of all the times Eddie tried to get us to California. If I'd gone, would he still be alive? He was on his way to convince us to go back with him. He had signed a big recording contract and wanted me to join them. I wanted to go, but we had just found out that Jen was three months pregnant. And now she wanted to get married. Sounded shitty for me to say it, but I was stuck like Chuck. There was no way. I really wanted to go, but it just wasn't possible.

"I made that sale today," she said with her eyes still closed.

"That's great," I said with as much enthusiasm as I could muster, which was really very little.

"I know I should have been there with you today," she finally said. She opened her eyes, turned to me, and smiled. It was the, *I'm being nice now, so everything is fine,* smile. "This was a big sale," she said. "The commission will get us that much closer to a down payment on our own house."

"That's great," I said again, keeping my eyes on the road ahead. "I knew that you would."

"God, I'm exhausted." She closed her eyes once more.

I took her hand and squeezed. "Let's relax by the pool when we get home. I'll rub your shoulders if you want." Staying angry would get me nowhere. Just be the bigger man and keep the peace. I could practically hear my mom whispering it in my ear.

She squeezed back and then quickly pulled away. "I'm going to bed. You have a guest to entertain." Apparently, she was through being nice.

I glanced at the rearview mirror. Jesse was gazing out the window. I knew Jenny felt threatened by Eddie, so I tried to forgive her for the way she acted towards him. I didn't understand why she was cold towards Jesse. It embarrassed me and made me feel bad for him. I rubbed my forehead, attempting to ease both my headache and my emotional state. I didn't understand how she could be so uncaring almost to the point of unkind sometimes, and I didn't like that part of her.

When we got back to our apartment, she did just as she said and went straight to the bedroom. She kissed me on the cheek and murmured, "Wake me when you come to bed." I said I would as she closed the door behind her. I wanted to go in with her and lie next to her slim, firm body. I wanted her to tell me we had done the right thing and that Eddie's death had nothing to do with us. I wanted her to put her arms around me and comfort me. I wanted her to be the person she used to be. But it had been a while, and that girl was long gone.

Still looking at the closed bedroom door, I asked Jesse, "Do you want to go out to the pool?"

"Nah. It's too cold. You have cable?"

"Yeah." I joined him in the living room and picked up the remote from the television stand and tossed it to him.

"What do you want to watch?" he asked.

"I don't care," I said as I went to put the beer in the fridge. As usual, there was no room. It was full of leftovers that had been leftover too long and way too much fruit and salad fixings for two people. It was an oversized stainless-steel refrigerator that I was still making payments on and there was no room for my beer. I sighed heavily and took the beers out one at a time and stuffed them between plastic containers of all sizes, keeping one out for each of us. I tossed Jesse his beer and fell into the other couch. He had the TV on Nick at Night, watching *The Twilight Zone*, which was okay by me. I liked old TV. I also liked old movies, old music, and old cars. My superpower would be time travel.

"Let me ask you something," I said. "Why was Eddie so hell-bent on me coming to L.A.?"

"I don't really know," he said. "Eddie spent a lot more time with the producers than the rest of us. Maybe he knew something we didn't." He took a long gulping drink of beer. "I do know he thought you and I could write hit songs together."

"So, what now?" I asked. It was hard to imagine writing a hit song. A song that everyone I knew would hear on the radio. How badass would that be?

"Either you come back with me to take Eddie's lead, or Suicide King is dead."

"Suicide King?"

"Yeah. It's the king in a deck of cards with a knife through his head."

"Yeah, I know what it is," I said. "I just didn't know it was the name of the band. We came up with that name when we were kids." Although I did wonder why Eddie never mentioned he'd used the name, the memory brought me a smile. We'd been playing penny poker with my family at one of the many sleepovers when my dad called the card the Suicide King. Eddie and I thought that was the coolest thing we'd ever heard. "I had forgotten about that," I said more to myself than to Jesse.

"Did you hear what I said?" He leaned forward to look at me. Although his question was abrupt and somewhat demanding in tone, he appeared tired and defeated.

"Yes," I said. "I did. But it's impossible. She won't go and I'm not leaving with a baby on the way. I'm sorry. I really am."

Jesse fell back into the couch. "Then I guess that's that."

I didn't reply. I wanted to go, and I wanted Eddie to be alive. If I could just go back a few months and do things differently. But what would I have done? Jennifer and I were not planning on a baby. Would I have left her if she wasn't pregnant? Why had I even stayed so long? Maybe if I'd gone out there, even just to visit, then he wouldn't have driven here. All I knew was, he believed he was taking us, or even just me, back with him permanently this time.

"Why can't someone else take his place?" I asked. "Surely there are all kinds of qualified musicians in L.A."

"Don't know. He never said. Miss Blake told him to come get you, and that's what he did...or tried to do."

Tried to do. The words hit me like a punch in the gut. Why couldn't any one of the events that led to his death been different? Why did the fucking idiot drive? Why didn't he get on a damn plane? Why didn't he just give up on me, like I had? Or had I given him false hope that I could be swayed? I never made it a secret that I wanted to be there. I just...I just couldn't.

"Who the hell is Miss Blake?" I asked, my irritability pushing its way back to the surface.

"Alexandra Blake. She's—"

"Alexandra Blake? *The* Alexandra Blake?"

Jesse nodded.

"What has she got to do with Suicide King?"

How could Eddie have failed to mention Alexandra Blake? She was practically a household name. She'd been in movies and had several songs on the Billboard Top 100 over the years. Probably dozens. Why in the world would somebody that famous and successful want me? It made no sense.

Jesse got up and went to get us another beer. I heard him opening and closing doors, so I followed him into the kitchen.

"Where the hell is your trash can?" he asked, looking around.

I took the empty cans from him and opened the trash compacter and tossed them in. He rolled his eyes and opened the fridge for the beer. "She's footing the bill," he said. "Not sure why. I guess Eddie sold her on the idea. But I think you were included in the deal. Again, not sure why."

I took a beer from him then walked over to the big sliding glass door that led to the balcony. I looked out at the Dallas skyline. I was living in an apartment that was beyond our means with the future mother of my child. I was always trying to make her happy. It was a constant struggle to do that and maintain my friendship with Eddie.

Jesse eased past me and slid the door open, causing a rush of cool air into the apartment. He stepped outside and lit a cigarette. "Nice view."

I followed him and pulled the door closed behind me. "You have a girl?" I asked. He nodded as he took a strong drag from his cigarette. He leaned against the side rail of the balcony so he could see me and the view of Dallas. "She have a problem with your music?" I asked.

"Not at all. She's waiting for the payday." He said this like he thought it was amusing.

"That bother you? Make you feel used?" I asked.

"No," he answered after some thought. "I had no prospects when I met her. Who knows, this all might be a bust too. I just get by now. I make decent money doing studio work, but not going to get rich off it."

"I don't know why Jenny is so against it," I said. "It's like another woman to her. Why can't I love both music and her?" It was so damn frustrating.

"Well, if ya can't please everyone, ya got to—"

"Please myself," I finished.

"That's right," Jesse said with conviction.

"Not when there's suddenly a kid in the picture," I answered with less conviction.

Jesse took another long drag on his cigarette. "Either way," he said, and blew out the smoke. "I'm going back in a few days. With or without you. Better for me if it's with you."

"If I didn't go when Eddie was alive, then why would I go now?" I asked Jesse. I meant for it to sound firm and decisive, but what I really wanted was a profound reason to go. One that not even Jenny could argue.

Jesse looked at me squarely. "*Because* he's gone. You do it for him."

That was a damn good reason for me, but I could already hear the argument. We'd had it enough times. I wasn't sure what, if anything, would change her mind. And now with a baby in the picture and all our family here...but I still couldn't let it go. Jesse was right. I wanted to do it. Now more than ever.

The day had been a long one and I was emotionally drained. I told Jesse I was calling it a night and tossed a pillow and some blankets on the couch in the studio. "Make yourself at home," I said, and went to my room.

I climbed into bed next to Jenny and gently touched her arm. She turned away from me without waking up. Sleep did not come as easily for me. I couldn't get my mind off Alexandra Blake. Why was she involved in Suicide King's recording contract? She was at her most popular probably twenty years ago. I might've even had something of hers on a cassette or CD. I slipped back out of bed and went back into the living room to see. One complete wall in our living room was built-in bookshelves filled with albums, cassettes, CDs, and even some books. I started with the albums. Everything was sorted alphabetically, except, of course, when Jenny didn't put something back where it went. I found Alexandra Blake's greatest hits CD and put it in the player with the volume turned very low. Her soft, sensual voice soon filled the room. I looked at the cover. Glamorous. She was glamorous while Suicide King was gritty or even grunge rock. The complete opposite. Why was she interested in this band? Why was she interested in me?

I thought of Eddie again. He was willing to do just about anything, short of selling his soul, to be a successful musician. He didn't care what anybody said or thought about it. The last time he and I played together was also the last time I played in front of a large crowd. I still played at a dive bar in Dallas on Wednesday nights, but that was the extent of it.

That last night was something we had looked forward to for months. We rehearsed night and day. We opened for a band that had moderate success around the country but were hometown heroes. They were a few years ahead of us in our high school. The newspaper did a big write-up on the show. The words stayed with me. *Don't count on Eddie Cooper or Cory Scott following any footsteps. Corbett Scott's performance was like watching a virgin stripper on the main stage.* I got sick with embarrassment every time I thought of it. *Cooper and Scott lyrics are about as deep as the kiddie pool and as meaningful as a mid-sex I love you.* There were a few more paragraphs about how bad we were, but I tried to shake the memories. I had thought we'd done well. But afterward, I lost all self-confidence. I quit writing and dreaming. All I could imagine was a life of rejection and disappointment.

Whenever I took the time to stop and think about how little I'd accomplished, I'd get a short burst of determination. That's how my studio grew into the room it now was. Among other things, I had seven guitars, an upright piano, and several notebooks filled with unfinished songs. But it never lasted. Doubt and fear always found its way back.

Eddie finally went to L.A. without me, but he never gave up on me. I was envious of his courage and confidence. It took him almost four years, but he did it. He had the recording contract. He was good and he knew it, regardless of what any critic wrote.

Eddie wrote letters and phoned me, always wanting Jen and me to go to California. He would fly in for a weekend from time to time to visit, always trying to restore my confidence. He had way more faith in me than I had in myself. He told me repeatedly that rejection was part of the process, but I didn't want to hear it. In his last letter, he said that he was coming to Texas and not leaving until Jen and I agreed to go back to L.A. with him.

He never made it. He was hit by a drunk driver while driving through New Mexico.

If I didn't find a way to get over my stupid insecurities and get my pregnant fiancée to L.A., all of Eddie's work and sacrifice would be for nothing. His death would be for nothing.

# 2

The morning sun burst through my window and woke me as it did every morning. I glanced over at Jen. The brightness of a new day never disturbed her sleep. I rolled over and put my arm across her. I slid my hand under her top and felt her hard, flat stomach. It was difficult to imagine a life growing in there. The thought of a baby delighted and terrified me.

For a pleasant but way too brief moment, I forgot about everything but Jenny and me and a baby. Then reality sucker punched me, and I wanted to go back to sleep myself. But I had a lot to do before going back to work in a few days. I got up, careful not to wake her, and did my morning exercises of push-ups and sit-ups. Normally, I would also go to the gym, but I didn't feel like it, so I just did extra at home.

After I forced my way through a hundred plus of each, I jumped into the shower that was crowded with numerous shampoos and conditioners for Jen's normal-to-oily and just as many for my normal-to-dry. Hers all mixed up, mine organized with each shampoo together with the corresponding conditioner. I resisted the urge to sort hers out.

After I dressed, I went to the kitchen and poured myself a glass of orange juice and started the coffee. Soon the entire kitchen and living room smelled like coffee, which always made me crave a doughnut. There would never be doughnuts in our kitchen. It was probably for the best. Jesse shuffled out of my studio, yawning and stretching. I poured and handed him a glass of juice, but he put his hand up and went by me to the coffee. "You sleep okay?" I asked.

"Like a baby," he said, as he took a mug from the cabinet and poured his coffee. "Comfy couch. That studio doesn't look like you've given up on music."

"I didn't say I'd given up music. I said I gave up on music as my livelihood. Anyway, most of that's going to my parent's house. Gotta start getting a room ready for the baby."

"That sucks," he said. "No offense, but I know that's like giving up a piece of your soul."

I shrugged. What could I say?

"Tell me that Takamine doesn't make you feel like Garth Brooks or that Les Paul doesn't make you feel like Eric Clapton," he said, pointing to the studio.

"Neil Young," I said. "Neil tells a story, and like the great Barry Gordy said, songs should always tell a story."

"Then tell me a story," Jesse said. "Play me one of your songs. I'm told you're pretty good."

"Yes, Cory, tell him a story." Jenny had come from the bedroom and was walking across the living room. I poured a cup of coffee and handed it to her as she stepped into the kitchen.

I looked over at Jesse and grinned because that's how I always dealt with her passive-aggressive side. I smiled and pretended it didn't exist. Jenny was threatened by my music. Maybe even jealous. She could be wrapped up in her own world, not caring what I was doing, until I picked up a guitar or sat at the piano, then suddenly I was ignoring her. She almost never came to my shows on Wednesday nights. Which was for the best, because when she did, she would get jealous at any attention given me and angry when my full attention wasn't on her. She knew she didn't have to worry about me with other women. I was as loyal as a hound dog. But she couldn't compete with the music, and that drove her crazy. It was in me and always would be at some level. No matter how much she tried to distract me from it, or how little she encouraged me or supported it.

"We're heading over to Mom and Dad's to clean out the garage," I told her. "I'll have most of that out by next week." I could have done it in a day but had lingering hopes that something would change. Maybe if I put extra effort into making her happy and she ended up liking Jesse...yeah, right. Who was I kidding?

"How long will you be staying with us?" she asked Jesse.

"I'm leaving tomorrow, but I can get a room tonight."

"Nonsense," she said. "You're welcome here." She turned to me. "What time will you be home?"

"I don't know," I answered. "By four at the latest."

"All right. I'll be home by then too." She headed back to the bedroom, sipping her coffee. "We can all go to dinner," she called over her shoulder as an afterthought.

"Looks like you're putting me to work," Jesse said as he refilled his mug.

I knew it took an effort for Jenny to invite Jesse to stay and I appreciated it. I made a mental note to stop for flowers or something on the way home. "It won't be that bad," I said. "Let me just take this garbage down and we can go."

"I got it," he said, as he reached down and pulled the compacted garbage bag out. He set it down and said, "I'll just throw on some clothes really quick first."

"Okay, I'll go say goodbye to Jen and meet you down there."

When I got to the Jeep in the parking garage, Jesse wasn't there. I drove down to the trash dumpster to find him playing with a stray dog. I pulled up next to him. He was kneeling, trying to get the dog to come to him, but she would get close and then dart away. "This dog is pyscho," he laughed.

I pulled the Jeep into a parking space and walked back to them. The dog, which I thought to be some sort of mountain dog mix, came up to me and then darted away in the same manner, so I followed her. She ran to the dumpster, barking and whining as she paced back and forth in front of it. I walked past her and looked in the dumpster, which was really gross and smelly just like a dumpster always is, to find a small black-and-brown puppy with a white chest and face. I reached in and scooped him up. The big dog went crazy, jumping on me and pulling at her puppy, so I put him down. She licked him clean, both of their tails wagging ferociously.

"What the hell," Jesse said. "What kind of asshole..."

Neither of them had a collar, and they both looked like they'd missed a few meals and a few baths. "Come on," I said as I picked up the big dog. "Grab him and let's go get them cleaned up and fed."

Jesse reached down and picked him up, not concerned about the pup being smelly or dirty, which I thought was cool of him. "Then what?" he asked, following closely behind.

"I don't know. But I can't just leave them here."

"I haven't known your girl very long, but—"

"Oh, hell no." I laughed at the thought. "We'll take them to my parents' house. My little sister will love them."

My little sister, Cari, was only five years old and a complete surprise to my mom and dad in their forties. I had been out of the house for about a year and my younger brother, Kevin, was away at college. They apparently took advantage of the situation. Cari was a funny kid. We never knew what would come out of her mouth. My mom was afraid to take her anywhere, worried that Cari would ask someone an embarrassing question or reveal some household secret. Mom would get so embarrassed, but Dad, Kevin, and I thought it was funny.

"Your parents will let you just drop off two dogs?" Jesse asked.

"No. But I don't know what else to do with them." As we approached the front door of my apartment, I reached into my pocket for the keys. The dog wiggled and slipped from my arms. "Anyway, they will be cake compared to the wrath we are about to face in here," I said as I struggled with controlling her and getting my keys at the same time.

"Then why the hell are we doing this?" he asked.

"What do you suggest we do? Just leave them out there?"

"I don't know." He shrugged. "I should have gotten a room."

"It's not like we're committing a crime," I said. "She'll get over it. Eventually."

The puppy was wriggling and climbing out of Jesse's arms. He pulled the puppy in close again and motioned impatiently for me to open the door. As I finally got the key out and started to put it in the lock, the door swung open. There was Jenny, dressed for work and looking like a movie star. We looked like homeless people and smelled like the garbage dumpster. She said nothing. Her expression said it all.

"Jesse did it," I blurted out. His head swung to look at me incredulously. At that moment, the mama dog, who I had decided to call Maggie from Elizabeth Taylor's character in *Cat on a Hot Tin Roof,* busted completely free from my grip. It all seemed to happen in slow motion. I could see the muddy prints on the light-gray carpet before she even entered the apartment. The puppy leapt from Jesse and followed suit. Maggie bolted into the apartment with the puppy not far behind. I didn't know what to do, so I called for them. Of course, they totally ignored me, so I went in after them. I cornered the puppy, but Maggie slipped by me and headed back towards the door. She started to jump towards Jenny in her light top and cream-colored skirt. I closed my eyes and waited for the impending doom. But it didn't come. I cautiously opened my eyes to find Jenny holding Maggie's front legs away from her.

"I have no idea where these dogs came from," she said as calmly as could be expected, "but please make sure they are gone when I get home." She dropped Maggie's legs and slid past Jesse to leave. Maggie tried to follow, but Jesse grabbed her.

"That wasn't so bad," I said. She didn't get nearly as angry as I'd expected. Maybe she did have a little kindness left in her after all.

"Jesse did it?" He raised an eyebrow at me.

"Sorry," I replied. "It just flew out."

"How is she getting to work?" Jesse asked. "I thought her car was in the shop." I could tell by his tone that he already didn't like her, which felt unpleasantly reminiscent of Jennifer and Eddie.

"Hm, I don't know." I went back outside to look for her and spotted her across the parking lot just as she slipped in and closed the door to Michael's car. "What the hell?" I mumbled. "She could have said something," I said to myself more than Jesse as I watched them drive away. I could have taken her. She should have said something.

"Come on," Jesse said, with a hand on my shoulder. "Let's get these dogs cleaned up and get out of here."

I followed him into the bathroom, where we put the dogs into the large, spotless white bathtub. "Grab some shampoo from the shower," I said as I filled the tub and struggled to keep both dogs still.

"Which one?" he asked looking at the assortment.

"One of the dry-to-oily ones, I guess."

"These dogs are going to have nicer hair than me. Think you spend enough on hair care?"

I glanced at Jesse's hair as I took the shampoo from him. Jet black and very straight and kind of long. He looked like a rock star.

By the time we finished bathing the dogs, the bathroom was a swamp. Jesse took them into the kitchen to find something for them to eat while I cleaned up. Then we loaded them up into my Jeep and headed to my parents' house.

"One down, one to go," Jesse said, as if the hard part was over.

"I have it all figured out," I said. "We'll find my little sister first."

"Ya know," Jesse said. "You're about as apple pie as they come. Now I see the angle."

"What do you mean?"

"I could never figure out why Miss Blake wanted you in the band so badly. You and Eddie sound somewhat alike, so why did she need you? Now I get it."

"You mean she wants me in the band because of the way I look?"

"Well, it helps that you can sing."

I thought about what Jesse said and how great it would be to play music for a living. I wished for a second that I had gone to California when Eddie did. When we were growing up, Eddie and I always talked of going to L.A., but Jenny wasn't having it. She urged me—or insisted, really—that I to go to the Air Traffic Academy instead. Then, she said I would have a good job while I pursued music. I always felt left out and a bit envious of Eddie. Playing on Wednesday nights was not pursuing a dream. But if I was honest with myself, I had to admit Jenny wasn't completely to blame. I was afraid of failure. My stupid insecurities let Eddie go alone.

The plan to find my sister first was a bust. My mom was in the front yard gardening when we pulled up. When she saw the Jeep pulling in, she beamed with a wide smile, until she saw the dogs. We left Maggie in the Jeep and Jesse grabbed the pup. The top was off, so I tied Maggie in with a rope.

"You just put those animals right back into your car, truck, whatever that thing is," she said, waving towards the Jeep as she walked over to greet us. "You haven't lived here, in what? Seven years? No more bringing home every stray." She hugged me and kissed me on the cheek.

I introduced her to Jesse and told her how we found the dogs. "What was I supposed to do? Just leave them there?" I said as I took the puppy from Jesse and held it out to her. "Look at that face. You would have done the same thing."

She tilted her head back and closed her eyes in defeat. Suddenly, the front screen door flew open, and Cari came racing out. "Coreee," she wailed with her arms outstretched. I knelt to catch her, but she put on the brakes. "Is he for me?" She turned to my mother. "Is he for me? Can I hold him? What's his name?"

My mother gave me a look to kill then turned to Cari. "Honey, we don't..." Cari's lower lip began to tremble. My mom heaved a defeated sigh. "Okay, but you are going to have to take care of him. Feed him, bathe him..."

She jumped up and down with excitement and held out her arms. Jesse took the puppy from me and handed him to her. Seeing a five-year-old with a new puppy was one of life's great joys. Finally, something to genuinely smile about. If only I could bottle it and throw it on Jen.

"What are you going to name him?" I asked her. Just then she spotted Maggie looking our way from the Jeep. Her eyes got big.

"Just the one," my mother said.

## 3

"I have something for Jenny," my mother sang out.

We were finished with the garage and getting Maggie tied back in. "What is it?"

She handed me the book *What to Expect When You're Expecting*.

"Thanks, Mom," I said. "I'm sure she'll love it."

"Get her something for morning sickness too, Cory. It's probably what's making her so cranky."

"Yeah," Jesse said under his breath. "That's it."

I gave Jesse a look. He shrugged and muttered, "Sorry."

I was pretty grubby from the work in the garage, but I said I would stop and get her something for the morning sickness to make my mother happy. She instructed me to get some ginger ale and maybe some tea.

I pulled into the shopping center and told Jesse I would hurry while he waited in the Jeep with Maggie. I ran in and got the ginger ale and tea as instructed and added her favorite candy, chocolate-covered orange slices.

"This is because I'm a nice guy," I told Jesse, holding up the ginger ale. "And the candy is because—"

"You're not fooling anybody," he said. "They're both because she's going to kill you over this dog."

I looked at her. She was on the floor between Jesse's legs with her head rested on his knee. "What the hell am I going to do with her?" I thought aloud, wondering how I was going to tell Jenny we were keeping the dog. Then I remembered her riding off with Michael and realized it had been preying on my mind the entire day, stuck there in the back of my thoughts while I tried to concentrate on the tasks at hand. "I think I'll go by her office," I said.

"She going to be okay riding in the Jeep with me and the dog?" Jesse asked.

"Oh yeah," I said. "She won't care."

"Mm-hmm," Jesse said. "Okay."

When I got to Jenny's office, Jesse waited in the car again while I went inside. I took the book and the candy with me to soften her up. It was Saturday so the receptionist wasn't in. I could hear Jenny's muffled voice coming from her office. I thought about different ways to explain why we still had Maggie. I'm usually even more excited about giving a gift than getting one, but I doubted the book and candy would soften her up at all. I was just going to have to put my foot down. It was my home too, after all.

As I got closer to her office, I could hear that she was talking to Michael. They seemed to be talking about work when she broke off and asked the time. I stopped, looked at my watch, and waited for her reply. I wasn't completely sure why I chose to stop and eavesdrop. Maybe I was interested in what they talked about when I wasn't around. Or maybe it would explain why she rode to work with him instead of asking me to take her.

"It's a little after two," Michael answered. "Why?"

"Let's get out of here. I told Cory I'd be home by five."

What the hell? She told me four.

"What if I don't have you home by five?" he asked her in a tone that I didn't like. A tone that suggested that maybe he was more than a coworker. Was I letting my anger towards her about Eddie influence my judgement?

"Oh, you'll have me home when I say you will," she replied. Flirtatiously?

I wasn't sure what to do. Did I walk in and stop what, if anything, was going on? Or was I being paranoid? Jenny had never really given me a reason to doubt her, so why was I? Was I being ridiculous? I reasoned that I must have been worried because I knew she was about to be mad at me about the dog.

"I could take you home now," Michael said with a hint of annoyance in his voice.

"Don't be like that," she said in a voice she had used to manipulate me hundreds of times over the years. "We still have over two hours together."

"That's what I get? Two hours a weekend?" Michael whined.

I clenched my hands into fists and leaned against the wall. It was clear now that I wasn't imagining things. Jenny was fucking around on me. Did I want to hear any more of it? No. I wanted to bust in there and beat Michael's ass. But I forced myself to remain calm and listen. When I did confront this, I wanted all the information. She would undoubtably play the victim and try to spin it all back on me.

"Are we going down that road again?" she asked, obviously irritated with him.

"Well why not?" Michael asked. "You told me you were leaving him. Is the baby really even mine?"

My stomach lurched. I alternated between anger and disbelief. One thing for sure was Michael was definitely getting his ass kicked. And Jenny...what a fucking lying whore.

"How many times do we have to have this conversation?" she asked. At least she was a bitch to him too.

"I just find it hard to believe that you have put Cory off that long," Michael said.

Put me off? Was he serious? Perhaps he should know that I fucked her that very morning. Okay, well not that morning, but within the last few days. That was a lie too. It had been many days. I was a damn fool not to have suspected something sooner.

"For the last time," Jennifer said. "I conceived that weekend that you and I were in Houston."

I looked at the baby book and the candy I was holding. For a second, I felt foolish standing there with them. Then anger overtook me again. Should I confront them? Or should I just leave? Just tell her to fuck off without explanation when she got home? Then I remembered the baby. How long ago was she in Houston? Had we been intimate before she left? When she got home? I felt unable to move. Trapped.

"You said you were going to leave him," Michael said.

"I can't right now. He just lost his best friend. He needs me." She said this as if trying to sound caring. Like she could pull that off.

"Then when?" he demanded.

"We've been together a long time. I need to ease into it." She was bored with the conversation. Thoughts of all the times she had been insensitive to my feelings went through my mind. I almost pitied Michael's dumb ass.

I didn't hear anything else. All that I'd already heard replayed through my mind. I tried to control my outrage, but my ears were ringing, and my hands were shaking. I couldn't think straight. So many thoughts were firing at me. Punch Michael in the face? Tell Jenny to go fuck herself? I needed to get out of there before I did something I might regret. I needed to think before deciding how to handle everything. But I couldn't think. I couldn't move. I stood there until they walked out and found me.

"Cory?" Jennifer stopped in her tracks. "What are you doing here?"

"I came to see if you needed a ride home," I said, trying to keep my voice steady. "But looks like that's not my problem anymore." Venom was rising in my chest. I held up the book and candy. "This was for you and our baby." Before I knew it, I had flung them both past her. The book hit the wall higher than I'd intended and bounced back, almost hitting her, as orange slices rained down.

She ducked out of the way and clutched her chest. "How long have you been out here?"

I looked her in the eyes, then I looked at Michael. He turned away, too much of a pussy to face me. I turned back to Jennifer.

She wasn't so beautiful to me anymore. "Long enough to know that you are a fucking controlling bitch that has ruined my life. You," I said, and poked her hard in the chest, "fucking killed Eddie. You might as well have put a bullet in his head." I turned away and paced back and forth. "I never cheated on you," I said. "Not even once." I'd had a constant ache in my chest since Eddie's death. That ache now felt as if it would choke me. I needed to get out of the building and away from her.

"Cory, wait," she said as I flung the door open and stormed off. "Please wait, I..."

When I got outside, Jesse and Maggie were sitting on the stairs. "Let's go," I said as I hurried past him. He jumped up and followed without saying anything.

After about ten minutes, he finally asked, "Everything okay?"

By this point, I was beyond angry. I needed to hit someone or something, so I drove to the batting cages. I gave the attendant an extra ten to let Maggie come with us. After hitting four sets of twelve pitches, I turned to Jesse and handed him the bat. "You wanna hit any?" He shrugged and took the bat.

After he hit twelve pitches, he turned to me. "You going to tell me what's going on?"

I tried to put my jumbled thoughts into comprehensible words. I wanted to spew out all the awful truths about Jennifer at once. I wanted Jesse to understand the depth of my anger and her betrayal, but no words seemed strong enough to adequately convey it. We turned in the bats and then walked back to the Jeep. I climbed in and slammed the door behind me. I reached for the steering wheel and gripped it so tightly my knuckles turned white. "I guess I'm just an idiot. I thought I was going to be a father."

"What happened?" Jesse asked as he got Maggie situated. "She's not pregnant after all?"

"No, she is," I said. "Just not with my baby."

He stopped fussing with the dog. "What the fuck? That's bullshit. She said that to you?"

I reached over and rubbed Maggie's neck to calm her, or maybe myself, and told him what happened.

"How do you know she's telling the truth?" Jesse asked. "Maybe she's lying to him."

"I don't know," I said. The adrenaline was wearing off, and now I just felt drained. "How does she even know whose it is? Mine? Michael's? Or is there some other guy she's fucking?"

"What are you going to do?" Jesse asked hesitantly.

"I don't know that either. Maybe it's all for the best. There's a bright side here somewhere." I started the Jeep and headed home. Home. What was I going to do about that? The thought of ever sleeping in the same bed with her or living my life with her at all made me sick.

"That you found out now," Jesse said.

"What?"

"The bright side is that you found out now. Not after the wedding and seeing the kid," Jesse said.

"I just can't believe she did this. I trusted her."

Jesse shrugged. "That's all you can do."

When we got back to the apartment, Jesse took Maggie down to the dog park and I started looking through Jenny's things. I wasn't sure what I was looking for. Evidence of some sort. I looked through desk drawers and boxes in the closet. I opened her nightstand and found an envelope from her doctor's office. Not sure of what I was hoping to find, I took a beat to prepare myself and opened it.

"Don't even bother looking."

I turned around to find Jennifer walking towards me. She took the envelope from me, but I immediately snatched it right back. "Why? Because I should just believe whatever you say?"

"I'm not even pregnant," she said.

"I don't believe you." I pulled the letter out and snapped the envelope to the floor.

"Then go ahead and read the documents. Routine physical. No baby. Just a healthy report."

I read the report and, sure enough, just a yearly exam with healthy results. "Why are you doing this?" I asked. For a moment, the anger settled a bit, and I felt betrayed. Finding out something that had been hidden from me for...I didn't even know how long, made me want an explanation. Something to make sense of it all. Something to make me feel better.

"I didn't want to lose you. I was afraid Eddie would talk you into going back with him once he had the recording deal."

"Then why Michael?" Anger found its way back to me with a vengeance.

"In case you left. You've always blamed me for missing out on a music career. If you're honest with yourself, you'll admit that you want that life. You want it more than the one I can give you. You've had one foot out the door for some time now. I was afraid to be alone."

"Why the hell are you telling him you're pregnant?" I shouted, pointing at the air as if Michael were there.

"I don't know," she yelled just as loudly. "I'm just trying to hold everything together."

"Well guess what?" I said. "You don't have to worry. I'm not going to tell him. You want to know why? I'll tell you why. Because fuck him. You two deserve each other."

"I was just trying to hold on to you both," she said as if that cleared everything up.

"I would have never left you, Jenny," I said, trying to calm myself. "I loved you and I was looking forward to starting a family." I knew I wouldn't have left Jenny, though I wasn't completely certain I was ready for a family. "Music was second to you," I added, knowing but not caring that it sounded lame and untrue.

"Loved? Was?" She started to cry. The tears infuriated me.

"Yeah, past tense. Did you think I wouldn't notice that you weren't getting any bigger?"

She gathered herself. I wasn't even sure the tears were real. "Convenient miscarriage," she said. "Once all this L.A. nonsense was behind us, I would claim a miscarriage. I thought that might bring us closer."

"How can you be so deceitful?" I asked, almost impressed with her natural ability. "How many others have there been?"

"I'm no fool," she said, looking at me like I was the bad guy in it all. "I know girls are always coming on to you when you play at that stupid bar."

"Don't even try to put this on me," I said to the spin I'd been expecting. "I never cheated on you. Not even close."

"I guess you can go to L.A. now." She threw up her arms dramatically like she was giving in. "Nothing keeping you here now." When that failed, she stopped the theatrics and attempted sincerity. She took my hands and said, "Maybe someday we'll be together again. After you get this out of your system."

After I get this out of my system? Thanks for believing in me, you self-centered bitch. "Yeah, right," I said, pulling my hands free. "Maybe." I shook my head at her audacity and looked away. I didn't want to see her lying cheating face.

She put her hand to my face and pulled so I was forced to look at her and said, "I love you."

I pushed it away. "It's hard to believe that I ever found you beautiful," I said. "I'll be out in a few days. You can stay with Michael till then."

With completely regained composure and no sign of tears, she said, "How do I know you won't leave me with nothing?"

"Because I want as little of you as possible," I said without doubt or hesitation. "Now get the hell out of here."

She turned to walk away. With her back to me she said, "Maybe in time we can work this out. I do love you."

"I don't think so. I don't love you." The words stung as I said them. But then I realized that I might not have loved her for some time.

"Alright," she said. And then she was gone.

# 4

"At the risk of sounding opportunistic," Jesse said, "you can come to L.A. now. You can stay with me till you get going." He talked about gorgeous beaches and cool clubs, sexy women.

We were sitting outside on the balcony. I fixated on the city in front of me because I knew I was leaving, and I wanted to remember the details. "I have to go back to work tomorrow. I'll ask for a transfer."

As I drove to work, I thought about California. I didn't want to think about Jenny, so I forced myself to think about L.A. and what life would have for me there. I wasn't really leaving any close friends behind. We had "couple" friends that Jenny would keep. I would miss having my parents and brother close by, and I worried about how Cari would handle it. I would call her every week and send her pictures and cards.

I had a ton of different emotions flowing through me. I felt insecure and scared, determined and strong, sad and lonely, excited and anxious.

First, I had to get the transfer. Then I had to tell my family. When I got to work, I went straight to my supervisor's office. I didn't want to risk losing my nerve.

"I saw on the bid list that there's an opening at Santa Monica tower," I said. "I'd like to bid for it."

He looked up from his mound of paperwork. "That's a level three. You're asking for a step down. Not up."

"I know," I said, shifting uncomfortably. "I still want it."

He looked puzzled and irritated. Like my intrusion exhausted him. We stared at each other for what seemed like a very long time. Finally, he opened his file drawer and handed me the forms. "Turn these in right away, and I'll see what I can do." Then he went back to his paperwork.

A few hours later, I took my first break and went to the break room to fill out the forms. One good thing about being an air traffic controller is the FAA makes you take several breaks a day. The television had a Joan Rivers talk show playing. She was interviewing former child stars that had become drunks or drug addicts. I liked old TV, so it made me kind of sad for them.

I signed the last page of my paperwork and immediately had a mini panic attack. What if I was making a big mistake? A wave of anxiety passed through me. Jennifer was suddenly no longer in my life. Eddie was gone too. I would be starting at a new tower and wouldn't know anybody. My whole life was going to be completely different. I'd worked with most of these people for several years. Although we all had our differences and quirks, we knew and accepted each other. The thought of being the new guy made my stomach hurt a little. But I was going to be in a band...a band that had a recording contract! Wait. I was going to be in a band assuming Alexandra Blake approved of me. I had a sick feeling that she might not.

Before I went back to my station, I called Jesse. He was still at the apartment. After what happened with Jen, he said he could hang around a few more days. I told him Maggie and I were going back to California with him. He laughed when I told him I applied for a demotion to get there.

I found it hard to concentrate the rest of the day, so I left a little early. I wanted to go to my parents' and tell them the news. As I drove home, I looked around knowing my daily routine was about to change dramatically. I had driven that same drive a million times. The GM plant on the right, shopping mall on the left, and a motorcycle cop hiding in the same place almost every time. The only variety to the drive was the weather. If you don't like the weather in Texas, wait a minute.

When I told my mom and dad about the transfer, the first thing they asked was if Jenny was going with me. I told them the whole story.

"It'll seem strange," my mom said. "You two not being together."

"I know," I said. I knew my mother was looking forward to a grandchild, but what could I do? "But it's for the best. I think we stayed together out of habit. We want different things." I found that as I explained it to my mother, I wasn't as upset as I could have been. I was angry for being lied to, and I was furious for her part in keeping me from Eddie and California, but I didn't miss her like I thought I would.

My brother came over, and we all had dinner together. Knowing it would be the last family dinner for a while, we dragged it out with dessert and conversation. Eventually, we ran out of things to say. I gave my parents and Cari hugs, and Kevin and I went out for drinks.

"You okay?" he asked me as we sat down at the bar. It was a dive bar that smelled like smoke and stale beer. At first, I had that ugh feeling that I was going to have to explain the smell on my clothes and hair to Jenny. When I remembered that she wouldn't be there, I had a small pang of sadness in my chest.

"Yeah," I said. "It all just takes some getting used to."

He nodded. "I'm not going say anything bad about her in case you guys get back together."

"I appreciate that," I said, and ordered two draft beers. I didn't care if he had anything bad to say about her; I just didn't want to talk about it.

"And two shots of Patron," Kevin added. "Chilled and dressed, please." When the bartender put the shots down, Kevin held his up. "To you, my brother. Let's get you hammered and laid." He licked the salt, downed the tequila, and sucked the lime, and I did the same.

The beers were served in frozen schooners and were so cold that they began to form a slush as soon as they were put in front of us. I took a big gulp and let the slush melt in my mouth. Kevin ordered two more shots.

It wasn't long before I was outpacing my brother in drinking, but I didn't care about that either. The band would start playing soon. I knew them all and I might or might not have been thinking about the lovely lead singer. She and I often jumped on stage during each other's shows. We had chemistry, so the audience liked it when we sang together, but that's as far as anything ever went. Would it feel weird to be around her now that I was single? Everything was safe before because everybody knew that I didn't cheat on Jen. I didn't want her to think I would automatically expect something now. The thought of nobody lying beside me at night anymore did make me feel a bit desperate. Desperation was not good. Maybe lustful was a better word. As I started to think of her body and what she must look like out of the leather jacket and tight jeans, she slipped between Kevin and me and ordered a round of shots.

"Hey, guys," she said cheerfully.

"Hey, Lisa," I said and motioned to Kevin. "You know my brother, right?"

"I do," she said. "How are you, Kevin?"

"Great," he said as shots appeared before us yet again. He clinked shot glasses with Lisa and said, "Thanks, darlin'." Then we took another shot of tequila.

"You coming up tonight?" she asked me.

I shrugged like it didn't matter to me either way. "If you want."

"Good, I'll see ya soon." She winked at me, and I watched her walk away in those tight jeans.

"She wants you," Kevin said.

"You think?"

I didn't hear his response. I was in my own world. It felt kind of weird thinking about being with someone else. I knew Jenny and I weren't together, but she was all I had known for so long. It felt like cheating. Then I came to my senses. Fuck that. If she found out, she could picture us together, like I did her and Michael.

I watched Lisa on the stage and forced Jenny out of my mind. The beer continued to flow while I listened and watched. She sang Pat Benatar, Joan Jett, and a few originals. To finish the set, I went up and we did the Neil Young song "Helpless." When the song was over, she pulled me backstage while the rest of the guys went to the bar.

She closed the door behind us. "Teddy and I split up," she said.

"I know. I heard." The alcohol was in full effect, and I wondered if I was slurring.

"I heard you and Jennifer did too."

"Yeah."

She leaned into me until my back was against the door and kissed me softly. "You need a one-night stand as badly as I do?" she asked.

Her neck tasted salty from the sweat of her performance, and I could smell her leather jacket and the jasmine scent of her shampoo. When I kissed her, she tasted like menthol cigarettes, which for some reason, I liked. I reached behind my back and locked the door, because at that moment, I needed a one-night stand more than anything else in the world.

I was late to work the next day and I was hungover. It was almost three am by the time I'd crawled into bed, and I had to be in at seven. My mouth was dry, and my head felt like it weighed an extra twenty pounds. I was finding it very difficult to care about my job.

"Climb and maintain one five thousand," I absently instructed a pilot.

"Verify altitude?" he replied.

I looked at my screen. Eastern 10, who just happened to be nearby at fifteen thousand, would not appreciate that. "Disregard American 12. Climb and maintain one three thousand."

"American 12, roger."

The FAA was right. I did need a break. Plus, there was a good chance I was going to throw up. I tried to remember how many tequila shots I'd done but had no idea. Jenny and Michael popped into my head for a second, but I immediately pushed them away. I thought of Lisa and remembered the taste of her lips, her soft skin...then I realized I wasn't paying any attention to my job. I called my supervisor and asked for a break. After reading me the riot act, since I'd only been at work for an hour and late on top of that, he sent someone to replace me.

I went to the bathroom and splashed cold water on my face. Five o'clock felt like days away. Quit being a pussy, I told myself. You can handle your alcohol. Then I threw up in the trash can. You are a pussy, Cory. But it did make me feel a little better. I went to the break room and got some gum and a Diet Coke from the vending machine. I was hungry but all the machine had was candy and chips. I wanted a Whataburger with cheese, extra mustard. Or a Taco Bueno burrito with extra salsa. I sipped my Coke and I realized I was still a little drunk. Uh-oh.

I couldn't go back to my station, and I couldn't let them know why. I was not a good liar. When I tried to bend the truth, I could feel the heat in my face as it reddened, and my eyes involuntarily darted away. I wasn't feeling well, that was the truth. I would focus on that. I was sweating and could smell alcohol emitting from my skin. I went back to the bathroom to wash my face and hands with soap. I pushed the pump for the soap and cringed, hoping it wouldn't dry my skin as I rubbed it all over my face.

When I told my boss I wasn't feeling well, he agreed that I looked like shit. He also informed me that my transfer was approved, and I had two weeks to report. Finally, something was easy. At least if Suicide King didn't work out for me, I would still have my job. A lower paying job in a more expensive city, but beggars can't be choosers, as my mother always said.

## 5

On the way home, I pulled through Whataburger and got Jesse and me each a cheeseburger, mine with extra mustard, and fries and a Coke. I made sure they put ketchup in the bag because Whataburger ketchup is what makes the fry. The smell of it filled the Jeep, and I couldn't help myself. I reached in for a few fries. The salt on my tongue was heaven. When the light ahead turned yellow, I stopped and took a big swig of the Coke with the crushed ice. I reached into the bag again for the ketchup cup.

The orange paper-wrapped burger smelled delicious. I peeled the top off the ketchup and dunked a cluster of fries, dropping a blob of it on my shirt when I lifted it to my mouth. I didn't even care.

"Used to Love Her" by Guns N' Roses came on the radio. I turned it up loud, remembering the "violent language" warning label the CD had on it when I bought it. Not sure why I liked the song. Maybe it just brought out the rebel in me.

When I got back to the apartment, Jesse was glad to see that I had brought the burgers. I filled him in on my day, which he thought was funny. I gave Maggie the last bite of burger and the small fries at the bottom of the bag. Jesse was tired of being holed up in the apartment, so he took my Jeep to do some running around. He said he would go and rent a U-Haul for the trip.

I turned the television on and stretched out on the couch. It was only moments before I dozed off. Not long after, there was a knock at the door, which I ignored figuring it was somebody trying to sell something. A few minutes later, Jennifer walked in. I sat up instantly and glanced at the VCR clock. I had been asleep longer than I thought.

"Hi," she said, stopping in the doorway, her keys still dangling from the lock.

"Hey. What's up?" I rubbed my eyes, trying to wake fully.

"I'm sorry," she said as she turned to take her key from the lock, struggling with it sticking. It was something I'd meant to fix but wouldn't bother to now. "I thought you would be gone. I'll just grab a few things and then I'll leave." When she finally got the key to let go, she went to the CDs and began looking through them.

"Those are mine," I said. "I'm leaving almost everything, but those are mine." It still hadn't completely sunk in that we were finished. Soon we would not be a part of each other's lives anymore.

"This one is mine," she said, holding up the Common Thread CD.

"No, it isn't." I got up from the couch and took it from her.

"You gave it to me for our anniversary."

"Anniversary of what? This relationship was a joke. I don't know how long you've been fucking around, but you were, so that voids this." I didn't really care about the damn CD.

"Does that mean you want all of your gifts back?" She took off her engagement ring that I was surprised to see she was still wearing.

"Yes," I said, holding my hand out. "As a matter of fact, I do." I would be in L.A. still paying for that stupid ring and her stainless-steel, top-of-the-line refrigerator that she had to have.

She turned and stomped into the kitchen. She flipped on the light and turned on the garbage disposal.

"What the fuck ever," I said. "You think I care?"

She turned the disposal off and put the ring back on.

I picked up the remote from the couch and turned the television off. I went to the front door and took the dog leash from the table. Jenny was still facing the sink, looking out the window. "I'm going to take the dog for a walk," I said. "Go ahead and take whatever you need. We're leaving for California in the next day or two. I'll leave my keys under the mat."

She didn't turn around, but I could hear her crying softly. "Can you ever forgive me?"

Unfortunately, the answer was "No."

When Maggie and I returned from our walk, Jennifer was gone, and Jesse had returned. The Common Thread CD was on the counter. Apparently, she kept the ring.

"Hey," I said as I unleashed Maggie. She ran to greet Jesse. "You get the U-Haul?" He gave Maggie a hug and began roughhousing with her. I knew why Eddie liked Jesse so much.

"Yep, it's due back at the U-Haul store in L.A. in a week."

"How much do I owe you?" The reality of money, or lack thereof, began to set in.

"Nothing. They gave me a credit card to cover our expenses."

"Who did?"

"Miss Blake and Jeff. I guess it's being added to the cost of recording."

I nodded. I still needed to close joint bank accounts and credit cards. It felt so final. I no longer had a job in Dallas and soon no bank account or home. I would not be able to see my family on a whim.

"What's wrong?" Jesse asked.

"Nothing," I said. "Just tired." I didn't have the energy to get into all that was wrong.

"You ready to take off tomorrow?" Jesse had gotten a beer and was kicked back on the couch with his feet on the coffee table. My initial reaction was to knock them off, but then I remembered that I wouldn't be eating anything there anymore.

"I need to tie up a few loose ends. Is it okay if we leave early the day after?"

That was fine with him. I wasn't sure how to handle the bank accounts. Dividing them equally seemed the fairest way. Not that there was a lot in them. When I called the bank to ask about closing the accounts, they informed me that we would both need to be present. Jenny wasn't in the office, so I left a message with the receptionist. If I didn't hear back from her, I would just have to take out half and leave the accounts open. Not a great idea, but not much I could do about it.

It turns out I didn't have to worry about that. Jenny called me back almost immediately. When I asked her to meet me at the bank tomorrow, her tone turned from pleasant and hopeful to cold and distant. It still made me feel bad to hurt her feelings. Even though she had lied repeatedly and cheated, I guess I still cared about her. Seeing her at the bank was not going to be easy. We would be taking the final step in ending our long relationship. It probably would have been a lot easier to forgive her and carry on like nothing had happened. Had we already been married, I probably would have done just that. But we weren't, and it was time for me to face my fears. If Alexandra Blake changed her mind about me once she met me, then I would find another way, regardless of how long it took me or how many rejections I had to endure. Eddie believed in me. I had talent. It was time for me to believe in myself.

After a restless night with very little sleep, I got up early and headed to the bank. I was ready to get it over with and focus on the future. I arrived a few minutes early, so I waited in my Jeep for Jenny. My nerves were growing more and more unsteady. It would probably be the last time I would ever see her since we didn't have a baby together anymore or anything else that tied us together. I kept glancing at the time on the dash. It would feel like a long time, but only be a minute or two since the last time I looked. I kept changing the channel on the radio, but it would just be another commercial. I started to dig in the glove box for a CD when a knock on the window made me jump. It was Jenny and waiting in the car next to mine was Michael. My stomach turned. I was pissed off at first, but I recovered quickly. There was no way I would let her know that he bothered me. And to think I worried about hurting her feelings just one day earlier. I turned off the ignition and opened the door.

"Hey," I said, as I jumped out of the Jeep. "Thanks for meeting me."

"Of course. I don't have much time though, we have—"

"No problem." I smiled and waved at Michael as I walked towards the bank doors. "Let's get this done."

She followed me in, and surprisingly, we were greeted right away. The professionally dressed lady took us to her desk. Thankful for small favors, I sat down and tried to appear relaxed. This would be over soon. The lady asked us for our check register so we could compare it to her computer and determine what might still be outstanding. I forgot the checkbook. Crap. Jenny looked at me expectantly.

"I forgot it," I said to the lady, feeling the burn of Jennifer's glare. "But I think I can remember."

"That's not how this is going to work," Jennifer said. "Leave the checking alone," she told the lady. Then she turned to me. "When everything clears, I'll mail you a check for half of whatever's left."

I knew I would never see a check. It didn't amount to much, maybe three or four hundred dollars, but I needed it. I had no idea what my expenses were going to be. Reluctantly, I nodded. She turned back to the lady.

"Go ahead and close the savings and give us each a check for half." The lady looked at me and I nodded again.

After the paperwork was done and we collected our checks, we headed back outside. The sun was out fully, and the mist had burned off. "Looks like it's going to be warm today," I said, as I reached into my pocket for my keys. We both stopped in front of Michael's car. I could feel him looking at us, but I didn't acknowledge it. We both knew this was goodbye. Jennifer's eyes began to fill, and she turned away.

"I want you to be happy," I said.

She nodded and touched away the light tears with the tip of her finger. I doubted she cared about my happiness, but perhaps I wasn't giving her enough credit. She stepped forward and put her arms around my waist and pulled me close. I gave her a final hug. She pressed her face against mine and said softly in my ear, "I love you. I always will." She pulled away and went to Michael's car. She got in and they drove away. She didn't look my way again.

I spent the rest of the day and into the night packing and loading the U-Haul. Jesse helped load boxes and as much as we could fit from my studio. I hated leaving the piano and most of the books and CDs behind, but we only had a small amount of space. Then we cleaned the apartment. I even cleaned out the refrigerator, tossing everything old and washing the Tupperware. It was after midnight when I fell into bed. The clock radio alarm was set for seven am.

It felt as if I had just shut my eyes when the clock radio went off. The music was loud with a lot of static. I reached over and hit the snooze. Nine minutes later, it blasted again. I sat up and turned it off.

Today is going to be a good day, I assured myself as went to my dresser for a pair of shorts and socks. I wanted to hit the gym for a brief workout before we left.

I headed for the kitchen to start the coffee, something I had been doing for many years. Then I remembered she wasn't there, so I went to the studio and poked my head in.

"Hey," I said. "You want coffee?"

"No thanks." Jesse sat up and yawned. "Let's pull through somewhere on the way out."

An hour later, Jesse, Maggie, and I had pulled through McDonald's and were headed to my parents' house for a final goodbye. My mom wanted us to come in for breakfast, but I told her we had just eaten.

After about thirty minutes of handshakes and hugs from my dad and brother, and hugs and tears from my mom and sister, we were finally on our way. My only regret was that it took my best friend dying to get me going.

# 6

As we drove along the highway, Jesse began telling me more about the band. He said that Greg, the drummer, was the only one not relieved that I was coming. "He thinks he should be our lead singer," Jesse said.

"Should he?" I asked.

"I dunno, I've never heard him sing anything more than backup."

"Why?" I asked.

"Miss Blake doesn't like him."

"Why?" I asked again.

Jesse shrugged. "He can be annoying."

Great. What if she doesn't like me? What if she thinks I'm annoying? I rubbed my temple. The whole thing was giving me a headache.

"Just get along with her." Jesse read my mind. "Whatever it takes."

"What else do I need to know?" I kept my eyes straight ahead and on the road, not wanting Jesse to see how unsettled I was.

Eddie had mentioned very little about anyone other than Jesse, and I was starting to wonder why.

"You just need to get along with someone who is difficult to get along with. Do that and you're golden."

Simple enough. I'm easy to get along with. Then I had a mini meltdown. Panic surged through me. I was in my Jeep driving across the country with a guy I had known less than a week. I had charged-up credit cards, eighty-nine dollars in cash, and a check for twelve hundred dollars in my wallet. Suddenly, I wanted to talk to Jenny and for everything to be the way it was before. Before the accident and before I knew about Michael. When I was blissfully unaware.

"You okay, dude?" Jesse asked.

"I don't know," I said. "What the hell am I doing? I should have flown out to meet her first. I should have—"

"Calm down, it's going to be fine," Jesse said.

"You don't know that. You don't know what she'll—"

"She will like you," he assured me. "She's heard you sing. Eddie had a video of you guys doing some show. She's heard you and she's seen you, and you're what she wants."

"Is Greg the only one she doesn't like?" I asked reaching for something.

"I'm going to be honest with you," Jesse said. "She's a complete bitch. But it's her studio, so she's the boss. Just sing what she wants you to sing the way that she wants you to sing it. Once we make a name for ourselves, we will have more say in things."

I didn't know what to say, so I stayed silent. There was nothing I could do about the circumstances, so I had to try not to think about it. For the first time, I forced the picture of Jenny and Michael into my mind instead of out. Whatever was in L.A. had to be better than dealing with what was going on in Texas. Jesse began small talk to distract me.

The Cure song "Friday I'm in Love" came on the radio, so I turned it up a little, but before I could listen to the whole thing, we started losing signal. Static began taking over, so Jesse reached into the back seat and pulled out a cassette holder. I glanced over his tapes. They were all from the sixties and seventies. I chose a Lynyrd Skynyrd tape.

"What can I say," he shrugged. "I was born in the wrong generation."

Since I liked older music and television as well, we passed the time asking each other trivia. I stumped him in the television category a few times, and he got me with the movies. He was easy to be around, and I found myself wishing for the umpteenth time that Eddie was with us.

It felt like we had been driving for a long time, but a glance at the clock revealed it had only been little more than three hours. We did need gas, however, so I pulled into the next station. Jesse flashed the credit card he'd used for the U-Haul and went inside to pay. While I waited for the pump to turn on, I put Maggie's leash on her, and we walked up and down the grass patch by the road. She stopped and sniffed every little thing but didn't seem to need to do her business. After a few minutes, I put her back in the Jeep and filled up the tank. Then I went inside to do my business.

When I got back to the Jeep, Jesse was in the driver's seat.

"Want me to drive for a bit?"

I was okay with that, so I jumped into the passenger's seat. He had gotten us each a bottled water and a sandwich. It wasn't one of those sandwiches that come in a triangular plastic container either. When I opened the bag, I was delighted to find that it was a handmade turkey and Swiss on wheat, with romaine lettuce, a fresh cut tomato, and the perfect amount of mayo.

"Damn," I said with a full mouth. "Good sandwich."

Jesse reached for his as he pulled out of the station. At the sound of my wrapper, Maggie had stuck her face between the seats. Jesse unwrapped his sandwich, pulled the cheese off, and handed it to her. She gobbled it up and swallowed it without even chewing.

"You don't like cheese?" I asked.

"Yeah, just giving her a bite."

I broke off a piece of mine for her and also gave her the last bite. Once she saw there was no more, she curled up in the seat behind me and fell asleep. My eyes grew heavy as I gazed out the window, and I soon followed.

I awoke a few hours later to Maggie whining and turning in the back seat.

"I'll pull in for gas," Jesse said. "I think she has to pee."

I looked in the back to find that the seats were covered in fur. She licked my face from my chin clear up to my forehead. It was gross, but I couldn't get mad at her. As Jesse pulled in, she grew more excited. When he came to a stop next to the pumps, I reached for her leash and jumped out simultaneously. Without waiting for me, she darted from the back seat and took off towards the road. Jesse and I both called for her to no avail. She was in full sprint. I ran towards her and called her name with authority, but she completely ignored me. She had spotted an armadillo waddling across the street and she was headed right for it. Cars were flying by, oblivious to us. My heart started to ache as I pleaded to whoever was listening, no, no please no. I can't fucking lose my dog too.

When she reached the road, I realized there was nothing more I could do. I stopped and closed my eyes waiting for the inevitable sound of my dog's last moments. The screech of tires from a car hitting the brakes filled the air, and then silence. I opened my eyes, praying she had somehow survived, to find Maggie also putting on the brakes at the last possible second. The light-blue sedan was so close as it passed by that it probably brushed the fur on the side of her face. The car somehow missed the armadillo as well. Maggie turned and galloped back to me as the armadillo disappeared into the ditch on the far side of the road. I knelt and gave her a hug and attached her leash. "You scared me," I whispered into her ear.

"Damn, dude." Jesse had caught up to us and was out of breath. He rested his hands on his knees and was shaking his head, obviously as relieved as I was. "Be more careful with her."

"Yeah," I said and hugged her again. "I will."

I drove next until we hit El Paso. Almost ten hours of driving and we were still in Texas. We checked into a small but clean motel that let us take Maggie in for an extra twenty dollars. I had brought her dog bed but let her on the bed with me. I was exhausted until my head hit the pillow, then suddenly I was wide awake. I got up and went out to the balcony with Jesse. He was leaning against the rail, looking at the brightly lit swimming pool and smoking a cigarette. We were the only ones out, and the only sound was the chirp of the crickets. The smoke from his cigarette drifted my way, but it didn't bother me. I asked him to tell me more about the band.

He started with Greg again. He said Greg used to be a lot more fun, but he got his girlfriend pregnant and married her. Jesse checked for my reaction. "It's okay," I said. "Go on."

"So anyway," he continued, "he's got a new baby and a new wife, and he's always stressed. All he cares about now is what's in it for him." Jesse dropped his cigarette butt and stomped it out. "Which is understandable but doesn't make it any easier to be around him."

Jesse had begun to feel like an old friend. I was comfortable around him, and I trusted him. He reminded me of Eddie in the way he was so easygoing. My heart hurt when I thought about Eddie, and I wondered if it would ever get any easier. It wasn't fair.

"Then there's Trent," he went on. "He is lazy and brilliant. He has a heart of gold but puts as little effort as possible into everything he does. Because he is so good at what he does, he gets away with it."

"What does he do?" I asked.

"Bass guitar mostly, but he can do it all. Write music, play the keyboards, lead, rhythm, sing. I think he can even play the trumpet or sax or some kind of horn."

"Why doesn't he sing lead?" I asked, fearful that it was yet another reason I might end up unneeded.

"He doesn't want to. He doesn't like attention."

I nodded, relieved. I could understand that.

"I'm going to take a quick shower, then go to bed," Jesse said. "I'm beat."

Jesse went in to take a shower, so I walked Maggie again. She still hadn't gone to the bathroom, and I didn't want her to go in the room or wake me up after I'd fallen asleep. She sniffed and looked around, but after twenty minutes of nothing, I went back to the room. I needed to call Jenny and give her Jesse's address and phone number, but I really didn't want to talk to her. I thought about calling Lisa, but we both agreed it was a one-night stand. That didn't stop me from feeling guilty for not calling.

I picked up the phone and punched in the phone number to my old apartment. I hoped she wouldn't answer, so I was relieved when the answering machine came on. I left a message saying where I would be if she needed to contact me for any reason. I didn't mention the checking account, even though it was my reason for leaving her the information.

I took a quick shower after Jesse. When I was done, the lights were off and he was asleep. I tried to stay quiet as I walked across the room and slipped into bed. Maggie was at the foot of Jesse's bed. I whispered and called to her. She took a flying leap across to my bed. Her front paws and about sixty pounds landed right on my stomach. I sprang forward with an "Umph." I was pretty sure the sound of me gasping woke Jesse, because I heard him laugh and turn over. She curled up next to me, and soon the two of them were snoring. I gave her a quick hug and was right behind them.

The morning sun forced its way through the mini blinds, and I could feel its heat on my face. I flipped over to face the other direction, not quite ready to face the day. Maggie inched up to me and put her nose on mine and puffed. Her nose was cold and wet, but I ignored her, hoping she would let me sleep a bit longer. It felt like such a chore to get up and walk her. I remembered that she hadn't gone yet and was probably about to bust, so I forced myself up and slipped on my jeans. She started turning in circles and doing a half bark, half whine as I put her leash on. We went outside, across the balcony, and down the concrete steps. She tugged and pulled and led me around the grassy area surrounding the pool.

"Go to the bathroom," I commanded. Nothing. Feeling frustrated with her, I tugged and headed back towards the room. Jesse was outside smoking.

"She won't go to the bathroom," I told him. "She hasn't done anything in almost two days."

"She doesn't want to go while she's on a leash," he said. "She's never had to do that, and she doesn't want to start now."

"What do I do? I can't just let her run free."

"She needs to learn. She'll go eventually. She can't hold it forever." He dropped his cigarette and stomped it out. "Ready?"

I followed him inside, where we finished getting dressed and gathered everything up. We decided to have breakfast at the coffee shop across the parking lot before we left. I put food and water out for Maggie before we walked over.

A pretty woman that reminded me of Michelle Pfeiffer in *Frankie and Johnny* took us to a booth and asked what we would like to drink. Jesse ordered black coffee, and I asked for ice water with lemon. I watched her hips swing back and forth as she walked away and hoped she would return. She did moments later with our drinks, but she only took our order and was gone again.

She stopped by a few more times and flirted with us while we waited for our food, and I wondered which one of us she would choose. Jesse had his longish black hair and blue eyes, while I had short hair and dark, serious eyes. All the time, people were telling me to smile, which I hated. I wasn't not smiling. It's just the way I looked.

It started to seem like the food was taking forever. Jesse began scribbling song ideas on a napkin, while my mind wandered. I thought about Jenny. Did she get my message, and would I ever hear from her? I hated to admit that I missed her. Or at least the comfort of not being alone. It was hard to remember not knowing her. Aside from losing my virginity at seventeen, and now Lisa, Jenny was the only girl I'd ever been with.

"Hey," Jesse said. "Where are you? What do you think?"

"Sorry," I said. "Just thinking." I looked at his notes on the napkin. There wasn't much there, but I liked what he had so far. It was something about how sex and lies keep us holding on. Hmm. Was he referring to me with Jen?

"Thinking about what?" he asked. "About leaving your girl and your friends and family and your job? For a demotion at work, to move to California, where it costs twice as much to live, to join a rock 'n' roll band?"

"It sounds crazy when you say it," I said.

He laughed. "Ya got balls. That's a good thing." Then he started teasing me about how long it took me to get ready in the morning. "You're worse than my girlfriend. How much stuff can you put in your hair and on your skin?"

It was true. Every morning I did a hundred sit-ups and push-ups and hit the gym if I had time. I used shampoo and two conditioners and then mousse. After I shaved, I washed my face with a moisturizing soap and put face cream on. It was a routine I'd had since I was a teenager. I was lucky that I never had to fight teenage acne like most of my friends. It was probably because I drank water, ate healthy, and took care of my skin.

Jesse's sourdough toast, fried eggs, bacon, and hash browns and my fruit and oatmeal finally showed up. The waitress unloaded it all onto our table and slipped me the check. After she walked away, I picked it up. "I wonder why she assumes I'm paying."

Jesse smiled big and took the check from me. He turned it over and tossed it on the table. On it was written her name and phone number with a little heart. "She's been flirting with you since we got here," he said.

"You think?"

He rolled his eyes.

"Is it rude if I don't call?" I asked.

"Do you want to call her?" he asked me as he poured ketchup and Tabasco sauce on his hash browns. They looked damn tasty, and the aroma of that Tabasco sauce made me want to reach over and scoop up a bite.

"I don't live here," I said. "I don't see the point, but I don't want to hurt her feelings."

"She'll live. Hand me the salt and pepper."

I scooted him the salt and pepper shakers. I took the pen she had left with the check and wrote "Just passing through" and put a smiley face.

"Feel better?" Jesse asked as he sopped up the yellow egg yolk with his toast and stuffed it into his mouth.

I felt a little better.

## 7

It was late by the time we pulled into town, so it was dark, but I could still see the palm trees along the highway. I hadn't realized there was such a variety, and I liked them all. They seemed so much more sophisticated than the trees in Texas.

Jesse wanted to go out for a drink, so we took Maggie to his apartment and dropped off the U-Haul. It was locked, so I wasn't too worried about anything being stolen. Unless, of course, someone hitched up and took the whole thing. I was more worried about leaving Maggie. She was in a new place and still hadn't gone to the bathroom, even after a twenty-minute walk around the complex. I filled a water bowl for her and put one of my tee shirts on her bed.

Jesse drove us to a club in Hollywood in his newish Toyota Supra, black with black leather interior and an upgraded sound system. It sat low and almost felt like sitting on the ground after two days straight in my Jeep. He opened the sunroof, turned the music up, and zipped out of the parking lot. We listened to Nirvana, too loud for conversation as he sped down the highway, his hair blowing madly from the sunroof wind.

Twenty minutes later, we were pushing our way through the crowded club. It was different from any bar I had ever been to. Almost everybody was wearing black, and it was difficult to tell the guys from the girls. Most had very light, almost white skin, black hair, and wore red lipstick and black eyeliner. Blue strobe lights dashed as "Ordinary World" played loudly. I made my way to the bar and paid five dollars for a beer that was room temperature. Seemed like a lot of money for a warm beer, but I would drink it anyway and probably more. I turned away from the bar to discover that I had lost track of Jesse, so I scanned the crowd for him. Someone, that I was pretty sure was female, slid up to me and spoke into my ear, asking me to dance. I didn't want to, so I said I had to go to the bathroom. She smiled knowingly and pointed to a lighted hallway. The sign above the entrance was neon purple and it just said, Head.

So even though I didn't need to, I went into the restroom, which was coed. The music was muffled, and the lights were very bright, a stark contrast to the rest of the club. Everyone looked at me strangely, so I was really glad I didn't have to go. I went back to the bar and bought a bottled beer this time, which was more expensive but slightly colder, then circled the place looking for Jesse. I finally found him sitting at a table with two girls and a guy. He introduced me to his girlfriend, Christy, her friend Amy, and Trent Austin from the band. Amy was Christy's roommate and the best-looking girl in the bar, which wasn't saying a whole lot, but she was definitely attractive. I wished it wasn't so loud so I could talk to Trent about the band, but that would have to wait.

Amy wore a skintight, skimpy black dress with clearly nothing underneath it. Her breasts were a bit larger than average and appeared to be very firm. The dress was so snug that if she got cold, her nipples might just pop right through. I leaned into her ear to ask if she wanted a drink, but before I had a chance to say anything, Christy took her by the arm and pulled her away. The two disappeared into the crowd.

"What do you think of Christy?" Jesse asked, shouting above the noise. Honestly, I was not impressed with her. She was thin and had long, dirty blonde hair and dressed sort of bohemian. The natural look I supposed, but to me she just looked like she needed a shower. I didn't want to be an asshole though, so I shouted back, "She seems great. How long have you been together?"

He held up two fingers and mouthed, "Two years."

I felt obligated to reply. "Cool. She's good-looking." I wasn't sure if he heard me, but he seemed pleased.

Trent saw a girl that he knew and went to talk to her, and Jesse went to get us a drink, so when Christy and Amy returned, I was alone with them. They both had full drinks, so I couldn't ask them if they needed one. I didn't want to deal with the bathroom again until it was absolutely necessary, so I stood there and tried to think of something to say.

Christy slid into a tall chair. She inched it close to me and asked, "Where's Jesse and Trent?" as she put her hand on my leg. She slid it down to my inner thigh briefly and then took it away. I supposed that was meant to turn me on, but it repulsed me instead. Amy inched in closer from the other side.

"What are you guys doing?" I asked. I had grown accustomed to the loud music and learned that if I talked below it, they could hear me.

Christy put her hand on my leg again. I wasn't sure if they were serious or just messing with me. "What part don't you understand?" she asked, giving me her seductive smile.

"I'm pretty sure Jesse will be right back," I said.

Christy shrugged and Amy said, "She's free to see other people."

I gave them each a skeptical look. Christy hopped from the chair and swung around to Amy. She lifted Amy's chin and kissed her right on the lips. I looked around. Nobody seemed to notice or care.

"Well?" Christy said as she wiped under her bottom lip with her finger.

I didn't know what to say. Luckily, Jesse came back with the beers and saved me. He set his on the table and took Christy to the dance floor. Amy looked at me expectantly, so I asked her if she wanted to dance. She said she did, so I took a huge swallow of beer and followed her to the floor.

It was a slower song, so I held her kind of close. She asked me if I wanted to go back to the apartment with her and Christy. I told her that I liked her but that I wasn't interested in Jesse's girlfriend. She thought that was sweet and kissed me. I liked the taste of her lipstick, so I licked my lips to taste it again.

The song ended and "Dream Attack" by New Order came on. Trent hit the dance floor, pulling along a girl with shockingly-white hair and dark-red lipstick. Amy and I went back to the table. Even though she was draped all over me, an Asian guy with half his head shaved and black hair hanging in his eyes from the other half asked her to dance.

"No tank jew," she answered, making fun of his English, which I thought was mean, but he didn't seem to notice. He nodded, still smiling as he turned and hurried away. It was an initial turn off for me, but I put it out of my head and focused on how short her dress was. I was feeling a bit full of myself from the two of them hitting on me, and I wanted to enjoy it.

Amy and I moved to a table further from the dance floor so we could hear each other better. She confessed Jesse really didn't know about Christy's infidelities.

"Then why did she kiss you back there? Jesse could have walked up at any moment."

"That's just the way she is," Amy shrugged. "She likes risk. Likes to see how much she can get away with." I wondered how much she and Christy actually messed around and made a mental note to make sure I had a condom before I did anything with Amy. "One time," she went on, "she had sex with a guy on the living room couch while Jesse was in the next room. Of course, he was out pretty good. He and Trent drank almost a full bottle of Jack."

"Hey, dude." Jesse snuck up from behind me and slapped the table. "It's almost closing time. Let's go to the girls' apartment. I have a bottle of Crown there."

"Okay," I said. "But I don't want any Crown. I can't drink the brown stuff." I didn't like whiskey or scotch. I got really drunk and sick on Seagram's Seven at my high school senior picnic, and ever since then, just the smell turned my stomach.

"I have beer," Amy said.

"Cool then," Jesse said. "Christy's riding with me. You ride with Amy?"

"Okay," I said. Like I could say no even if I wanted to with her standing right there. I figured he was happy to see Christy again after his time in Texas, so I didn't mind too much.

Amy drove an RX7 which was really uncomfortable for my tall frame. Plus, she was playing loud techno music that was giving me a headache. I asked her if she minded if I changed the channel. I found the Garth Brooks version of "Shameless."

"I guess I forgot I had me a Texas cowboy," she said with a drawl.

"There's worse things than being a country boy," I said, although I didn't consider myself a country boy. I wasn't sure if this was flirting or small talk. I was going back to her apartment, but Jesse and Christy would be there.

"I didn't say it was a bad thing," she said.

I couldn't think of anything clever to say, so I asked her to pull into a drugstore. I didn't want to be presumptuous, but I did want to be prepared. She pulled in and threw the car in park but didn't turn it off. I asked her if she wanted anything to drink or anything else. She said she didn't need anything. I debated on whether to let her know why I had her stop. She did invite me back with her and Christy, after all. I grabbed a six-pack of Corona as a cover and bought the small package of condoms.

"I told you I have beer at home," she said as I climbed back into the car.

"I was in the mood for Corona," I said.

She threw the gear shift into reverse and put her arm around my shoulders as she looked to back out. Her face was close to mine when she said, "You didn't get any condoms?"

"I might have," I answered.

She kissed me firmly but briefly, then put the car in forward and took off. It was a quick drive to her apartment from there, which we rode without any more conversation. The radio had ended up back on the techno music.

When we got to her apartment, Jesse and Christy were nowhere in sight. There was a guy sleeping on the couch, and the television was on very low volume. "That's my brother," she explained as she flipped on the light and went over to the couch and shook him. "Wake up," she told him. "Go sleep in my room, I have company."

I was in the kitchen putting the beer in the refrigerator, but I did not want him going to her room. "It's okay," I said through the opening from the kitchen to the living room. "Stay up and have a beer." I opened three Coronas and took them each one. Her brother sat up and rubbed his eyes and took the beer. He had thick scruffy hair and a few days' beard. He wore a flannel shirt unbuttoned with the sleeves cut off and jeans with holes in the knees. He took a big gulp of beer then set it on the coffee table that was littered with mail and dirty dishes and a huge, multicolored blown glass bong. He took a baggie from his shirt pocket and began stuffing the bowl.

"Make mine a joint," Amy said.

I was glad she did too, because it would have been a turn-off to see her sucking on that ridiculous bong. Moments later, he handed her a joint, and I watched her put it between her lips and light it. She took a deep hit and held the smoke in her lungs and then exhaled slowly. She offered it to me, but I was good with just the beer. I gave her a few more minutes with it before I leaned into her and said, "Let's go to your room."

Amy nodded and began walking towards the stairs. She took my hand and pulled me along. I looked over my shoulder at her brother, who was still thoroughly wrapped up in his bong project. I followed her up the stairs and into her bedroom. She shut the door behind us without turning on the light. There was a soft glow through the window from an outside light. The red numbers on the clock radio read 3:16 am, and for a second, I worried about my dog at Jesse's apartment. I hoped that's where Jesse and Christy went. As Amy moved towards me, I felt a rush of nerves pulse through me and wished that I'd downed a few more beers. She put her arms around me and slipped her hands under my shirt. They were warm against my skin. I pulled her in for a kiss, soft at first, but then more aggressive. The flavor of lipstick was gone, and she now tasted like Corona and marijuana. She pushed me gently onto the bed and fell on top of me. The nerves disappeared.

The smell of ammonia roused me from my sleep. I was disoriented, and it took a second to remember where I was. The bed was empty next to me, and I could hear the washer and dryer going. I glanced over at the clock radio. It was a little after nine. I jumped out of bed and pulled on my jeans. The sound of a vacuum cleaner drew closer. I found it odd that she was up early cleaning, and it reminded me of waking up at my parents' house on a Saturday morning. As I located my shirt and shoes, Amy opened the bedroom door and turned off the vacuum.

"You should be a model," she said looking at my chest.

"Thanks," I said and slipped on my shirt. "Can you give me a ride to Jesse's?"

"Sure. Why are you running off so soon?"

I had morning breath and smelled like smoke from the bar. I wanted a shower and fresh clothes. "I need to check on my dog," I said.

"Oh. Okay." She seemed surprised. "Yeah, come on. Let's go." She went and grabbed her keys, and I slipped on my shoes and followed her out.

I hadn't meant to spend the night, but I didn't want to ask for a ride the second we were finished. My plan had been to give it a few minutes and then let her know I needed to check on Maggie. But then, of course, I fell asleep.

It took about twenty minutes to get to Jesse's apartment. Even though I didn't like her choice in music, I was glad when she turned the music up in the car. I wasn't in the mood for small talk.

When she pulled into the lot, I thanked her for the ride. I didn't want her to come in but suddenly realized that I didn't have a key. I looked around for Jesse's car but didn't see it. I hoped it was in one of the garages because I didn't know what I would do next if Jesse wasn't there. "Do you mind waiting until I make sure he's home?"

She said she didn't mind, so I jumped out and sprinted to the door. I was relieved to find that it was unlocked and waved to Amy, then opened the door and shouted for Jesse. Maggie jumped from the couch and bounded for me. She was crazy excited to see me. I found her leash as Jesse came flying from the bedroom.

"Hurry up, dude," he said as he pulled a black tee shirt with The Cure written across it over his head. "We were supposed to be at the studio an hour ago."

"I have to take her for a walk and take a shower."

"I already took her down to the dog park," he said, as he stooped over to scratch her. "And she was a good girl, weren't you, Maggie?" He looked back up at me. "She still wouldn't go on the leash, but we left quite a bit behind at the dog park." He tucked his shirt into his jeans, then changed his mind and pulled it back out. "Move your ass," he said. "We gotta go."

"Okay, okay," I said. I had two days' growth and smelled like the bar, but at the very least, I was going to brush my teeth. I wasn't happy even leaving the apartment in that condition, much less arriving like that on my first day to meet the others, but what could I do?

## 8

On the way to the studio, Jesse told me that he and Christy had gotten into a huge fight, and that's why they didn't come to the girls' apartment. He didn't say what they fought about. Just that it was for most of the night, and it took a lot of apologizing.

"What could you possibly have done that was so awful?" I asked, thinking of what Amy had told me about Christy.

"I don't really know. I was drunk, so I probably said something that pissed her off. She has a temper. Once she gets mad, it's a lot of work to talk her down."

I hadn't known Jesse for very long, but he seemed like an easygoing, nice guy. They were fine when they left the bar, so whatever he did, it was after that. I wanted to tell him what Amy told me. "Why do you put up with that?" I asked.

He looked over at me and grinned almost shyly. "Cuz, I love her."

I nodded, not sure what to say.

"Jeez, slow down," I said to Jesse as we took the stairs in leaps. "We're already late, what's a few more minutes?" He didn't slow down. If anything, the reminder that we were already late made him go even faster. We flew up the stairs, ran around the corner, and burst through the door. Everyone stopped what they were doing and looked up at us.

After what seemed like an eternity of silence, Greg, the drummer, did the badum-tish then said, "Looks like our new member is trying to make a good first impression." I already didn't like him. He was overweight and had a sarcastic look about him and was probably an asshole.

Jesse apologized and strapped his guitar on, which made me realize I didn't bring one. Heat traveled up my face.

"Christ, look at the three of you," Greg said.

I knew I looked rough and that things were already not going well. Jesse's eyes were a little red, and I think he might have forgotten to comb his hair. Trent sat in the corner with his elbows on his knees and his face in his hands. His eyes were closed, and he might have been asleep.

Not knowing what to do, I stood uneasily and took in my surroundings. I noticed that Jesse's guitar was a bright cobalt-blue that matched his eyes, which I thought was cool. Greg did not look like one would expect a drummer to look. He looked like a banker or an accountant. I noticed that Trent looked very young, maybe not even old enough to have been in the bar. He had a kicked puppy look about him that made me want to give him a hug.

Jesse looked past me and muttered, "Damn."

I turned to a man who I assumed was Jeff and…Alexandra Blake. I knew Alexandra Blake from her music and movies. On her CD cover, she was glamorous, but in person, she was all business. Her hair, which had been wild curls on the CD, was pulled up in a tight bun, and large silver hoops dangled from her ears. Her attire had gone from sparkling silver to a black suit with a low-cut white blouse underneath. I had always liked her but not thought much about her. She was a celebrity, and I was not one to be starstruck, so I wasn't sure what hit me in that moment. She had a presence that made me forget anybody else was in the room. I couldn't take my eyes from her. It was as if time stopped. The last time I had felt removed from reality like that was when I heard Jen with Michael. That felt awful, this was incredible. As she walked towards me, I locked eyes with her and held out my hand. "I'm Cory," I said as she shook my hand. "I'm sorry we were late. It's my fault, and it won't happen again."

"Where is your guitar?" she asked, her dark-brown eyes without emotion.

"I...forgot it." Damn, why did I have to be so absentminded? And why did I have to smell and look like I slept in a bar? I could smell the alcohol from my skin and wondered if everybody else could too. She smelled like she had just walked through a mist of the sexiest perfume...and was there a hint of vanilla? I was thankful I'd at least brushed my teeth.

"Do you plan on coming in drunk every day?" she asked. "You smell like booze and heaven knows what else."

"No," I said, trying not to laugh. Damn, sometimes I found the strangest things amusing, but I couldn't help it. I felt joy just standing close to her. "I mean, I'm not drunk, I just—"

"Have you gone over any of the material?"

"No," I said again. She was clearly irritated with me, but all I could think of was The Doors song "Hello, I Love You." She said something else, but I didn't hear her. All I could hear was the song running through my brain as I imagined her luscious, long legs wrapped around me.

"Mr. Scott, do you understand?" she said.

I hadn't heard a word she said. I looked her in the eyes and gave my best grin. "Perfectly," I answered. I was certain I saw something from her before she turned, and I watched her walk away, hips swaying ever so slightly.

Jesse put his hand on my shoulder and said, "Don't worry, we'll go over some stuff tonight, and tomorrow you'll knock her dead."

I ran my fingers through my hair, which insisted on springing back up. "She's absolutely gorgeous."

"You'll get over that soon enough," Jesse said, shaking his head. "Let's get out of here. You have a lot to learn by tomorrow."

Greg walked past us. "Another wasted day," he said, giving me a look on his way out.

With my mind still on Alexandra Blake, I followed Jesse.

"Hey, wait up," Trent called as he ran to catch up to us. We stopped and waited. When he caught up, he bent over and put his hands on his knees to catch his breath. He must have run all of fifty yards. Finally, he stood up and flipped his hair out of his eyes. "Miss Blake is really mad at you guys," he said. "I overheard her and Jeff talking." Trent looked at me. "She said you better have the voice of a goddamn canary or you can haul your arrogant ass back to Dallas. That's exactly what she said. 'Goddamn canary'."

"She said I was arrogant?" I asked, pleased. Rarely was I accused of arrogance. Shy, yes; arrogant, no. My confident act must have been convincing.

"That makes you happy?" Jesse said. He shook his head and laughed. "Let's get going; you need to learn the material."

"What about Miss Blake?" Trent asked. "You don't have anything else to say about that?"

"Yeah," I answered, as I opened the door to Jesse's car. "She's heard me. She knows that I sing like a goddamn canary." Then I got in and shut the door, determined not to let anybody else's opinion stop me ever again.

On the drive back to his apartment, Jesse played a blues compilation CD. We listed to, among others, Albert King, Billie Holliday, and Stevie Ray Vaughan.

"I have the room," Jesse said. "You're welcome to use it. You can chip in on the rent when you go back to work or when we start making money."

Ugh. Back to work. I hadn't thought of the tower since I left and wasn't thrilled to go back. "Why do you have a two-bedroom apartment?" I asked.

"I had a roommate. Just never replaced him when he moved out." He looked in the rearview mirror at Trent, who wasn't paying any attention to us. "He stays there sometimes," he said to me in a lowered voice.

"Okay," I said. "I appreciate it. I'll sleep on the couch if he needs to stay over."

"He can sleep on the couch," Jesse said lightly. "You're going to pay rent. Eventually."

When we got back to the apartment, I took Maggie to the dog park. While she ran around in the enclosed area, I jogged around the outer perimeter. After we both had run several miles, we went back to the apartment. I felt like I hadn't taken a shower in weeks. Along with the smoke and stale beer smell, I could now add sweat. Crap. And I still needed to unload the trailer. I put the shower off yet again. Jesse and Trent helped me unload it, and three hours later, I was finally under a steaming hot shower.

An hour later, I emerged from my new bedroom clean and refreshed, in jeans and a Texas Rangers baseball tee.

"There he is," Jesse announced like a smart-ass. "Mr. America. Is that record time? It takes him over an hour to get ready to go absolutely nowhere."

"Ha ha," I said. "Mr. Funny. I just need to call my parents to let them know we made it okay." After Eddie's death, I promised myself I would stay in closer touch with my family.

Jesse pointed to the phone and went back to softly playing his guitar. Trent was in the recliner with it kicked back as far as it would go and smoking a joint. I was surprised that Jesse didn't mind him smoking inside. Generally, the apartment was clean and orderly, but now it smelled like weed. Trent sucked on the joint and exhaled without removing it from his lips.

I called my mom and reported that we had arrived safely. My dad was at work, but I could hear Cari yelling in the background that she wanted to talk to me. My mom put her on the phone, and I promised to send some pictures and call again. After about ten minutes, my mom took the phone back and hesitantly told me Jenny called her. I patiently listened to reasons why I should forgive and work it out before I told her that would not happen.

"You know that for a relationship to last there has to be forgiveness," she said.

"Yes, Mom, I know. But we weren't married, and we want different lives."

"Let me just tell you one more thing," she said. "Your father and I have been married for thirty years, and the only reason is forgiveness. I have done him wrong more than once, and he has made his share of mistakes. The only way it lasts is if you work through it and stick it out. I'm not telling you this to push you back to Jennifer. I'm telling you this so that you think carefully before committing to someone again."

"Okay, Mom. I will." We hung up without my mother knowing how much her statement impacted me. Did she just say they had cheated on each other? Had I been naive in believing that their marriage was as easy as they made it look? She was right. People break up all the time because someone cheated or lied or did something else "unforgivable."

"Are we ready?" Jesse asked.

"Yeah," I said and went over to Trent. I reached down and pulled on the lever, making the recliner and Trent spring forward. He jumped up, flipped his hair from his face, and punched me hard on my arm.

It hurt but also made me laugh. I got him in a headlock and said, "Why don't you cut this mop?" His hair was always in his face; that would drive me crazy.

"What are you? My father?" he answered from his headlock.

"You guys need to cut it out," Jesse said. "We have a lot to do."

"Okay, okay," I said, letting go of Trent. He gave me one more punch before picking up his bass. He also picked up an almost empty bottle of Southern Comfort from the coffee table and took a swig. I declined when he offered it to me.

I fell back into Trent's spot on the recliner and said, "Okay, let me hear this stuff."

Jesse began playing his guitar and softly sang a song that I immediately recognized as the work of Eddie Cooper. I could see Eddie at the piano smoking one cigarette after another. He claimed he only smoked when he drank or when he wrote but seemed like he was always doing one or the other or both. When Jesse finished the song, he asked me what I thought.

"He sometimes played it at a faster tempo," he added, before I could answer.

"I like it," I said, and I meant it. Eddie had talent.

We spent the rest of the day and into the night going over the songs for the album. Trent sang one that he wrote called "Need Your Love" that was very Nirvana-esque. Jesse sang two that he co-wrote with Eddie, and I would be doing lead on the rest. We went over them all a few times, then focused on a song called "Last Train Out" that was expected to be the first release. It was written by Greg, and it needed work. Finally, after several hours of rehearsing it, I had to ask.

"Who decided this would be our release? And why?"

They looked at each other and shrugged. "I assume Miss Blake," Jesse said.

"She decides everything," Trent added.

"Okay then." I took a deep breath. Last thing I wanted was another confrontation with her. "We have it down as good as it can get the way it is. I think we should either make some edits or practice "Hard Times Again." I know Eddie and I wrote it, but it's good. It should be our first single."

"Doesn't matter to me," Trent shrugged.

"I don't want to spend time on changing anything just yet," Jesse said. "Let's do "Hard Times Again" a few more times." So, we did. And it was going to be a hit; that I knew.

After we played it for the last time, I went to the fridge for a beer. I grabbed one for each of us and fell into the couch. Trent had claimed the recliner again, and Jesse pulled the patio door open and stood outside smoking a cigarette. I noticed there was a large area of grass between our apartment and another building in our complex.

I got up and grabbed Maggie's leash and took her out through the patio. We walked around for several minutes. I wanted to teach her to mind in hopes of avoiding any more close calls. After a bit, I took the leash off. I would allow her up to about ten feet away before calling her back.

"Look at that," I said to Jesse. "She's a good dog."

"Yeah," he agreed. "But keep an eye on her. I don't want her homeless again."

"For sure," I agreed, and we went back inside for another beer.

"You think Miss Blake will like me?" I asked Trent as I tossed him a beer and sat on the couch. Jesse's and Amy's apartments were similar in layout, except the bedrooms were upstairs at hers and down at Jesse's. But both had small kitchens that opened to a short breakfast bar.

"I don't know why she wouldn't," he answered. "Just do as she says, and she'll leave you alone."

I didn't want her to leave me alone and I didn't want to call her Miss Blake. "How did she become involved? This isn't her kind of music."

Jesse was sitting at the small breakfast table. "I think she was looking for a project," he said. "It's been a while since she's had anything of her own. Her music is outdated. I suppose that's why she hired Jeff to help. He's been involved with some big names. He's hinted that we may go on tour and open for one of them."

Trent nodded. "Yeah, wouldn't that be cool?"

"What about my job?" I said.

"You said you didn't like it," Jesse said. "Quit. Miss Blake and Jeff can get you some studio work."

I thought about that. Would that mean I would see more of her? I began to fantasize about the taste of her lips. She had nice full lips. I laughed a little at myself. I had spent all of two minutes around her and I had already fantasized about her long legs and her full lips. I couldn't remember anyone ever affecting me so intensely before.

The phone rang, and while Jesse answered it, I turned to Trent. "Hey, is there a library close by?"

"Yeah. Why?"

"I just need to pick up a few books."

"I volunteer there on Thursday mornings," he said. "You can come with me this Thursday if you want."

That was a couple of days away. I wanted to learn more about Alexandra Blake now. I've always been bad about wanting what I want immediately. Patience has never been my strong suit. "Yeah, I'll go too. What do you—" I was about to ask what he volunteered for when Jesse hung up the phone and announced that Amy and Christy were coming over.

"How much beer is left?" I asked Jesse.

"Not much. I can run to the store."

"I'll go," I said. "Want me to get something to throw on the grill too?"

"Yeah. Here, let me give you some money." He pulled out his wallet.

"I got it." I wasn't paying rent yet. I didn't want to mooch food too.

Trent held up the empty Southern Comfort bottle. "Get some booze too."

"Ride with me and get what you want," I said. He nodded and got up to follow me.

"I'll throw some potatoes in the oven," Jesse said. Then he grinned and said, "We'll fill everyone up on tators so we don't spend so much on meat." He was silly when he was happy. His band was complete again and things were good with Christy, so he was a happy guy.

"Good idea. I'll get stuff for a salad. That's cheap too," I said.

"Wait," Jesse said. "Let me see if I have that already." He opened the fridge and pulled out a head of iceberg that was limp and browning and a sad, already cut, slimy Roma tomato. He held them up. "What do you think?"

Trent turned his nose up at it and I said, "I think I can afford two dollars for fresh."

"I want to stop at a music store first," I told Trent as we drove off in my Jeep.

" 'K. There's a Sam Goody just down the road." He pointed and said, "Turn right when you get to the stop sign, then it's in the strip center on your right."

I followed his directions, and in a few minutes, I was looking for Alexandra Blake tapes or CDs. I found the one I already had in CDs and a few others in tapes. I took both tapes and went to the magazine section. I looked through all the entertainment magazines, but nothing about her. She hadn't been popular for at least ten years. I took the tapes to the checkout. While the checkout girl was struggling with the plastic security holders, Trent walked up.

"Find anything you can't live without?" I asked.

He shook his head and turned to the girl. "Hey, Olivia."

She smiled big. "Hi, Trent."

"Evan leave anything for me?"

"No, sorry," she answered apologetically, like she really wished Evan would have left something to please Trent. She finally got my tapes out and took my credit card.

When we got back to the Jeep, I put one of the cassettes in. About halfway through the first song, Trent looked at me with great distaste. "Why the hell are we listening to this?"

"I'm just trying to learn all I can about her."

He raised an eyebrow. "Why?"

I thought about telling him but then decided to keep my infatuation to myself for the time being. "I just want to succeed, and you guys say she is the one that can make or break me." He seemed to accept that.

When we got back to the apartment, Amy and Christy were watching *Less than Zero* on cable. Trent and I each mixed an

Absolute Citron and tonic while Jesse got the steaks and chicken breasts ready for the grill. He put Saran Wrap under and over them and then pounded the steaks and chicken with a tenderizing hammer. Then he took each one and carefully dried it with a paper towel and seasoned it heavily with salt and lightly with pepper.

"These won't take long," he called over his shoulder. "You mind throwing together a salad?"

I washed the lettuce and tomato and dried them with paper towels. I took a large knife and started slicing up the lettuce. Jesse came back inside, leaving the door open behind him. The grill was already filling the apartment with delightful aromas.

"You're going to brown the lettuce slicing it with a knife," he said. "You're supposed to tear it apart."

"First of all, we're going to eat it all in a few minutes, and second of all, is that what happened to the brown slimy mess you had in the vegetable drawer?"

"No," he laughed. "Just not sure how long it's been in there."

I was doomed to live with people who didn't throw food out when it was no longer eatable. "Where'd you learn to prep the meat like that?" I asked him.

"Cooking shows," he said, as he put the cut-up lettuce and tomato in a bowl.

After we had a large bowl of salad prepared, we went outside. Maggie was licking the grease droppings behind the grill. I made a mental note to hang a can to catch the grease.

Amy came outside and started hanging on me, which got on my nerves a little. I wasn't really interested in anything with her. I realized between her and Lisa that I was not meant for one-night stands. I felt guilty for not calling after, but also not sure that my call was even wanted. It was an uncomfortable dilemma. Now here was Amy making it clear that she did want more, and my thoughts were elsewhere.

When the steaks and chicken were finally done, Jesse brought them in and dropped one on everybody's plate. Chicken breast for the girls and me and steak for Jesse and Trent. The chicken was tasty and moist, but when I saw the blood ooze onto the plate from Jesse's rare steak, I regretted opting for the chicken. I turned to look at Trent's steak. It was well-done. What a shame to ruin such a beautiful thing.

Christy and Jesse looked almost domestic attending to everyone's needs. Christy brought everyone except Trent a baked potato. She had cut a potato up for him and made him French fries, which made me think for the moment maybe she wasn't so bad. He shook salt and pepper on them then dunked each one in ketchup. I licked my lips and almost reached over and grabbed one.

By the time we fished eating, it was almost ten. We'd all had three or four drinks, and I was ready to go to sleep. I wanted to be fresh and alert when I saw Miss Blake the next day. So, when Jesse suggested we play nickel-dime-quarter poker, I declined.

"Come on, old man," he said. "It's barely ten and we don't have to be there until eleven tomorrow."

"Few more drinks?" Trent asked. "I'll get up early with you to practice your song again."

"It'll be fun," Amy chimed in.

"Okay, all right," I agreed. Trent's puppy dog face made it hard to say no. "You guys know how to play Guts?" I asked. None of them did. This was going to be fun.

# 9

Jesse went to his bedroom and returned with a large pickle jar filled with change. He and Christy scooped out change, while Trent, Amy, and I each bought twenty dollars' worth from him. Amy and Christy cleared the table, and Trent made us all fresh drinks. Jesse put CDs in the player, while I stacked my coins and checked that the deck had all the cards.

Once we were all seated, I said, "Okay. Everybody antes a nickel." I tossed a nickel to the center of the table. Everyone did the same. I explained the rules to the game, apparently in too much detail, because I'd completely lost Trent's attention and Jesse was rolling his eyes like I would never shut up.

"Sounds easy enough," Christy said. "Let's play."

Amy put her hand on my thigh. "Yeah, I think I can handle it. Let's play."

"Wait, there's more rules," I said. I didn't like Amy's hand on me, but I couldn't very well push it away. I was in a good mood from meeting Alexandra and was looking forward to seeing her again the next day. So, I chose to ignore Amy's hand in hopes she would stop. But if Christy tried that bullshit again, I would make a scene.

"Oh my God, let's just play," Jesse said impatiently.

I dealt the cards. Trent won with a pair of twos. "Trent take the pot, the rest of you put in twenty-five cents."

"But I have a straight," Jesse said. "In poker—"

"Remember, straights and flushes don't count," Trent said.

"That's dumb," Jesse said as he tossed in a quarter.

Christy laughed, "Don't be a sore loser."

"Just put your quarter in," Jesse said, pointing irritably at the change in the center of the table.

Christy and Amy put their money in. "Remember, now the pot is seventy-five cents," I said as I shuffled.

I dealt again and happened to glance at Jesse while he looked at his cards. I almost laughed aloud when I saw the joy on his face. I hoped for it to be as good as he apparently thought it was, but it wasn't meant to be. "Amy wins with the eight kicker," I announced. "Christy and Jesse, seventy-five cents each."

"Man, this can get expensive fast," Jesse mumbled.

"Yeah," Trent said. "Now it's a buck fifty if you lose. How much you think is in that pickle jar, Jess?"

"You worry about you," Jesse replied. "Deal the cards, Cory."

I tossed Jesse the first card and dealt around. "Buck fifty if you lose," I reminded them. Once again, my cards were a mess. Jesse and Trent remained in. Jesse showed a pair of threes and Trent had a pair of eights.

"What the hell!" Jesse gave Trent the evil eye. It just wasn't Jesse's night.

Trent laughed. "Dollar fifty to you, Jess."

"Yeah, yeah," Jesse grumbled. "I need another drink."

Trent downed his and said, "Me too. Anybody else?"

My drink was still about a quarter full, but Trent took it anyway. Christy and Amy decided they wanted frozen drinks, so they went to the kitchen to make margaritas. I was left alone at the table. I stacked the coins in the pot neatly, then did the same to everybody's pile. Through the whir of the blender and the clinking of ice in glasses, I barely heard the phone ring. I stood to answer it when Trent called from the kitchen. "Make your drink stronger?" God no.

"No." I went into the kitchen. "It was good the way you made the last one." I hovered over him to make sure he didn't get heavy-handed and forgot all about the phone.

Once the drinks were made, we all headed back to the table. "Hey," Christy said. "Who messed with my pile?"

"Cory, did you stack everybody's pile?" Amy smiled and put her arm through mine, acting like she really knew me. It didn't take a rocket scientist to know it was me...the only one left alone in the room. Why did that annoy me?

I forced a smile. "We ready?"

"When is it my turn to pick the game?" Christy asked.

"When someone beats the dummy hand," Jesse barked.

I bit my lip not to laugh. Jesse took the change from his pile and slapped it into the middle of the table. The coins spun around, so he slapped them down again. I dealt again, starting with me. This time I had a pair of fives. Only Amy dropped out. The rest of us flipped our cards over. Jesse had a pair of nines, but Trent had a pair of jacks.

"Buck fifty to all of you suckers," Trent sang out joyfully, as he pulled the change in.

"Okay," I said as I shuffled the cards. "This time—"

"We know," Jesse grumbled. "It's four fifty if you lose. We get it."

All I could think was he's going to get a worry line between his eyes if he keeps frowning like that. I took a big gulp of my drink and tossed the cards. Amy peeked at her cards like she was afraid of what she'd find. Trent picked each one up as it landed in front of him like he could hardly wait to see how they would magically fit together. Jesse waited for all three to land, then snatched them all up to see what misfortune was to befall him next. Christy looked blankly at hers, completely unsure at this point of what constituted a good hand. I glanced down to find a pair of aces. Only Amy folded. I laid my hand on the table. Two aces and a jack. Jesse rolled his eyes and tossed in his cards.

"I think that beats me too," Christy said and showed her cards to Jesse.

He took them from her and threw them face down. We all turned to Trent. A mischievous grin spread across his face as he slowly laid down three tens.

"Asshole," I teased him as I counted the four fifty from my dwindling pile.

"So, what happens if we lose now?" Christy asked. "I don't have thirteen fifty if I lose again."

"You have to get more money outta the pickle jar," Trent sang out.

"But then what? This could get out of hand," she said.

"You could fold," Jesse said, visibly irritated.

"If I fold, I can't win."

"That's right," Trent agreed. Jesse gave him a look. "Well, she is right," Trent said.

"Shall I keep going?" I asked.

"Yes, you shall keep going." Jesse huffed. "The pot is right."

I shuffled the deck and slid Christy the first card. She looked at it like it might jump up and bite her. Jesse waited for all three cards to look and then immediately mucked them as if he'd been singled out for misfortune by the poker gods.

"What now?" she asked.

"You play against the dummy hand," I said. "Whatta you have?"

She slowly turned her hand over and laid it down. A pair of jacks and a ten. I reached for the dummy hand. "Okay, here we go," I said. I turned the cards over one at a time for suspense.

When she lost, Jesse sprang from his seat. "Oh my God! This is insane."

"This takes all of my money," Amy said as she counted out the last of it. "What do I do now?"

"You can just watch," I said.

"I'll be damned," she said, jumping from her chair. "Where's my purse?"

"Fuck," Jesse said incredulously. "There's twenty-seven dollars in the pot. When will it end?"

"When somebody beats the dummy," Trent answered.

Jesse glared at him. "I know that."

"Should we just call it?" I asked. Jesse was getting irritable at his bad run. He was trying desperately to control his results, but

Lady Luck wasn't having it, and I was kind of worried he and Christy would start fighting.

They all looked at me like I was crazy. "No!"

"Okay then, twenty-seven if you lose and a new dummy hand."

Everybody dropped out but Christy.

"What are you doing?" Jesse cried. "Wait, what do you have?"

She flipped over a pair of tens. Jesse buried his face in his hands. Then he looked up and grabbed the dummy hand. He looked at the hand and a smile spread across his face as he put the cards on the table one at a time. A jack, a queen, and a four. She beat the dummy and scooped in the twenty-seven dollars. You would have thought she won the lottery.

As the night wore on and the alcohol flowed, we all got tired and grumpy. A little after three, I finally said I was going to bed. Jesse and Christy agreed, and they went to his room. I figured Trent would sleep on the couch again, which would leave me with Amy. I just wanted to sleep. Trent surprised me, though, and said he was driving home.

"That's a really bad idea," I said. "You've been drinking heavily all night."

"I can take him," Amy offered.

My escape. But she had been drinking as well. A lot. "I don't think that's any better," I said. I could call them a cab, but who knew how long that would take. Why can't you just flip off alcohol when you're done with it?

Trent finally agreed to stay, so he turned on the TV and got comfortable on the couch, which again left me with Amy. Most of the alcohol had worn off, and though I was still a little buzzed,

I was tired more than anything. Not sure what else to say, I told her that I was going to take a quick shower. When I came out of the bathroom, she was sitting on the bed, leaning against the headboard and looking at a magazine.

"I can drive or stay out there with Trent if you want me to," she said.

I felt bad that I had made her feel unwelcome, but I didn't want to lead her on either. "Whatever makes you comfortable," I said.

She put the magazine down, jumped off the bed, and came over to me. She smelled like tequila and cigarette smoke, which was exaggerated by me being freshly showered. She was a beautiful woman that could probably get almost any guy she wanted.

"I want to sleep with you," she said, standing very close to me.

"Okay," I said. "Help yourself to the bathroom. I think there are some extra toothbrushes under the sink." I slid by her and went to set the alarm. She stepped into the bathroom, and moments later, I heard the shower.

As I got into bed and pulled up the blankets, I realized that in spite of myself, I missed my bed in Dallas and maybe even Jenny a little bit. I missed not knowing what she had done, and things being simple and predictable. Which led me to Alexandra Blake. I probably wasn't prepared for what she expected of me. I felt silly for thinking for a moment that she would be interested in me. Earlier in the evening as we all laughed and had fun together, I could hardly wait to see her again. Now, alone in the dark with the buzz fading, it seemed stupid of me. I started to drift off to fantasies of her when Amy slipped into bed next to me. I glanced over and could see the outline of her breasts and the blanket covering her below the waist. She smelled fresh from the shower, and I sleepily hoped she didn't use my towel to dry off. She started kissing my chest and made her way south. I didn't do anything to encourage her advancement, but I didn't stop her either. I felt ashamed of myself for missing Jennifer, wanting Alexandra, and having Amy. I played Suicide King songs in my head until she was finished, and then I fell asleep.

## 10

"Wake up," Jesse yelled from the hallway. "We can't be late again."

I glanced over at the clock radio. It was already almost ten, but I knew I set it for eight. After looking more closely, I found that I set it for 8:00 pm. Damn, I needed to get the hell out of my own way.

I suddenly remembered Amy and looked over to find that she wasn't there. Maybe she already left? I jumped out of bed and threw on some shorts and a tee. I put on my running shoes and went to find Maggie. I figured I had just enough time to take her out and then get ready to go.

When I walked into the living room, Christy, Jesse, and Trent were at the table eating. The smell of bacon filled the apartment. Maggie was at Amy's feet in the kitchen. I whistled for her, but she wasn't leaving cooking bacon, so I had to drag her out.

"You ready to go?" I asked Jesse as I pulled on Maggie.

"Waiting on you," he answered.

I got Maggie outside and put her leash on her, and we went for a run. I hadn't said anything to Amy. Not so much as a nod. I was being a jerk and I knew it, but I couldn't seem to help myself. I just wanted her gone when I got back. I wasn't going to have time to prepare for the studio and I blamed her. It was my own fault, and I knew that in my heart, but I didn't care. I had no idea what to expect from Miss Blake and wished that I had spent more time rehearsing and less time drinking and playing cards.

When I got back, Christy and Amy were walking to their car. I walked up to Amy and said, "Hey, I have to hurry and get ready. I'll call you later."

She leaned against the car and crossed her arms. Christy winked at me, then got inside and started it up. I wasn't sure what the wink was for. Was she just being friendly? Or was it in reference to her offer the first night I met her? Though I was antsy to get inside, I stood and waited for Amy to say something.

"I had fun with you last night," she finally said.

I nodded anxiously. "Yeah, me too."

"Then I'll see you later?"

I didn't want to get into anything, any type of discussion with her. "Sure."

She came in for a kiss. I made it a quick one then dashed inside. Jesse and Trent were ready to go and waiting on me.

"We don't have time for your full routine," Jesse said as I breezed past him.

There was no way I was going back to that studio looking anything less than my best. I wanted Alexandra Blake to want me, but first, I needed her to accept me. I needed her to know that I took the band seriously. I was able to shower and dress and get us out the door in record time.

When we got to the studio, Jeff came up to me and said that Miss Blake wanted to see me. I looked past him and saw her sitting in her office. She looked perfect. Every hair was in the right place, her clothing accentuated every curve, and even her expression said all was right in the world. I bet people never told her to smile. I wanted to be near her, but at the same time, I was too nervous to move.

"Go on," Jeff said. "She's not as scary as she seems."

I took a deep breath and buried the insecure little Texas boy and walked in the confident L.A. man. "You wanted to see me?"

She looked up from her work and gave me the once-over. "You look much better today. Have you gone over the material?"

I told her that I had.

"Very good," she said, making me feel like that little boy seeking approval. "I trust that I won't be disappointed when I hear for myself."

Again, I wished I had spent more time with the songs. "I'm sure you'll be pleased," I said, surprised at how sure I sounded.

"Good," she smiled. The smile sent electricity through me. "I was just looking at some photos," she went on. "Eddie spoke very highly of you."

I looked at the photos in front of her. On top of the pile was an old one of Eddie and me at our infamous last show. "He was a good friend," I said, feeling a beat of sadness. How cool it would have been if we were on this adventure together.

"He was a very talented musician. I heard recordings of you both, and I just hope you can do alone what we planned on the two of you doing together."

I didn't know what to say. There was no way I could do that.

"You didn't make a very good first impression yesterday," she said.

Be strong, Cory, be confident. "I know," I said. "I'll make it up to you today." Think positive, Cory, think positive. I was positive she could see right through me.

"So, then you're ready?" she asked.

"I am," I said. "What do you want me to do?"

She spun her chair around and stood. She was wearing a dress, and I caught myself eyeing her legs. Her long, smooth, strong legs. "Have you ever been in a recording studio?" she asked as she walked slowly towards me.

My heart began to pound so fast and hard that I felt it in my ears and thought surely she could hear it too. I hated to admit it. "No, I haven't."

"But you're sure you'll make it up to me today?" she said, suppressing a smile. Did I amuse her? No, I decided as she moved closer, she wasn't amused. She stopped so very close to me that I could smell the freshness of the soap on her skin.

I worried that if I spoke my voice would betray me and sound weak or timid. I cleared my throat and said, "Yes, I'm sure," with all the confidence I could summon.

The thrill of a new attraction hung thick in the air between us. I wanted to take her in my arms and throw her back into a movie-worthy kiss, but instead I stood as still as a marine with a drill sergeant in his ear.

"Just tell me what you want me to do," I said, remembering Jesse's advice.

"I assure you that I will do just that," she said. My face burned with awkward want. Why couldn't I be smooth and know how to turn this moment into something more?

"Follow me," she said as she wrapped her fingers around mine and lightly tugged. It sent a jolt up my arm, but she let go as soon as I took a step towards her.

She put me in the booth and handed me headphones. I wanted to pull her in that damn booth with me. I took the headphones. It felt like slow motion as we made eye contact.

"I want to hear you sing the lead on "Hard Times Again," she said.

"We're doing "Hard Times Again" ?" I asked, doing my best to shake the sexual tension and pay attention to her words.

"Is there a problem?" she asked, still giving me the suppressed smile look. Her beautiful brown eyes were dancing.

"No, not at all." I was relieved and elated. I had thought we were going to do Greg's song. Maybe she knew as much as I did that it stunk at its current state. I didn't come down from my high until we were on about the twelfth take. I looked out at the guys. Trent tossed his hair out of his face and nodded his approval. His dull green eyes had slight purple circles underneath them as if he hadn't slept in days. Jesse was pacing nervously, and Greg was sitting in the corner looking pissed off. When she instructed me to start again, Greg got up and went to say something to her. I couldn't hear them, but I figured it was because we weren't doing his song. Sooner or later, all of them had to be recorded, so I didn't understand his anger.

It was apparent they were arguing. I didn't know if I should come out of the booth or wait there. Alexandra appeared calm when Greg pointed at her, then threw his sticks across the room and stormed out. I took the headphones off and stepped from the booth. I was mad at Greg for talking to her like that and wanted to put him in his place. Trent went to pick the sticks up and sat on the couch. He tilted his head back and closed his eyes as if he were going to take a nap. Jesse and Jeff went after Greg, so I held back, not wanting to make matters worse. Alexandra went into her office and shut the door. I wanted to go in after her, but instead, I went and sat next to Trent.

"Don't worry," he said without opening his eyes. "This happens a lot."

"What do you think of her?" I asked, unconcerned with Greg's outburst.

"I think she can be unreasonable sometimes," he said. "But she's giving us an opportunity, so I guess it's her right."

Just then, Greg came flying back into the room, no less incensed than when he flew out. "I don't know what the hell I'm even doing here," he said as he smacked the cymbals on his drums. He didn't seem to be talking to anybody in particular. "I'm working with three fucking thugs, a prima donna, and a goddamn fag."

Trent turned to me. "I'm not a thug."

"Hell no," I said. "Jeff's gay?"

He shrugged. "I don't think so."

Jeff was not far behind Greg. He charged in and got right in Greg's face. They both began yelling, neither one listening to the other. Jesse tried hopelessly to calm them down while Trent and I just watched. Greg was an asshole, that I knew.

"What do you think?" I said. "About Miss Blake."

"I just told you. She's unreasonable," Trent said. "I don't know what they're arguing about, but Greg is wasting his energy. Why do you keep asking me about her?"

"I think she knows what she's doing, and Greg is wasting our time," I said.

"Greg started all of this," Trent said. "And now he sees it all slipping away. She should just let him sing his song and let's move on."

"You think that's what this is about?"

"I don't know. But I know that would shut him up."

Alexandra came out of her office as calm as if nothing had happened. She instructed Jeff and Greg to go in and closed the door behind them. I watched through the window. Jesse came over and plopped down on the couch next to me. Trent and I looked at him to clue us in.

"It's my bad," he said. "I suggested to Greg we do a little rewrite on his song. Then when he heard you guys start with your song, he came unglued."

I didn't really care why Greg was upset. I was happy to be there, and I felt like he should feel the same. Finally, he seemed to calm down, and he and Jeff left the office. I wondered what was said to appease him and if he was going to get his way about the songs. Alexandra closed the blinds to her window and shut the door. Jeff called us back to work. Damn, I wanted to be in that office with her.

When we were finished for the day, she pulled me aside. "You did very well today," she said. "Are you feeling comfortable with everything?"

"I'm getting there," I said. We were standing in the hallway, and I found myself wishing she had taken us to her office. In the hallway she would not be concerned with anybody hearing us, which left me strangely disappointed.

"I have something scheduled for the band this weekend," she said. "Should I cancel it?"

"No," I said sharply. "I'll be ready." I would make sure I was ready. I wouldn't let any opportunity to be around her slip away.

She smiled politely. Politely. Did I imagine the chemistry between us? I wanted a real smile. I didn't know how yet, but I would figure out how to get it. "Wonderful," she said. "Then I'll see you tomorrow." She started to walk away, then she looked over her shoulder and gave me a look that said maybe I hadn't imagined everything. "Don't forget your guitars."

"I think she likes me," I said to Jesse on the way home.

He looked at me like I was an idiot. "Don't count on it. She likes what you can give her."

"What can I possibly give her?" I asked.

"Hopefully, a hit record."

"I see that as she's giving me something," I said. "Let's rehearse tonight. I want to sound better tomorrow."

"No way," Jesse said. "I'm tired. The girls are coming over, and I'm grilling fish."

"I don't want to see Amy tonight," I said. I told him that I needed the practice to be ready for the weekend, but he said he was grilling fish and that was that.

"Okay, fine," I said. "I'll call Trent and see if he wants to go out."

Jesse then informed me that he needed me to be there for Amy. We argued for about two minutes before I gave in and said I'd stay home. "I'm still going to ask Trent to come over," I said.

Amy and Christy were already there when we got home. Trent showed about an hour later with the movie *The Doors* and a case of Amstel Light. I started to think I should forget about my two-week break and get back to work, if only to get some rest.

Jennifer always asked me why I liked to drink so much. I liked the taste and the way it made me feel. When I was buzzed, I wasn't shy or insecure about anything. In fact, I could be down-right cocky. I liked that feeling. The next day wasn't always so great, but you take the bad with the good.

Trent put the beers in the fridge, keeping one out for me and one for himself. He tossed me mine as he fell into the couch next to me. He picked up the guitar that was leaning against the end table and started strumming it. Just on the other side of the sliding glass door, Jesse was at the grill. He was gentle with the fish filets as he removed them from the grill and slid them onto a plate. Maggie waited patiently for any droppings or handouts.

Trent started playing the acoustical version of "Stairway to Heaven," but it was hard to listen because Amy and Christy were fussing in the kitchen. They seemed to be debating who should clean up the kitchen. Finally, Jesse went in there and told them to shut up he would clean the damn kitchen. I thought that was funny, but Christy gave me a dirty look, and Amy told me I was insensitive. I thought that was a stupid reason to call me insensitive and told her so. She proceeded to tell me that I was being a jerk while Christy started in on Jesse. "This," I said, "is from spending too much time together." That did not go over well either.

Trent stood up and switched from Led Zeppelin to Bob Seger's "I Feel Like a Number." Then he tossed the guitar on the sofa and walked out, mumbling about how tiring we were. The bathroom door closed and locked behind him.

Christy and Amy looked at each other, and Christy said, "Now see what you've done?" and they resumed bickering. I went into the kitchen and navigated my way around them to grab another beer from the fridge, then went outside with Maggie. I threw an old tennis ball into the field for her. It was gloriously quiet for about thirty seconds before Amy came out. She put her arms around my waist and apologized for being irritable. I wondered what I had done to make her feel so free about touching me. I wanted to remove her arms because at that moment I felt nothing for her.

I took a long drink of beer and threw the tennis ball again, pleased that Maggie would retrieve it and return. Sometimes she dropped it, sometimes I had to pry it from her mouth. When I threw the ball, it effectively shrugged Amy off me. She went back inside without saying anything more, and I felt like an asshole yet again.

I turned and leaned against the balcony to look inside the apartment. Christy glanced up and our eyes briefly met. I had to ask myself if maybe I didn't like her because I was somewhat like her. She pushed the limits to see what she could get away with. Maybe to a degree, I did the same thing with Jennifer. I took the dog home, knowing she wouldn't want her. I invited Jesse to stay without checking with her. I didn't get my way about California, so maybe I demanded my way about everything else? Jennifer thought it was only a matter of time before I would go to L.A. Maybe she was right about that. I suddenly realized that maybe I did push her into the safety of someone else's arms.

The grilled fish started to sound pretty good, so I went inside. I headed to the bathroom first and bumped into Trent on his way out.

"Sorry," he mumbled, as he tried to get by me.

Not sure why I enjoyed messing with him so much, I stood firm in his path.

"What are you doing?" he asked.

His eyes were glassy, and he had an almost imperceptible trace of white on his nose. "You have something on your nose," I said.

He wiped across his nose and looked at his hand. He licked the minuscule spot of white. "Stuff's expensive," he said, and forced his way by me. I got out of his way and watched him join the others.

I went into the bathroom and looked around to see if Trent had left anything in there. I wasn't sure what I was going to do with it if I found it, but it turned out not to matter. He used up or kept on his person whatever he had.

When I got back to the living room, Jesse and Christy were outside groping each other and Amy was at the table painting her nails and smoking a cigarette. Trent was in the recliner with his foot on the floor spinning it around. Apparently, dinner was a less formal occasion this evening. I went into the kitchen and made myself a plate of mahi mahi and grilled zucchini and ate standing by the sink.

My mind wandered to Alexandra Blake, and I wondered what she was doing at that very moment. The thought of her there hanging out with us amused me. I couldn't picture her playing Guts or drinking beer with us. Which posed the question: What did I want from her? Did I want her to step down into my world? Or did I want to disappear into hers? Anything more than a fantasy seemed hopeless. I finished eating, rinsed my plate, and went into the living room. The clock on the VCR read 8:06 pm. I put *The Doors* movie in and tried to watch it, but my mind was still obsessing with Alexandra. What would she be doing at eight at night? Would it be something as simple as watching television? Dancing at a nightclub? Having sex? What was she doing at that exact moment that I was thinking of her? Was there any way in hell she was thinking of me?

Amy slid onto the couch next to me and kissed me on the cheek. I patted her on the leg awkwardly. Not only was I not interested in her following me to my room again, but I also wanted her to leave me alone right now with my thoughts.

The apartment suddenly smelled like something frying, so I looked up to find Christy in the kitchen again. I wondered what she was cooking, and then realized she was making French fries. I wanted some of those fries. A few minutes later, she brought Trent a plate with a piece of fish and a pile of fries with ketchup squirted on them. "Eat some dinner," she said. "I made you your French fries."

Trent took the plate without saying anything, ate a few of the fries, and then picked up the fish and gave the entire thing to Maggie. She gobbled it up before Christy even had a chance to object. Christy snatched the plate from Trent's grip, causing messy fries to slide right off the plate. Maggie gobbled those up too. "I give up on you," she told him. "That was an expensive piece of fish." He didn't respond. "Whatever," she said as she turned to storm off. "Don't expect me to make you French fucking fries ever again," she said from the kitchen. She dropped the plate into the sink, making a clanging sound that brought Jesse inside. He looked around as if saying, now what?

"Come on, Amy. Let's go," she said as she grabbed her purse and went for the door.

Amy stood up and said, "Why do guys have to be such dicks?" and followed Christy out. Jesse gave us both a scolding look and followed them.

"What did I do wrong?" I said to Trent.

He stood up and said, "Want to go to my house?"

# 11

"Damn, I forgot the beer," Trent said.

I pulled into a convenience store so he could buy more. Although he hadn't had much to drink, I told him I would drive, and he could get his car later. I had very little experience with drugs, so I didn't know if the white powder would impair his driving. I figured if I drove him home, then at least he wouldn't go out and get into any trouble.

Although I was in a band and hung around a lot of musicians, I never got into any drugs. I didn't mind if people smoked weed around me, but I always made it clear that I wasn't into anything hard-core and didn't want to be around them. My mother's real father, not the man that raised her or that I called Grandpa, but her biological father, was a drug addict. It was drilled in our heads since we were old enough to understand English that drugs would not be tolerated. My parents even took Kevin and me to the police station when were little and had the officers give us a good scare.

A few of my high school buddies got into various drugs, one of them heavily. We drifted apart when it went from joints to needles. I saw him a few years later after he'd gotten his life back together. He had false teeth at twenty-one. No thanks.

I didn't judge Trent. I just didn't want anything bad to happen to him.

When he got back in the car with his beer, he immediately opened one and turned up the radio. The expression he gave me when we realized that the Alexandra Blake tape was still in made me laugh. I found the Nirvana tape for him and turned up the volume. We drove the rest of the way with "Smells Like Teen Spirit" blasting.

When we pulled up to his house, we needed a code to enter. I punched in the numbers as he told them to me, then the gates swung open, and I pulled up the long steep driveway. Trent instructed me to pull up to the front door to park.

It was dark outside, so I couldn't see exactly what the house looked like or how big, but it was sure something. Trent jumped out of the Jeep, and I grabbed the beer and followed him. He punched another code to unlock the enormous, heavy wooden front door. As soon as we stepped into the foyer, the housekeeper came running up demanding in Spanish and broken English that we move the Jeep. Something about his dad getting angry. Trent ignored her and kept going, so I continued to follow him. I smiled at the woman apologetically.

As we walked through the living room, I saw who I assumed to be Trent's mother sitting on a gray sofa with her legs tucked up next to her. She had a remote control that she continually flipped the channels with in one hand and a drink and cigarette in the other. She looked really tired, like if she were to sleep for a few days she would be very attractive. As we walked through the room, she watched Trent without emotion. He glanced her way but said nothing. Just as we were about to pass her, she said, "Trent, be a dear and make me another drink, would ya, honey?" He stopped abruptly, which made me run into him. He turned and went to the bar while I stood there awkwardly. She looked at me and smiled. I wasn't sure if it was meant as a seductive smile or just a friendly one. Either way, I felt sorry for her because it was just a sad smile.

As Trent mixed his mother's drink, he asked her, "Where's Bryan?"

"He's at Monica's house," she answered as she looked me over. "He'll be home next week."

Trent went to his mother and set her drink on the coffee table so abruptly that some splashed onto his hand. He licked it off and said, "Come on, Cory, let's go upstairs." He looked at his mother with disgust then headed up the stairs.

I shook his mother's hand and told her it was nice to meet her. She held on for a few seconds too long before giving it a final squeeze. Trent had already disappeared up the stairs by the time she let go.

When I made it to the top of the long spiral stairway, he was waiting for me. "Coo coo ca choo," he said.

"Stop it," I said and gave him a shove. "I was just being polite."

"Whatever you say," he said as he took off down the hallway.

When we got to his room, he opened the door and flipped on the light. It was just a desk lamp, so it was still pretty dark. He locked the door behind us, then flopped onto his bed. He pointed to the beers I was still carrying, so I tossed him one. He got comfortable, took a swig, and said, "Shit. I forgot to turn on the stereo. Toss me that remote."

I took the remote from his dresser and tossed it to him. He pointed it to his Nakamichi sound system and turned it on. Nirvana filled the room much too loud for conversation. He watched the red and green lights until his eyes fluttered and he fell asleep. I put the beers on his dresser, then took his and put it on his nightstand.

Trent's bedroom was as big as the master bedroom in my parents' house, and it had its own bathroom. The room was very neat and clean, which I guessed was probably the work of the housekeeper. Over the bed hung an original abstract oil painting of red, yellow, and shades of blue guitars. On his desk, there was a picture of Trent with who I guessed to be his younger brother. There were also three art books, one with papers sticking out. I opened it to see that the papers were sketches. Really good sketches of naked men. I sat down in a comic book print over-stuffed chair and started flipping through the books. One of them was instructional, and the others were pictures of famous works.

Trent stirred and called for me. "Cory, you still here?"

"Yeah," I said.

He sat up and rubbed his eyes and turned down the volume. "Sorry," he said. "How long was I out?"

"Only about twenty minutes," I answered. "That your brother?"

He looked at the picture and then at me, seeing that I had seen his sketches. I worried that maybe I had violated his privacy, but his eyes were expressionless. "Yeah," he finally said. "That's my brother, Bryan, though he would never admit it. He's at my grandmother's house. He stays there a lot." Trent pointed over his shoulder to the painting. "Bryan painted that. He loves art and is really good at it. I'm trying to learn about art so we have something in common." I nodded and he went on. "I used to read Dr. Seuss to him when he was a kid. He hates me now."

"I'm sure he doesn't hate you," I said, though how could I know?

"Trust me, Cory. Bryan hates me."

"Why?" I asked. "What did you do?"

"I have some pot. Want a joint?"

I told him that I didn't, but he got up to roll one anyway. He sat at the desk and concentrated on it like he was performing surgery. When he was done, he lit it and took a long drag. He looked at it with admiration and handed it to me. I took it and watched him. He tilted his head back, closed his eyes, and slowly blew out the smoke. When he opened his eyes, I handed it back to him.

Suddenly, somebody started banging on the door. Startled, I jumped out of my chair as if I'd been caught doing something shady.

"Open the door, Trent," demanded the man.

Trent stubbed out the joint and put it and the ashtray in his desk drawer. "My father," he said as he went to let him in. Why do rich people always say father and middle-class people say dad? What did poor people say?

"What the hell is going on in here?" he demanded. "Why was the door locked?"

Trent said, "Nothing. We're just hanging out."

Trent's dad was big and wore an expensive-looking suit. His gold silk tie was tied snugly against his neck. I pulled my own collar from my neck, feeling discomfort for him, and wondered why he didn't loosen it. I looked up from his tie to see that he was glaring at me. I held out my hand and introduced myself. He ignored my gesture and said, "I don't need my son hanging around you guys. We have enough trouble as it is."

Not knowing what to say, or who he thought I was, I took a step back.

"You have the wrong idea," Trent said to him. "Cory is the ideal son. He played football and baseball in school and even has a real job. Tell him about it, Cory."

Trent's dad looked at me expectantly. "I work for the FAA," I said meekly, wishing I was someplace else.

"Yeah," Trent said. "He only hangs out with me because he has a thing for Miss Alexandra Blake."

"Is that right," his dad said, like he didn't know what else to say. "Where's your mother?"

"In front of the TV."

"What else is new," he muttered as he turned to leave. "Leave the door open," he said and pushed the door all the way against the wall before he left.

Trent watched him leave and then turned to me. "You do want Miss Blake, don't you?"

I nodded. I wanted her desperately.

"You just want to fuck her?" he asked as he stood and shut the door.

"I don't know," I admitted. "I just know that I think about her all the time." I'd thought about every inch of her body, and

I knew from these fantasies exactly what she looked like under those expensive clothes.

"It doesn't bother you that she's way older than you?"

"No, not at all," I said. "I don't think she's that much older." I didn't care about any of that at this point, because at this point, she was still just a fantasy.

"It doesn't bother you that she's Black?" he asked. He thought for a second and then said, "Light skin, but Black nonetheless."

"No," I said. "Should it?" Her skin was a beautiful caramel that I longed to touch and taste.

"I don't think so," he said as he retrieved his joint. "All people feel the same in the dark. What about your parents?"

"I think they would be more concerned about her age. You know, the grandkids thing." My parents? Grandkids? Are you fucking kidding me? This woman wasn't going to give me the time of day. Damn reality invading my fantasies again.

He lit the joint. "Well, what about that?"

"I don't know," I said, suddenly feeling a bit down. "I haven't thought that far ahead. She doesn't even know I feel this way." She had to know. We shared something today. I wasn't sure what, but it had to be something. "I doubt she would see me the way I'd like her to." Disappointment washed over me like a cold shower. What were the odds that something like this would ever work out?

"I don't get it," Trent said as we both sat again, him on the bed and me on the chair. "But the heart wants what the heart wants."

"She fascinates me," I admitted. "She is so confident and independent...and sexy as hell." And a part of almost every thought and dream.

"People can be deceiving," Trent said and blew smoke my way. "People are rarely what they seem."

"What do you mean? Are you not what you seem?" I asked. Trent seemed so young and empty. Being around him made me feel protective of him. I wasn't sure why. He just seemed to need it.

"I don't know. How do I seem?" he asked.

"Empty," I said without thinking.

"I guess sometimes people are what they seem." He smiled as if he were joking, but we both knew better. Trent had laid back down and was having trouble keeping his eyes open. I sat back quietly in the comic print chair, depressed at the whole damn thing. Things weren't right in this household, and a romance with Alexandra Blake was impossible. Once he was asleep, I threw away the evidence of the joint and pulled his black Doc Martins off. I turned the light off and shut the door behind me.

Most of the lights in the house were off. The hallway was dark, the only light coming from under a closed door. I ran my hand along the wall hoping to find a light switch, to no avail. The glow and the muffled sound from the television guided me down the stairs. I stepped softly, hoping to leave without Trent's mom seeing me, but she spotted me and asked me where I was going.

"I'm just going home," I said. "Trent's asleep."

She took a long drag from her cigarette. The orange glow traveled down the cigarette as she sucked on it. She blew out the smoke and said, "Why don't you have a drink with me first?"

She was actually a very sexy lady, but she was Trent's mother, and that made her offer seem weird. "I can't. I have someone waiting for me. Can you make sure the gate is open?"

She knew I was lying. She stared at me for what felt like a very long time before she stood and went to punch in the numbers. "You're free to go now," she said.

She had the same expressionless green eyes as Trent. "Thanks," I said and left, wondering exactly when she had lost her self-respect.

When I got back to the apartment, I was glad to find that Jesse was there alone. "You still in hot water?" I asked.

"No, but she decided to stay at her apartment tonight." He put down the magazine he was reading, clearly still irritated.

"I don't know what it is about him," I said. "He does something crappy like that and I feel sorry for him."

"You're wasting your energy. He's never going to change."

Jesse's magazine was the latest edition of *Circus* with Kurt Cobain on the cover, which made me think of Trent. Should I save it for him, or had he already seen it?

"Mrs. Austin hit on you?" Jesse asked.

"No," I lied, imagining my own mother that lonely.

# 12

On Thursday morning, I met Trent at the library where he volunteered. I still hadn't had an opportunity to talk to Alexandra about anything but the band, so I wanted to look up everything I could about her. When we walked inside, he and his guitar went his way, and I went mine. There wasn't really a good reason for going to the library with Trent. I could have looked everything up on my own. Maybe I just didn't feel as stalkery with him there? I promised myself I would learn what I could and then just man up and talk to her.

Some digging in the magazine archives turned up articles in *Rolling Stone, People,* and *TV Guide.* She had been big in the seventies and done a few movies in the mid-eighties, but not much information on any recent activities. If only there were a single place where a person could look up everything about something. I wasn't sure what I was even looking for or hoping to find. A "how-to" article on romancing a celebrity? This was crazy. It was time to go find Trent...after I checked the book section.

The book section produced a "tell-all" book about Miss Alexandra Blake. It was over three hundred pages long. If I checked it out, would that approach the very definition of stalking? After flipping through it and looking at all the pictures, I started at page one.

After about fifteen minutes, I conceded that the book would take hours, if not days, to finish. If only I could scan it in a few minutes. I put it back on the shelf and started to go look for Trent, but then went back for it. I walked away once more before finally taking it from the shelf again. What if she found out I checked it out? Would she be angry? Would she look down on me? Or would she just think I was cheap because I didn't buy it? After skimming through it for about fifteen minutes more, I put it back on the shelf for the last time. I would buy the book.

Trent was reading Dr. Seuss to preschoolers when I found him. When he saw me, he stood up, put down the book, and picked up his guitar. He finished the book by playing the guitar and singing the words. The kids clapped their hands with delight.

"That's pretty cool," I said as we walked through the library.

"I love Dr. Seuss," Trent said. "He's a genius. Nobody else like him. All you can do is copy him." Then he rapped a verse of *Green Eggs and Ham*. An older lady whispered to her husband as we passed by, "Drugs." The husband nodded in complete agreement.

"What do you want to do now?" Trent asked, his eyes squinting from the sun.

"I want to run to the bookstore. Then whatever."

"Where's everybody else?" he asked.

"Jesse and Christy are out running around. I think Amy's at work."

Trent nodded. "I know where there's a party."

I looked at my watch. Eleven twenty.

"It's a carryover from last night," he explained as if that cleared it all up.

"Our studio time is at three. How about we go to the bookstore, then get some lunch, then head to the studio?"

"Go ahead," Trent said. "I'll see you at the studio." Then he started walking to his car.

Damn. Technically, there was no reason why I shouldn't expect him there at three. He hadn't missed any time. Why did I doubt him? It nagged at me as I walked to my Jeep. Fully intending to go to the bookstore, I pulled out of the library parking lot and headed that way. Then I ignored the no U-turn sign and flipped back to follow him.

Twenty minutes later, we pulled into the driveway of a small white house that was in dire need of paint and lawn care. The bushes were completely overgrown, and the yard was dry dirt with a few weed patches here and there. The house was an eyesore in an otherwise middle-class, clean neighborhood. "What happened to the bookstore?" Trent asked, as we walked to the door.

"I'll get there," I said. "Where are all the cars? I think the party may be over." There were two other cars in the drive and a few more on the street.

Before he knocked on the door, Trent said, "Guess we'll see." He leaned against the porch rail and said, "Why are you here? You aren't going to drink or anything before we go to the studio."

"Just to hang out with you," I said.

"You mean to babysit?"

"No. Just hang out."

"You know I'm going to do what I want to do. You being here doesn't change that."

"I know," I said.

"If you go in there, there is a good chance you'll come out smelling like weed. Or at the very least, cigarette smoke. Miss Blake won't like that."

"You're right," I said. "So why don't we blow this off and go get some food?"

"I'm going in there," Trent said. "You can go get food. I will be at the studio by three. I promise. I keep my promises...I promise." He smiled at his cleverness.

"I'm already here," I said. "Let's go on in."

Trent knocked on the door, and a few minutes later, it swung open. For a second, I thought I was face-to-face with Steven Tyler. Trent laughed. "This is my buddy John," he said to me. "He fronts an Aerosmith cover band." I nodded. That made a lot more sense.

John apparently liked to stay in character because he was shirtless and wore leopard print spandex pants. "Nice to meet you," he said, taking my hand and shaking it vigorously. "You guys should have been here last night," John said. "It was insane." He threw out his arms and his eyes got big for emphasis.

"I totally forgot," Trent said. "And you should put on some jeans or something. I can totally see your junk." You totally could.

"Yeah, yeah, no problem," John said. "You guys want a drink or something?"

We walked through the living room, which had beer bottles strewn about as well as a few half empty bottles of Jack Daniels on the coffee table. A couple of guys were in the living room watching television. The living room had gold shag carpet that looked like it was installed in the seventies.

"What time did it break up?" Trent asked as we all pulled up a chair to the kitchen table.

"Man." John shook his head like he couldn't believe it. "The cops showed up around two and then again this morning at sunlight. We weren't even being loud or nothing."

"You should tidy up the front," I said. "You know, so it looks like the other houses on the block. You want to blend."

"That's a good idea." John lit up. "Yeah." He nodded emphatically. "Thanks for the advice."

Trent went to the refrigerator and brought back three beers. He set a bottle of Corona in front of me. "We'll be right back." John took a beer from Trent and followed him. I watched them walk down the hallway and until they disappeared into another room. I knew what they were doing, but I didn't know what to do about it. I opened the Corona and took a long drink.

The front door opened and slammed, and in walked a guy that looked like he'd been yachting. He stopped when he saw me. "Trent here?" he asked. I nodded and pointed down the hallway with my Corona bottle. Yacht Boy went down the hallway and into the same room. A few seconds later, John came back to the kitchen.

"You hungry?" he asked.

I was starving. "No, I'm okay."

John opened the refrigerator and filled his arms with sandwich fixings and closed the door with his foot. He dumped the items onto the table and dropped two pieces of white bread directly on the grimy, fingerprint-smudged table. He squeezed mustard on the bread and slathered a glob of mayonnaise into the mustard. When he pulled the plastic container of the bologna open, I could see that it was slightly green around the edges. He pulled out a piece of bologna and pinched off the green with dirty fingernails and tossed it to the trash can behind him. My stomach turned. Finally, he pulled the plastic wrapper from his cheese slice and laid the slice onto the slimy bologna. I started to tell him to dry off the bologna with a paper towel but stopped myself. John slapped the piece of bread on top and lifted the sandwich to his mouth and took a huge bite. He seemed satisfied with the results.

I jumped from my chair and called for Trent. I'd had enough. I was there to keep an eye on Trent, and he was in a bedroom doing God-knows-what while I watched this fool make a bologna sandwich. He stuck his head out of the other room. "What?"

"Let's go," I said.

"Okay. Hang on." He popped back in the room, emerging a few seconds later with glassy eyes and a bottle of Jack. Just how many bottles did they need?

I started to insist that Trent ride with me but, after thinking about it, determined it was better if I followed him. We had only been at John's house for about an hour. If I took him back after the studio, he could end up driving after several hours of partying.

We went back to the apartment to let Maggie out and find something to eat. When I set a bowl of soup in front of him, he turned his nose up and pushed it away. "I'm not hungry."

"You want something else?"

"No."

"French fries?"

"I'm not hungry...Dad."

I took the soup and put it on the floor for Maggie. "I have to take her for a run. Be right back and we can ride to the studio together. Okay?"

He nodded, so I grabbed the leash and took her to the dog park. We did our usual run and went back to the apartment. Trent was gone. I hated Trent on drugs. Aside from the health concerns, he was an asshole when he was high.

When I got to the studio, I was disappointed to find that Alexandra wasn't there. Trent showed up on time as promised. I didn't bother asking why he left the apartment. Like he said, he was going to do what he wanted to do.

When I asked Jesse why Miss Blake wasn't there, he said that she was probably taking care of the details of the show. "Let's get to work," he said. "We only have tonight and tomorrow to get ready."

I agreed and we worked hard all afternoon. She showed up about halfway through the rehearsal, which I of course was happy about, but the others all moaned, knowing it would be a longer workday.

Once again, she had me do things over and over again. Jesse and Trent got antsy, while Greg complained that I wasn't as good as they all had hoped.

To this, she stopped and said, "Trent and Jesse, find something to do. Greg, why don't you call it a day."

Trent and Jesse looked at each other, clearly not sure what they were to do, and Greg gave her a "Whatever" look.

"That was not a request," she said, mainly to Greg.

We all stayed silent, waiting to see if there would be another blowup. Greg apparently thought better of it and left, shaking his head and muttering to himself.

She returned her attention to me and patiently explained what she was looking for. Whenever she sensed me doubting myself, she would squeeze my hand and encourage me.

We had been working on a song called "Her Tears" when she stopped everything. Standing close enough for me to feel her breath she said, "I need you to dig deeper. I know you have more." She touched my chin and lifted so that our eyes met. "Don't pay any attention to them. There's nobody here but you and me. Sing to me like you mean it."

So, I did.

"Perfect," she said. "Absolutely perfect. Jeff, I think we should add some girls in backup. Anybody available?"

The guys were ready to go. They didn't like her. They saw her as demanding, controlling, and condescending. I saw her as someone that believed in perfection and that believed in me.

"Nobody available at the moment," Jeff said. "We can schedule it. Or...you could do it."

"I guess I don't have a choice," she said. "I want it done now." She looked at all of us and said, "This is going to take a while. You boys can stay or go."

Jesse and Trent were happy to go. I, of course, stayed. I was a little bit surprised when she was as tough or maybe even more so on herself than she ever was on any of us. It was the same grind of doing it numerous times until she felt it was perfect. Also, turns out she was right. Adding a strong female voice for backup brought the song to a whole new level. When she and Jeff were finished, parts of the song sounded like she and I were singing to each other, which I thought was really cool.

"Thanks for today," I told her as we were leaving. It was late and had been a long day.

Jeff walked by and said, "Good job today, Cory."

"Yes, very nice," she agreed, as she locked the door behind us.

Jeff stopped and looked back at us both. Realizing we weren't going yet, he raised an eyebrow and said, "I guess I'll see you guys tomorrow."

Jeff's look of judgement was unimportant to me other than my fear she would be put off by it.

"You're welcome," she said when he was far enough not to hear us. "I'm proud of what we're doing." I could tell she was tired but not quite ready to go. She seemed to be waiting for me to say something.

"Me too," I said, wishing I had something profound to offer. It was my opportunity, but instead I stood quietly. Although I still felt the sexual energy between us, I now wanted more. I wanted to hear her talk to me, and I didn't care about what. I just wanted to hear her voice. I wanted to spend time with her. I would have stood in that parking lot for hours just to be near her, but I feared that if I asked her to go for a drink or dinner and she turned me down, my fantasies would be shattered.

"I want you to know," she finally said with renewed energy in her voice. "You have something special. Remember that when you are on stage." She squeezed my hand. "You have a lot to be excited about. Forget about the past and enjoy it."

She knew about me and my fears. I wasn't sure how I felt about that.

Her driver had pulled up and was waiting quietly by the back-seat door, which he opened as soon as she turned that way. I wanted to stop her, but I just watched her slip into the car. She smiled at me as he closed the door.

"Today's the big day," Jesse said. "We rehearse all day and party all night. I'm looking forward to playing with you. We're going to kill it."

The show was really to see how we performed together more than to promote us, but we were excited about it all the same. The studio day in and day out was becoming a grind.

I finished the last of my sit-ups. "Yeah, I know. This'll be the first time for me to be around Miss Blake away from the studio."

Jesse rolled his eyes. "You need to forget about her. This is important tonight. We're counting on you."

Jesse was probably afraid that if we stunk, I would lose my confidence and drive again. He didn't need to worry.

"You're always rolling your eyes at me," I said. "I got this. No worries."

"I just don't get you. She's a freaking control freak."

"No, she's not," I said. "She just demands perfection."

He rolled his eyes again.

"Do you do that on purpose? That eye rolling thing?" I teased him.

"Just finish getting dressed. I'm ready to go."

I took Maggie for her run and then showered. I decided not to shave, opting for the five o'clock shadow look instead. I rubbed leave-in conditioner in my hair, giving it a short, tossed look. After giving myself a final once-over in the mirror, I said out loud, "You got this, Cory."

Jesse was right. We rehearsed most of the day. The bar was more of a concert venue with bars. It reminded me of Billy Bob's in Texas. The show was to start at nine, and we didn't start wrapping up the rehearsal until almost five. The doors were to open at 7:00 pm, so we would have time to relax and have a couple of drinks.

As we finished the last song, I looked around for Alexandra. She was at the sound system talking to Jeff. The extent of our conversations had been only about the music and what she wanted me to do. I trusted her judgment, so I didn't mind following Jesse's advice to do what I was told. However, I did have a few ideas I wanted to share with her, preferably outside the studio. I watched them and wondered what they were talking about. She nodded a few times, then touched him on the shoulder and headed towards the exit. What? She wasn't going to say anything to me before she left? Hell no.

I set my guitar down and ran after her. When I caught up to her, I realized I had no idea what I was going to say. I slid in front of her and blocked the door.

"Did you need something?" she asked, startled.

"Yeah, they say you're not coming tonight." I realized as I said it that it sounded accusatory. "I mean, tell me you're coming tonight." I smiled, trying my best to look irresistible.

"I'm afraid I have other obligations," she said. "Don't worry; you're ready. You'll do fine."

"I was really hoping you would be here," I said, hoping it didn't sound as pitiful to her as it did to me.

"I'm sorry, I can't," she said. "As I said, I have another commitment."

My heart sank. I just knew she was going to be with another guy. "I need you here," I said, knowing I only had moments to change her mind. "It's my first show with the guys," I said. "It would really help me if you could be here."

She tilted her head and seemed touched. "You really want me here, don't you?" Her eyes were bright with amusement, and I began to feel foolish.

"I wanted to talk to you about a few things," I said. Then I tried to change my tone. Act like it really wasn't that important to me. "But it can wait."

She touched my face with the back of her hand. "You can barely see your dimples with that shadow. Don't grow it any thicker." Then she slipped past me and out the door. Her driver stood waiting for her.

Once I recovered from the thrill of her touch, I called after her, "So does that mean you're coming?"

She put on her sunglasses and slid into the car. "I'll see what I can do." The driver shut the door, and all I could see was dark-tinted glass. He went around to his side and got in and drove away. I felt my cheek, remembering the softness of her touch.

"You ready for a drink, Casanova?" Jesse had snuck up and shoved me playfully.

"Yeah," I said, jolted back to reality. "I'm ready."

"Not so fast." Greg walked up. "Jeff wants to go through a few songs one more time. You didn't really ask her to come back, did you?"

"In fact, I did," I said.

Jesse shook his head and muttered under his breath, "Here we go."

Greg pointed his finger in my face. "If she gives me any shit, I'm outta here."

I wanted to slap it away, but I held my temper and just backed up. By this time, Trent and Jeff had joined us. "I can play drums," Trent said, and I thought Greg was going to hit him.

"Break it up, guys." Jeff held up his hands. "If she does come back, it's just as part of the audience. Let's knock out a few more songs and then have a round of drinks. They're on the house as part of the agreement, so you can order what you want."

"Cool," Trent said. "Let's get this done."

We got back to work, ignoring Greg's fury for the moment. Considering the tension between Greg and the rest of us, and the fact that I had only been in the band a short while, we sounded pretty good. We did a Pink Floyd song that Trent sang and sounded awesome, and Jesse did an old Springsteen song that he killed as well. Trent had "Need Your Love," and I did the rest. My only problem was that I could sound like anybody from Frank Sinatra to Axl Rose, so sometimes I would forget my own voice and slip into somebody else's. An hour later, Jeff finally released us for drinks.

Greg's wife and baby walked in as we all sat at the bar. Seeing him with his family made me temporarily forgive him for being an asshole. The bartender brought us a pitcher of beer and said,

"Sorry, I'm told beer only. But I can throw a couple of pizzas in the oven for you."

"You guys go ahead," Trent said. "I need to run and take care of something."

Greg and Jesse looked at each other like, uh-oh.

"I'll go with you," I said. "I need to find something healthier than pizza anyway." Damn, but I wanted that pizza fresh out of the oven.

"Where are we going?" I asked Trent as we walked across the parking lot.

"I just need to drop off some money I owe. Then we can get you something to eat."

We got into Trent's extremely cool 1965 black Mustang Fastback. It had two thick white stripes across the hood, top, and trunk. He also drove a new BMW, but I liked the Mustang.

About fifteen minutes later, we pulled into a really seedy-looking motel called the Proud Parrot. The stucco was painted bright blue, and all the doors were red. The street sign was an old-fashioned neon sign that simply said MOTEL with an arrow pointing to the parking lot. The side of the building facing the street had a parrot and the words Proud Parrot painted on it.

Trent pulled into a spot in front of one of the red doors and said, "Wait here. I'll just be a minute."

The sun would be setting soon, so I hoped Trent would indeed be only a minute. I locked both doors and looked for a song on his ridiculously expensive radio. The U2 song "One" soon filled the car. His ever-present ice chest was in the back floorboard, so I helped myself to a beer. Three songs and then I would go in after him.

Thoughts of the show began to fill my head. If I was awful, would that ruin everything? Why in the world had I insisted Alexandra Blake be there? Wait, I wanted her there...didn't I? My stomach gurgled, and I realized that I didn't know what I wanted. Two more songs passed and no Trent. A song came on that I liked, so I gave him till the end of that one. Still nothing. Each song was about four minutes long, and four had come on, so that was over fifteen minutes. One more song or about twenty minutes seemed long enough for about any conversation. At the end of song five and a few ads, he was still not out, so I went to the door and knocked.

There was no answer, so I knocked louder and called for him. Music was playing inside, but it didn't sound so loud as to drown me out. The sun was setting, and we were in a bad part of town. It was time to go. I tried the door, but of course it was locked.

Two guys staggered up to the room next door. They both had long greasy hair and dirty clothes. One of them nodded and said, "Hey."

I gave a meek wave and nod and said, "Hey," back to them. I worried they might want to help, so I waited for them to go into their room before I continued knocking. My knuckles began to turn red. I was getting irritated and scared. Why the hell wasn't anybody answering?

Finally, the door slowly opened a few inches, and someone peered out and said, "What?" All I could see was one dark-brown bloodshot eye with a dark circle underneath. He held the door close, causing most of his face to be covered by his arm.

"I'm looking for Trent," I said, and pushed forcefully on the door. The guy tumbled back, and the door flew open, banging against the wall and back. I stopped it and stepped in.

"Wow," the guy said as he pulled himself up. "You're strong, dude."

Nobody else was in the room. I flipped on the light switch and said, "Where is he?"

"He's in the can," he said, pointing over his shoulder with his thumb. "He fell and hit his head."

I knocked the guy back down, just out of frustration, and went to the bathroom. The door was locked but flimsy enough to kick open. Which I intended to do if he didn't answer. After one round of pounding, the door opened. It was Yacht Boy. I stepped in to find Trent standing at the counter looking at a cut on his forehead. His hair was matted down with thick red blood, and the hand towels around him were soaked bright red. He kept dabbing at it as if that would stop the bleeding.

"You have to keep the towel on it," I said. "Apply pressure." I moved Yacht Boy aside and stepped in. "What happened?"

"Hey, watch it," Yacht Boy said.

I ignored him. "What happened, Trent? You need to go to a hospital."

"Nah," he said. "It doesn't hurt."

"Because you're high," I said calmly. I wanted him to know the gravity of the situation, but I didn't want to freak him out.

"I can take him," Yacht Boy said. "Come on, Trent, I'll drive you."

"We have to get this handled and get back to the club," I said. "Let's go." I took Trent by the elbow and pulled him to me. He followed surprisingly easy, so I kept going. The guy in the bedroom stepped back and out of our way, but Yacht Boy followed. Once I had Trent outside, I turned to them. "You guys should be ashamed," I said. They just looked at me without expression. I glanced past them to see that the nightstand had a needle set up. Yacht Boy had long sleeves on, but the other guy wasn't wearing a shirt. When he saw me looking at his tracks, he put his hand over them. I suddenly noticed that he smelled like sweat and so did the room.

I put Trent into the passenger seat, then ran around to the other side. "Let me see," I said as I slid into the driver's seat. I pulled the towel away from his forehead. Almost immediately, the blood flowed out again. "Hold it tight," I said. "We're going to the hospital."

"We can't go to the hospital," he said. "It'll take hours. Call Amy. She's a nurse, she can sew it up."

"Amy's a nurse?" I realized I never even asked her anything about herself. "What about the pain?" I said. "She can't prescribe anything."

Trent thought about that for a second. "I like painkillers," he finally said.

"Right. I'll call Amy."

We weren't far from her apartment, so I just drove to it. Pay phones were filthy. When we got there, she was on her way out.

"I was just leaving for the show," she said as she turned back to unlock the door. "What the hell happened?"

"Yeah," I said to Trent. "What did happen? You never told me."

"When I told Mike I didn't have any money on me, he pushed me. I tripped over something, a pair of shoes I think, and fell. I hit my head on the corner of the TV stand on the way down."

"The corner of the furniture was that sharp?" Amy asked as she opened the door. Trent and I sat at the kitchen table while Amy went to get supplies.

"A piece of the corner is broken off, so it's kind of sharp. I'm not sure if that's why it cut me or if I broke it off with my face." The whole side of his face was swelling and turning blue.

Amy came back into the room with an armful of supplies. "We need to have it looked at," she said. "I can stop the bleeding, but we need to make sure there is no internal damage."

"It's really not as bad as it looks," Trent said. "I swear. I just grazed it."

Amy and I looked at each other. Finally, she said, "You go on to the show. I'll take him to the ER. I know the staff. If all is well, I'll bring him to the club in a few hours."

Trent nodded, so I gave Amy a big hug and said, "Thank you." I jumped up to go and said to Trent, "I'll see you in a few hours." As I closed the door behind me, I turned back and said, "By the way, which one was Mike? The shirtless one or Yacht Boy?"

"The shirtless one. Yacht Boy is Evan."

I nodded and shut the door. My head was spinning I was so mad at Trent and his idiot friends. By the time I got to Trent's car, my mind was racing with what I would say and do. I started the car, sped out of the parking lot, and headed back to the hotel. Those morons needed a beating like they had never seen. Then reality set in. The guys wouldn't be able to go on with both of us missing. It took everything in me to do another illegal U-turn and not drive back to that piece of shit hotel.

# 13

"You were supposed to keep him out of trouble," Greg said again.

Jesse just shook his head and looked away. Jeff was on the phone trying to find a replacement.

"I know," I said. "I should have gone in with him." I turned to Jeff. "I can play bass. Not as well as Trent but good enough till he gets here." I didn't want to play bass, but we were running out of time.

Jeff looked at Greg and Jesse. They shrugged, so he hung up the phone.

I picked up Trent's guitar, and everyone sucked in their breath. I played some bass lines. The Clash, Deep Purple, Cream, The Beatles, and Metallica. "I got this," I said, sounding more confident than I felt.

"Not like we have a choice," Greg said.

Jeff looked at his watch. "It's ten after nine. I can stall another ten to fifteen minutes."

"Go introduce us now," I said to Jeff. "I need to get out there before I think too much about it." My last live performance crept into my head. If the critics hated me then, what made me think they'd like me any better now? On top of everything, I had to play bass.

"Don't worry," Amy said, charging into the room, dragging a stitched-up Trent behind her. "We made it. You guys are going to be great." She slid up next to me and pulled my face in for a kiss.

"What the hell?" I said. "How'd you—"

"I told you, I work at the hospital. I got him straight through." She looked at Trent. "He looks like hell, but he was right, superficial."

Jesse went to Trent and lifted his hair. It was bandaged up, so he couldn't see much. "Man, you better start watching yourself," he said. "Or you're going to end up dead."

"I could use a drink," Trent said.

"They give him painkillers?" I asked Amy.

She shook her head. "Just Tylenol 3."

"Okay for him to drink?" I asked her.

"Probably not the best idea."

"I'm definitely having a drink," Trent said.

"Not going to look so good on the CD cover," Jeff said.

Greg laughed. "Miss Blake's going to be so pleased."

"She here?" I asked them all.

"I wouldn't count on her showing up tonight," Jeff said. "Don't take it personally."

"Why would she?" Jesse said. "Think about it, Cory. She is wealthy and famous. You're...not."

"Let's just get started," I said. "Can you go introduce us?" I asked Jeff.

He nodded and went on stage. The L.A. bar scene knew Suicide King with Eddie. If they didn't like me, I didn't know what my future with the band would be. Jeff told the crowd about Eddie and how we grew up together. He told them that I came to L.A. to keep Eddie's dream alive. They sounded receptive. As Jeff left the stage, Jesse, Trent, and Greg went on. I strapped on my guitar but felt weighed down.

"You said you were ready," Jeff said. "Go on. They're waiting for you."

My heart raced, and I felt like I might throw up. Would everything come down to this? If I thought I was good again and it didn't go well, how would I ever be able to trust my own judgement?

"Here," Jeff said, handing me a shot of something. "Drink this, then get your ass out there."

I took the shot of whiskey and nodded as it burned my chest. "She's going to be sorry she missed this," I said, and went on stage as if I'd done it hundreds of times before.

We opened with "Hard Times Again," then Jesse and Trent did their songs. We did "Knockin' on Heaven's Door." I started with the Eric Clapton version, then got antsy and went into my Axl Rose voice. It took the guys a second to catch up, but when they did, we sounded great. The crowd loved it. The girls liked the heavy metal sound coming from a clean-cut, apple-pie-looking guy, and the guys just loved the rock 'n' roll.

The whole time, I kept my eye on the front door. Each time it opened, my heart raced with anticipation, hoping it was her, then sank with disappointment when it wasn't. By the end of the first set, I had to admit to myself she wasn't coming. I left the stage feeling good about the performance but bummed that she wasn't there to see it.

I took a beer from the backstage refrigerator and fell onto the couch. I put my feet up on the coffee table and downed half the beer.

Greg said, "Looks like you've been stood up. What a shame."

I put my feet down and sat up to look at him. "What is your problem with me?"

Jesse stepped between us. "Come on, Cory. You didn't really think she would come, did you?"

I fell back into the couch, forgetting about Greg. "No, I guess not."

"Maybe something came up," Trent said. "Maybe she just couldn't come."

"Yeah," Greg said. "Like her book of the month came in."

"Why do you care?" Jesse asked. "You have Amy, and she can get just about any guy she wants. And you could probably land any of the girls out there." He pointed to the club. "The only difference between Alexandra Blake and any of the others is she has money."

"So, you think she's not interested in me because she has money and I don't? You think if she didn't have money, she would be interested in me?"

"This whole thing is so stupid," Greg said. "You're infatuated with her because she's rich and famous. If she wasn't, she would be just like anybody else. The funny thing is she's just an okay-looking, middle-aged has-been. And no offense, but she's also Black. And a complete bitch."

"I just don't see her the way you guys do," I said, ignoring Greg's remarks since his opinion meant nothing to me.

Just then, the door swung open, and in walked Christy and Amy.

"You guys were great," Christy said, as she walked up to Jesse and put her arms around him.

"Incredible," said Amy, coming my way. When she came in for a kiss, I turned my face so that it landed on my cheek. "The girls out there love you," she said. "You should have seen the looks on their faces when I told them I was with you."

I forced a smile. Jesse gave me an I-told-you-so look. "Girls that don't look twice at you ordinarily suddenly love you when you're on stage," I said as I tossed my empty beer can into the trash. "We ready?"

I walked up to the microphone with a touch of arrogance from the several beers I'd downed. The crowd was screaming, and I felt like a star. As soon as they settled down, I said, "This next song is one that I know all you guys can relate to. You know what I mean when I say the unattainable woman?" The guys all hooted and hollered, and the girls all smirked as if they were that woman. "The woman that you would die for. The woman that if you could have her just once, you'd give up all other women." Then I started The Beatles song "I Want You" and led into Trent's song "Need Your Love." Trent took over the vocals, and I did a guitar solo. The crowd went wild. The guys gave each other high-fives, and the girls screamed and held up their drinks. I had won them over, and it felt good.

When the show was over, I was really pumped because I knew that we had done a good job. I only wished Alexandra had been there to see it. I felt silly for thinking she'd be there just for me. She probably forgot all about it the minute the driver shut her car door.

Trent hung his arm on my shoulder. "You were awesome tonight," he said.

"You were," Amy agreed. "Christy and I just ordered a few pitchers of beer. You coming out to the table?"

"I'll be out in a few," I said. "I just want to call my parents first."

"Aw," she said. "That's sweet." She kissed me and said, "Hurry up, though," and bounced on out.

I picked up the phone to call Texas when I heard the back door to the alley open. I turned to find Alexandra Blake leaning in the doorway. She was wearing a red sequined evening dress, her hair wild and curly, and she looked absolutely stunning. Like she did on the CD cover. I hung up the phone, unable to speak.

"Am I the unattainable woman?" she asked with a sexy grin.

I took a step towards her. I was so happy to see her that I wanted to scoop her up and hug her, but I stopped myself. "As a matter of fact, you are," I said. "How did you hear that?"

"I was backstage during the second set," she said, knowing it was like handing me a gift.

"I had no idea." I was stunned and delighted. "I'm so glad you're here. You want a drink?" I looked around to find something to fix for her.

"Yes, I do," she said. "But not here. I have practically a full bar in the car. Would you like to join me?"

"Yeah, of course. Let me go tell the guys I'm leaving." They were not going to believe it. I couldn't wait to tell them. And fuck you, Greg.

"They'll figure it out," she said.

"Okay." I jotted down a note and followed her out. I felt bad for ditching everyone for about two seconds.

The driver held the door open for us. It wasn't the same car she had left the studio in. It was a limousine. "You must have had a big event tonight," I said as we both climbed in. Sam Cooke was playing on the radio.

"Not really," she said. "What would you like to drink?"

"Anything is fine. Whatever you're having." I really didn't care. I was in a limo with Alexandra Blake.

She poured us each a glass of red wine. She took a sip, and I took a gulp. She looked absolutely breathtaking. Everything was perfect. Every hair in place, nails neatly manicured, and she had a beautiful smile. I felt completely self-conscious with my faded, torn jeans and tee shirt. I was sure I was sweaty from the show as well, while she had that faint smell of perfume that made me want to take a bite of her. She probably felt like she was hanging out with her gardener.

"You look really great," I said. "Were you someplace special?"

"Actually, it was rather dull." She looked directly into my eyes when she spoke. I loved her easy confidence.

I downed my wine.

She laughed. "Maybe you would rather have beer?" She handed me a bottle of beer and held her wine up for a toast. "To the rest of the night," she said.

I clinked her glass with my bottle, then sat back and took a deep breath. She was with me because she wanted to be. She wanted me there with her, and I didn't need to worry about my clothes or anything else. I took everything in and paid attention to every detail in case it was the one and only time I would have with her. All my fears and doubts about her world or mine I would push aside for at least this one night.

Alexandra ran her hand along the back of her neck and lifted her hair so that it fell over the seat behind her. She leaned back, closed her eyes, and smiled contently. I couldn't take my eyes off her. Her skin was smooth except for a few small laugh lines around her eyes and mouth. She didn't look middle-aged to me. My eyes wandered down her long neck and smooth brown chest. I imagined how soft her skin must feel. I could almost feel the warmth of it as I envisioned slipping my hand under the strap of her dress and down to her...

"What are you looking at, Corbett?" she asked, amused that she had caught me.

"I'm just—"

"Admiring my dress?"

"Exactly." I knew my face was red with embarrassment, but I didn't care.

She took my hand and rested it on her chest for a few seconds, then she lifted it to her mouth and left a lipstick kiss. I wanted to kiss her more than anything in the world, but I was afraid to move. We locked eyes for what seemed like a long time. Either she realized she would have to make the first move, or she wanted me even a fraction of how much I wanted her. Or maybe she was just fine being in charge. She put her hand on the back of my neck and pulled me to her. She put her lips to mine and pressed firmly but only for a second. It was all I could do not to jump on top of her.

I took her hand and held it to my face. It was as soft as I remembered. She watched me as I did this, and I was amazed to find that it felt right. At that moment, we were just two people attracted to and at ease with each other.

I knew it was late, probably well after two am. "Where are we going?" I asked.

"Las Vegas," she said with the sparkle of a secret. "Now don't ask any more questions about that."

The woman I had spent every waking moment fantasizing about just kissed me. I didn't care where we were going or why. I was with her and didn't want it to end. I leaned back and tried to relax. It was late and had been a long day. I should have been exhausted, but I was amped. I was freaking headed to Las Vegas with Alexandra. I could hardly wait to see the look on Jesse's and Trent's faces. They were going to be as amazed as I was.

"Okay if I fix a drink?" I asked.

"Of course, whatever you like."

I fixed a Tanqueray and tonic to calm myself. I downed it and fixed another. She watched me with a calming smile. I had never been so infatuated and intimidated, and I think she knew it.

I tried to relax, but I couldn't imagine why we could possibly be going to Las Vegas. Certainly, it wasn't just to spend time together. We didn't need to drive four hours for that. Maybe she was doing a show? I took a gulp of my drink and figured there was no use speculating. Only time would tell. I glanced over at her. Her eyes were closed, but I wasn't sure if she was awake or had fallen asleep. There was a cellular phone in the car, but I was afraid if I tried to call Jesse, I would disturb her. I knew I could count on Jesse to take care of Maggie. Maybe I was going to do a show there? No, that didn't make sense. My mind was jumping all over the place.

Alexandra put her hand on my knee. "We have about four hours of driving ahead of us," she said. "Don't you want to get some sleep? You must be tired. You've had a long day."

"Sorry," I said. "I didn't mean to disturb you."

"You were really good tonight. I'm very proud of you."

"Thanks," I said. "I wish I had known you were there."

"What would that have changed? Maybe your 'unattainable woman' speech wouldn't have gone as well."

I thought about it and wondered if that was why she waited for me. I announced to the entire club that I would do anything to have her just once. If I'd known she was back there, I certainly would not have done that. "I don't know," I said. "I'm just glad you made it. And I'm glad to be here with you."

"I'm pleased you're here as well," she said and playfully added, "although, I would be sound asleep in a warm bed in Las Vegas by now had you not insisted I come to the concert."

"But you would be there without me," I reminded her with my first hint of confidence.

"There you are." She smiled big. "I knew there was a self-assured young man in there somewhere."

The gin was taking hold, and my inhibitions waned. We talked about the band and about Eddie. We talked about Greg's song "Last Train Out." We both had ideas on how to fix it. Our ideas took it from an amateurish simple song to one we both believed could be a hit. We talked about music, movies, books, and about almost everything else, except ourselves. I didn't want to think about her being a celebrity or my boss or anything else that gave me a reason to doubt we could be together. For that moment, I chose to believe that it was all possible. She smiled easily with me, and it filled me with joy every time she did.

Sometime around four o'clock, my eyes began to get heavy. As much as I fought it, because I didn't want to miss a thing, I dozed off.

I felt like I'd been asleep for about ten minutes. The driver was shaking me. "Excuse me, sir, Miss Blake is waiting for you."

I sat up and blinked a few times. The driver held out a key. It was dark, so I was a bit disoriented, until I realized we were in a parking garage. "What time is it?" I asked.

"It is eight thirty-five, sir. Miss Blake is waiting for you." He held out the key again.

I was sore from sleeping in the car, and my mouth tasted like old gin. "Where is she?"

"In the room, sir."

"You don't have to call me sir...I'm sorry, what's your name?"

"Marco," he said.

"You don't have to call me sir, Marco." I took the key. "Do I look as bad as I think?" I might have been slightly hungover. Probably due to drinking beer, wine, and gin.

"You look like a rock star," he said.

"Hmm. Okay. Which way to the room?"

"Follow me."

I followed him through the parking garage into a back entrance of the hotel. We went down a long hallway and took the elevator to the top floor. I caught a glimpse of myself in the elevator mirror. I looked about the same as I did that first day I'd met her. I was definitely not a morning person.

When the elevator opened, Marco told me to have a good day, then pressed for the doors to close. I stepped out of the elevator and went down the hall to the room. I started to use the key but decided to knock instead. I ran my hand through my hair, trying to make it as presentable as possible. There wasn't much I could do about my morning gin breath. I would just have to keep my distance. I took a deep breath and knocked on the door.

# 14

As I waited for Alexandra to open the door, I wondered what she looked like in the morning. I doubted I would know anytime soon. She probably never let anybody see her looking less than perfect. What if she did open the door looking as rough as I did? Was I supposed to act like I didn't notice? I pictured her with her hair a mess, no makeup, scratching her backside, and yawning with morning breath. It made me laugh, though it was probably not a good idea to laugh at her this early in the process. The truth was it wouldn't bother me a bit. In fact, I would be glad that I wasn't the only one looking less than perfect. Why was I thinking about something so irrelevant anyway?

The door swung open, and of course, she was showered and changed and looking fantastic. Her hair was pulled back, and she wore a cream-colored business suit. Her freshly showered scent made me want to wrap my arms around her and bury my face in her neck. I, of course, was still a mess.

"As usual, you look great," I said. "But I don't have anything to change into."

"I've taken care of that." She stepped aside and motioned for me to come in. I followed her into a room that was ridiculously extravagant. An entire wall was glass doors that opened to a balcony overlooking the Las Vegas strip. There was a full living area with a grand piano, a full bar that was about five feet long, and a huge television. I assumed the bedroom was behind one of the closed doors. Hmmm...one bedroom or two? She opened the door to the bathroom and said, "Do hurry. We have an appointment to make."

I went into the bathroom without question. She pulled the door closed after me. The bathroom was as big as a master bedroom. The sunken tub looked like it could fit three people. Ew, I pictured that and peered into it to make sure it was really clean. It was spotless. Thick white towels hung from tubes that had water rushing through them. I touched the tube to find that they were warm from the water. Insane. I reached in to turn on the walk-in shower. Water sprayed from all four directions.

As I undressed, I saw that Alexandra had a blue suit laid out for me, along with shoes, socks, boxers, and an undershirt. I peeked in to see the size of the suit but didn't see anything. There was also a white shirt with no size and a pink tie. Pink?

The shower was a moment in heaven. Warm water hit me from all angles. I used shampoo and conditioner that I'd never heard of and shaved with a razor that cleared my shadow swiftly and completely. I washed every inch of my body with soap that not only smelled delicious, but also left my skin feeling soft and healthy. I could have stayed in the shower for days, but she had told me to hurry, so I wrapped it up quickly. The towels were softer than I had ever felt and were warm from the tubes. Send in food and I could have lived in that bathroom.

I brushed my teeth with an electric toothbrush and rinsed with mouthwash. She'd forgotten nothing. I dressed and looked in the mirror. She was right; the pink tie worked. The suit and shirt fit perfectly. I hadn't worn a suit since high school graduation and certainly didn't remember it looking this good.

When I opened the bathroom door, Alexandra stood from the piano and came to me. She beamed like a proud parent. "Perfect," she said.

"Thank you." I tightened my tie even more. "How did you know what size?"

"I have my ways," she said as she looked at my hands. "You must quit biting your nails."

"It's not a bad habit or anything," I said. "I just do it when—"

"They need to be trimmed?" she said with amusement. "Well, stop. We'll need to get you a manicure, and I'm guessing a pedicure."

"I don't think—"

"And don't start now." She winked as if to say she was joking, but not really.

"Where are we going?" I asked

"Just a quick meeting," she said. "And then the rest of the day is ours to enjoy. We'll head back to L.A. tomorrow."

"What kind of meeting?" I asked, not really concerned with her answer. I was busy wondering about the one- or two-bedroom thing.

She gave me a look that basically said don't worry your pretty little head about it and motioned for the door. I followed her without worrying any more about it. When we got downstairs, Marco was waiting for us. Inside the limo there was coffee, mini bagels, and fruit. "I'm sorry about breakfast," she said. "I'll make it up to you at lunch."

I was starving, so I ate what was there without complaint. She had coffee and a few bites of fruit. Then she took a folder from her bag and began going through it, jotting down notes. I started to wonder if I got to keep the suit. Not that I would have anywhere else to wear it. Unless I was going someplace with her. Would I need a suit frequently with her? If so, that meant that I would be wearing this same suit every time. I probably couldn't wear my high school graduation suit with her. Damn, was I going to have to buy an expensive suit?

Alexandra put her hand on my knee. "What's on your mind?"

"I was just wondering where we're going," I said.

She thought a moment and formed her words carefully. "I must tell you, Cory, I have big plans for you."

"Okay. What kind of plans?"

"Let me back up a bit," she said. "Sometimes in this business, a person becomes successful simply because someone sees something special in that person."

"Okay."

"I saw something in you. All I had to go by was an old video and some photographs. So, I was a bit nervous when you showed up that first day looking...well, not your best."

"Sorry about that," I said, and gave a sheepish grin.

She smiled back and reluctantly added, "But you were still adorable, so we marched on."

She thought I was adorable. Even when I looked like hell. How about that.

"You have something special, and we are going to squeeze it for all it's worth," she said as she ran her hand through my hair and messed with it until it pleased her.

"What about the other guys?" I asked.

"Don't worry about them," she said. "They can come along for the ride."

I wasn't sure what that meant but decided to drop it for the moment. I wondered if the kiss in the limo had been all I'd hoped it was. Right now, she was all business, and it made me feel like a child being driven to school. If I told her how I felt about her, would she send me back to L.A. right after the meeting? Would she distance herself from me?

"I'm glad that you see something in me professionally," I said.

She had gone back to her paperwork but looked up when I spoke. "It sounds like that is going to be followed by however. Is something else on your mind?"

"I'm more interested in you than what you can do for my music career," I said quickly before I could change my mind about speaking up.

She took my hand. "I know," she said with a simple, beautiful smile. "I'd suspected right away that you'd formed a crush on me." She touched my face and said, "It's sweet, don't be embarrassed. I may have had some feelings of my own." She took a deep breath and said, "However, you're still going to be famous, and you're going to make us both a lot of money." She lifted my chin and leaned in to kiss me. I wasn't going to let it be another short, inconclusive peck this time. I pulled her to me and kissed her with the passion and desire that had been growing in me since I first laid eyes on her.

When it was over, she took one of the white cloth napkins and wiped away her lipstick from my mouth. "I can't have you going into a meeting wearing my lipstick," she said. My whole body tingled, and I knew that I would do anything she asked of me.

We pulled up to a tall, mirrored building. In its reflection, I could see the limo park and Marco jump out and walk back to open our door. He took Alex's hand and helped her out, then I slid out after her. The tingling had subsided and now I felt sick, not knowing what I was walking into.

I followed Alex into the building. We rode the elevator in silence to the twelfth floor. My reflection in the shiny silver doors took me by surprise. The blue suit and pink tie remained foreign to me. For half a second, I thought it was another guy in the elevator with us.

"What are you grinning at?" Alex asked, talking to my reflection.

"I'm just not used to dressing like this," I said as the doors opened.

As we stepped off the elevator, she looked at me and straightened and tightened my tie. "You look splendid," she said. "Just agree with everything I say in here. Okay?"

I nodded and followed her down the hallway. "Splendid," I said softly to myself. I couldn't remember anyone ever saying I looked splendid before.

We went into an office, and Alex told the receptionist who we were. The lady told us to have a seat, so I started to walk to the waiting area. Alex took my arm and pulled me back. "I don't think you heard me correctly," she said to the receptionist. "I am Miss Alexandra Blake," she enunciated as if the lady really had not heard correctly. "Let Mr. Buchanan know we are here."

The lady looked like she wanted to punch Alex in the nose. She looked at me like I might be helpful. I just shrugged. She picked up the phone and talked quietly into it. I was sure I heard the word bitch. When she hung up, she fake smiled and said, "Go right in."

"Thank you," Alex said, and in we went.

An older guy with thick silver hair and bright blue eyes opened the door to greet us. He gave Alex a light hug and kissed her on the cheek. "You look beautiful as always," he told her as we walked in. It was a corner office with a view of Las Vegas. Alex introduced me to him, so I held out my hand. He didn't take it. Instead, he put his hand to his chin thoughtfully. He looked me over and said, "You're right, Alexandra. The group will be here any minute. I don't think we'll have any trouble."

Alex put her arm on my back, beaming with pride like an FFA student with the prize bull at the state fair. "Let's sit down," she said and nudged me towards the chairs at the large glass conference table. As we started to sit, three more people walked in. Alex went to greet them. I wasn't sure what to do. Sit, stand, or go with her to greet them? I noticed a bar by the window and wished I could fix a drink. New rule. Any more meetings and she was getting me buzzed first.

Alex, Mr. Buchanan, two new guys, and a new lady walked over to the table. Alex introduced me to them individually. While they all began to sit around the table, Alex took me by the elbow and instructed me to sit next to her. She had a knack for making me feel twelve years old. I tugged on my shirt collar. It was too tight, and it was too warm in the room. I started to worry that I would sweat in the shirt that wasn't mine.

Once we were all seated, Mr. Buchanan opened his briefcase and pulled out a manila envelope. He took out four 8x10 black-and-white photos of me in jeans and a white tee shirt. They were all taken at the studio. He passed them around the table. Each of them studied the photos and looked me over. Alex was sitting back, totally relaxed with a poker face. I shifted uncomfortably.

Finally, the woman said, "I didn't like the idea before, and I don't like it now."

Alex ignored her and turned to Mr. Buchanan and said, "What do you think, Vince?"

He grinned. "I like it. How about you, Sam?"

The name Sam reminded me of Trent's version of *Green Eggs and Ham*.

Sam nodded and said, "It could work."

Alex smiled smugly and turned to the other man. "How about you, Dave? What do you think?"

"Well," he said as he looked at Alex and then at the other woman. "I think it's an option, but nothing to rush into."

Alex leaned forward and said, as coolly as if she were offering coffee, "Don't be a pussy, Dave. Answer us."

I almost fell out of my chair. I wasn't expecting that. The lady rolled her eyes, but Sam and Vince seemed amused. I was definitely amused.

Dave threw up his arms and said, "I think it's brilliant." He turned to the woman. "I'm sorry, but I do. I think we've hit on something big."

Alex stood and motioned for me to follow her, which I did. She opened the door, then turned back and said to Dave, "I hit on something big." She winked at him and we left.

When we got to the elevator, I asked her what was going on.

"I'll explain everything at dinner tonight," she said. "Right now, I'm feeling lucky. Let's go play some blackjack."

"I'm starving. How about you explain it to me over lunch?" I said.

"I did promise you a nice lunch, didn't I?"

As Marco drove us, she explained that she spent a lot of time in Las Vegas because of all the shows she had done over the years. "And," she added, "I have actually learned to gamble fairly well."

The restaurant was in the lobby of our hotel and looked expensive. We both ordered a grilled salmon and spinach salad with a lemon basil vinaigrette. She ordered unsweetened iced tea, and I had my ice water with lemon. The salads tasted fresh and delicious. Even though I was anxious to hear her plan, I engaged in small talk with her. I listened to her every word, interested in her thoughts on things big and small. As we finished our meal, the waiter asked if we wanted coffee, dessert, or a mid-afternoon cocktail.

"We're in Vegas," Alex said. "Would you like a drink?"

"Sure," I said, not wanting our conversation to end. "I'll have a Corona."

"Of course," the waiter said. "May I see your ID, sir?"

The minute he asked for it, I realized I had left my wallet in my jeans. I was so distracted by the bathroom's luxury I completely forgot about it. "Damn," I said to Alex. "I forgot my wallet in the bathroom." It was bad enough that I would look like a deadbeat, but Alex probably felt like she was with a teenager as well. "I can run up and get it." I started to stand.

"Nonsense," she said and put her hand on my leg. "We'll go up together." She looked up at the waiter. "That will be all for now."

"Sorry about that," I said, hoping my face wasn't turning red.

"It's okay. Why are you embarrassed?"

"I'm not, I just—"

"You are," she said as she took my hand and squeezed it. "It's cute the way your cheeks turn pink when you're embarrassed."

Okay, so cute was good...right?

"I'll be right back," she said. "I'm going to run to the ladies' room."

I watched her walk away, mesmerized by her sultry, sexy sway. She went past the restrooms and around the corner. About two minutes later, the waiter showed up with a glass of wine and a Corona.

"Can I get you anything else?" he asked as if nothing had happened.

"No, I don't think so. Thank you."

"Look at that," Alex said as she sat back down. She took a sip of her wine and began explaining her plans for me. "Vince is a publicist in the Las Vegas area. The other three are executives from Intrigued Inc. They have a new high-end men's cologne. The idea is that the cologne is for you when you are in jeans and a tee shirt on stage with Suicide King or in an expensive suit having dinner with a beautiful woman. That is a drastic over-simplification of course, but basically, your picture will be on billboards across the country for the cologne and for the band."

My picture on billboards across the country? I didn't even wear cologne. It was hard to imagine. "I don't know what to say," I said.

"Say thank you."

"What about the other guys? Will they be included?"

"They have their part, and remember, if you are successful, that makes them successful. I'm already lining up a show for you boys out here once the recording is wrapped up."

"What about my job? I'm supposed to start back next week."

"You simply won't have time. I have an advance for you as well as a weekly stipend. If you need more, let me know. I can arrange for some studio work until all of this takes off."

"So, let me make sure I understand. The guys will be there for at least the on-stage part of it. Right?"

"Yes. Of course."

"Okay." It was all sinking in very slowly. "Wow, this is crazy. I need another drink."

Alex waved the waiter over and ordered another round. Eventually, the shock wore off and her excitement became contagious. She shared her plans and ideas with me and listened when I had input. It was hard to believe that things would unfold as she said they would, so I tried to keep my expectations in check. I wanted to call my parents and Jesse and Trent to share it with them but decided that waiting for some things to materialize would be better.

We finished our drinks and strolled through the casino. It was my first time in Vegas, so the sounds and lights fascinated me. Ultimately, we found our way to the blackjack table. The minimum bet was a hundred dollars a hand, so I, of course, stood back and watched.

Alex seemed to know what she was doing when she pushed out two black $100 chips. The dealer tossed each player two cards. When it was her turn, she flipped over two eights and said, "Split." Suddenly, she had four hundred dollars on the table. The dealer gave her a three on one hand and a two on the other. The dealer had a five showing. Alex said, "Double down," and put another two hundred on each hand. Now she had eight hundred dollars in play. I prayed to the blackjack gods for her. The dealer delivered a four and a six, so she had a fifteen and a sixteen, respectively. Not great results. I bit the palm of my hand as the dealer turned over a ten for herself. She had fifteen, and the rules stated she must take a hit until she had at least seventeen. Alex remained calm while I was about to jump out of my skin. A small crowd had gathered to watch. The dealer dealt herself a jack. Twenty-five. She busted and Alex won. The crowd and I cheered. Alex laughed at me and asked if I wanted to play.

I did want to play. But not with her money, and I couldn't afford it...yet. Upon my hesitation, she told the dealer to color her up and we stepped away. She took a purple $500 chip from her stack and handed it to me.

"I'll take it out of your advance. We can go play together at a lower limit table."

After a few seconds of thought, I handed her back the $500 chip and took two black $100 chips. "You'll take it out of my advance?"

"Yes. Of course. It'll be fun. You know the rules?"

"I know them," I said. "You don't mind playing at the cheap tables?"

"Not at all. But maybe we should run up and get your driver's license."

"Oh yeah."

"We can change clothes too. Get into something a little more casual. I have a few more things for you, or if you'd rather, your clothes from last night should be washed and ready."

When we got back to the suite, my clothes were clean, but Alex seemed disappointed that I wasn't choosing the expensive jeans and shirt she had for me. So I wore that instead. We were very different; that was without question. But I figured if I could get used to things a little more her way and she could a little more mine, we could make it work. The intimidation I had felt was dissolving, and I was truly enjoying her company.

I made us each a gin and tonic while she dressed in the bedroom. It was a brand of gin I had never heard of, but it tasted okay. I squeezed extra lime and put extra ice in hers.

"We ready?" she sang out as she came out of the bedroom. She had let her hair down, so it was back to the wild curls. I didn't think her clothes were any more casual than what she was wearing before but figured if it was comfortable to her, that's all that mattered.

"We are," I said as I took her the drink.

She took a sip. "Mmm, very good."

As she stepped away, I took her hand and pulled her back into my arms. It was an impulse that surprised us both. Relieved that she didn't resist, I said, "I'm having a great time with you."

The drink splashed a little onto her wrist. Feeling a bit bolder now, I lifted it to my mouth and kissed her hand and wrist, tasting the gin with her skin. She watched me and said, "I'm having a nice time with you as well." She kissed me gently on the lips. "Now don't forget your wallet."

"Oh yeah, that's right." I darted into the bathroom to grab it. "I almost forgot it again," I said as I walked out of the bathroom and put it in my back pocket. On the way out, I noticed a phone on the end table. I really needed to call Jesse, but Alex had my hand and was pulling me after her, so I just kept going.

We found a $5 table, and we each bought in for two hundred. Our stacks went up and down for about an hour. Then I went on a run and suddenly had over $400. The cocktail waitresses were bringing drinks as fast as we could drink them. The free drinks were costing us $5 each in tips, but we didn't care. When the cards started going the other way, we colored up our chips and left the table. I gave Alex back her $200 and still had over a hundred left.

"I think I'm a little drunk," Alex said.

"Me too. You want to get some dinner?"

"I don't know," she giggled. "I might want another drink."

I almost laughed at her giggle, and it made me want to hug her. Alexandra Blake was a tad drunk. It was cute, but I decided it might be best to sober her up some. "How about a drink with dinner? That steak on the menu looked amazing."

"My superstar wants steak, then steak he shall have," she said.

Although nothing was guaranteed, I felt like celebrating. I was spending personal time with Alex, that was enough in itself. I also had a recording contract and possibly a modeling contract. The only thing I didn't have was the money to treat Alex the way she was used to. At least not yet.

"I don't want you worrying about money," Alex said as we sat down and began looking at the menu. "I know you're a bit old-fashioned."

"I'm not old-fashioned," I said. "I just don't like feeling like an opportunist. I don't want you to think you have to pay for everything."

"This trip is a business expense." She reached across the table and touched my hand. "So don't worry about that. When we get back to L.A. and you get your advance, you can take me out to dinner."

A guarantee I would be with her again. "Promise?"

"I do. Now, what kind of steak are you thinking? I believe I'll have the filet."

"I'm celebrating," I said. "I'm having the bone-in ribeye."

We both ordered our steaks medium-rare. Alex instructed the server to inform the chef that the steaks were for her. "He knows exactly how I like them," she explained. "I hate it when I order it medium-rare and it comes out over or undercooked."

I agreed. The steaks were delivered absolutely perfect. As the waiter placed the plate before me, my mouth began to water from the aroma. When I cut into it, the deep-pink middle was cooked flawlessly. Not overdone and not even the slightest bit raw or underdone. The first bite of rich tenderness made me realize that I had been craving it since I deprived myself of steak for chicken at Jesse's.

"How is it?" Alex asked.

"So good that I forgot you were here for a second."

She laughed. "Wonderful, I'm so glad you like it."

I had intended to drink water to shake off the buzz, but the beer tasted so good with the steak that I couldn't resist. Alex appeared to feel the same about the wine. When we were finished eating, I suggested a walk down the strip. I told Alex it was my first time in Vegas, and I wanted to see it at night. The truth was I wanted to make sure she wasn't drunk when we got back to the hotel room. I didn't know if anything more was going to happen between us, but if it did, I wanted her to have a clear mind. And I really didn't mind seeing the strip anyway.

I bought us both a bottle of water at the hotel shop on our way out. After being inside the casino for the entire day, the night air was a welcome reminder of the outside world. The distance between casinos proved to be much further than I had imagined. Looking down the strip, the casino lights contrasted against the dark sky and seemed close, as if they were one after the other. As we walked, the next casino seemed to just get further away.

When we came to a crosswalk and went to cross the street, our hands brushed against each other. I took the opportunity to hold her hand.

"You're blushing again," Alex said.

"Is this okay?" I asked, lifting our hands.

"Of course. It's nice." She gave me a perplexed look. "Why don't you have a girlfriend?"

I told her all about Jennifer.

"That must have been very painful," Alex said. "Are you angry?"

"I'm not angry," I said. "I was at first, but then I realized she was just trying to hang on. I should have been stronger. I should have broken it off with her when I realized she wasn't the one. It was really all I had known and thought that was all there was."

"That's very mature of you," Alex said. "Most would harbor some anger."

"I don't want to waste time with that. Like I said, I was partly to blame. I stuck around when she could have been finding someone that loved her the way everyone deserves to be loved."

"What about you?"

"She fulfilled my needs...physically, at least. I see now that I stayed with her out of a misguided sense of commitment. Honestly, I was never really drawn to anybody else." I glanced at her as we walked. "Until you."

"That's sweet," she said. "But you expect me to believe you were never attracted to anybody else?"

"I didn't say I didn't find other women attractive or sexy. I said I wasn't drawn to them. I had made a commitment, and like I said, I thought that was it. Once the relationship was over, I was with a few others, but it was just sex."

"You're about to have women throw themselves at you. You're going to be the country's most eligible bachelor," she said. "I'm not sure you know what's in store for you."

"I don't want you to take this the way it's going to sound," I said. "But I'm used to women coming on to me."

"I bet you are," she said, giving my hand a squeeze.

When we got back to the room, it was a little after eleven, and she had some messages waiting for her. I wasn't sure what to do while she looked through them, so I went into the bathroom and took a shower. When I got back to the living area, she was on the couch looking through some papers. She put them aside when she saw me.

"Great news," she announced as she jumped from the couch.

"What's that?" I asked.

"Mmm, you smell delicious," she said and gave me a hug.

"Thank you." I wrapped my arms around her. "What's the good news?"

"The modeling is a go. Things are unfolding just as I planned. There's only one little hiccup, but nothing to worry about."

"Wow, that's amazing. This all feels so surreal...wait...what's the hiccup?"

She squeezed my hand as she pulled away from me. "They don't want to use the band for the rock star part. They just want you."

"Why? What does it matter who's playing around me?"

"It's all about the money. If we include the others, they open themselves up to contracts with four of you instead of just one. We can use models. It's fine. This is for you anyway. The band still has my full commitment for the music."

Were Jesse and Trent going to see it that way? "I'll have to talk to them," I finally said.

"Sure. Of course. But please remember, your success ensures their success."

I nodded as if I agreed because I knew that she was going to do things her way.

"This is good news," she said. "Don't look so glum."

"I'm sorry, you're right. It's incredible. Thank you," I said, trying to mask my concern.

"How shall we celebrate?"

I looked at my watch. "It's midnight, but we are in Vegas…"

She pulled me towards the bedroom. "That's not what I had in mind." She playfully pushed me into the bedroom. "I'll be right back," she said and disappeared into the bathroom.

I heard the shower start and imagined her naked body under the steam and hot streams of water. Everything else was forgotten.

## 15

When I woke up, Alex was already in the bathroom getting dressed. I sat up and looked around the room. A few days earlier, I was in a library looking at her tell-all book, and now I was actually with her. I reached for the phone and called Jesse. Trent answered.

"Hey," he said. "Where the hell are you?"

"In Las Vegas," I said. "With Alexandra Blake."

"Are you fucking kidding me? No way. Like, *with* her with her? Or just there with her?"

"We're heading home today. So I'll see you when we get back. Can you make sure Jesse is taking care of Maggie?"

"Yeah, yeah, for sure. Hey, my brother Bryan is coming home tomorrow. Let's hang out, okay?"

"I thought you said he hated you."

"He does," Trent said. "But I'm trying to fix that."

"Okay, we can do that," I said. "But I gotta go now. Tell Jesse I called." I was ready to get off that phone and go find Alex.

I hopped out of bed and slipped on my boxers. The bathroom door was open just a tad, so I knocked and called to her.

She opened the door and stood before me totally naked. I found the absence of tan lines extremely sexy.

"Wow," I said. "You are so beautiful." I put my arm around her waist and pulled her to me. I buried my face in her neck. "You're built like a twenty-year-old model," I said, practically chewing on her neck. She smelled and tasted so good.

"Hardly, but thank you," she said and pulled away. Looking at me skeptically, she said, "Do you even know how old I am?"

"No, and I don't care."

"I'm forty-four," she said and waited for my reaction.

"Okay." I wasn't sure how I was supposed to respond. Was I supposed to act surprised, implying that she looked younger? Or would that be bad like I thought forty-four was old?

"And you are?"

My first instinct was to lie to close the gap. "I'm twenty-seven," I said truthfully. "Twenty-eight in September. And you just turned forty-four." I remembered her birthday was in March from the tell-all.

"I thought you didn't know my age?"

"I just don't care. It doesn't matter." I looked up and down her slender, brown body. "All I care about right now is that you're naked. Can we discuss this later?"

"Yes, we can."

On the ride back to L.A., I was like a teenager that had just had sex for the first time. I wanted to touch her the entire time. Alex seemed amused by this, but after about two hours, she took my hands and said, "I absolutely adore your enthusiasm, but I need to get some work done."

I decided to take the opportunity to finally write a letter to Eddie's parents. At the funeral, I stayed distant, and I didn't go to their house afterwards. I was a coward and felt bad about that now. If I had gone to L.A. with him, he wouldn't have been driving back for me. If I would have let Jennifer go, she would have been spared years of insecurity and possibly even have a family now. I owed the Coopers an explanation, and possibly even Jenny. I took a pen and a spiral notebook from Alex's bag and started with the Coopers.

The letter began with an apology for not being there for them. I wanted to ask their forgiveness for Eddie's accident but couldn't find the words. I found myself straying and jotting down thoughts. The thoughts turned into lines and then verses.

"What are you so engrossed in?" Alex asked.

"A song," I said. "About Eddie. It's called "Cooperstown." Think we could make room for it?"

"We're almost finished. How quickly can you have it ready?"

"I'll get Jesse and Trent to look at it when we get home. Tomorrow soon enough?"

"I'll listen tomorrow. Sound fair?"

I nodded and we both went back to work.

As soon as we entered the Los Angeles area, Alex called Jeff from her cellular phone. After she hung up, she told me they were waiting for me at the studio. She said that she would drop me off and then she had some appointments to make.

"I had a wonderful time with you," she said. "Thank you."

She was thanking me? "Yeah," I said. "So did I." Wait, was she saying that it was just a fling? Was she preparing me for the real world? I wanted to say something to make sure she knew it was more than that to me, but I didn't know what to say.

"Las Vegas can bring out the adventurous side of a person," she said. "Don't you agree?"

"I don't know," I said. "I guess so." I felt unnerved, like she was distancing herself from me now that we were back to reality.

When the car pulled into the studio, I closed my notebook and reached over to kiss her goodbye. She turned her head so that I ended up kissing her on the cheek. Just like I had done to Amy. As I sat back, I looked up to find Marco holding the door open, and he, Jeff, and Trent standing there looking at us. Jeff was clearly pissed, and Trent was obviously entertained. I looked back at Alex. She smiled politely and said in a hushed voice, "I'll see you soon."

I got out of the car and Jeff got in, giving me an annoyed look. Marco shut the door quickly and jumped back into the front and drove away.

"Dude," Trent laughed. "What the hell are you doing?"

"I'm not sure," I said as we watched them drive away.

When we got inside, Jesse and Greg both looked like they wanted to hit me.

"Welcome back," Jesse said. "You could have called. We didn't know what was going on."

I looked at Trent. He shrugged and said, "I forgot."

"I did call," I said. "And left a note."

"I guess it doesn't matter now," Jesse said. "Let's just get to work."

"Like hell it doesn't matter," Greg said, looking at Jesse like he'd lost his last ally. "We lost the whole weekend thanks to him." He got in my face, pointing his finger at me. "Who do you think you are? You are a fucking nobody taking advantage of a bad situation." Greg knew that he hit a sore spot with me. He continued. "Your best friend is dead because of you, and now you are trying to take advantage of that."

My hands curled into fists, and it was all I could do not to hit him. "You don't know what you're talking about."

"Like hell I don't. You think you can do whatever you want because Eddie was your friend."

That was it. "Look, you pudgy son of a bitch." I poked him in the stomach. "I *can* do whatever I want."

We were in a standoff. "And why is that?" he asked, his face contorted into an angry, ugly mess.

I backed up and leaned easily against a desk. "Because I'm fucking the boss."

Greg's face turned red, and I thought he was going to kill me, but I was ready for the fight. Jesse put his hand over his mouth and said, "Oh shit." I knew then that Alex was behind me. What the hell? What was she doing back so soon?

At this point, I didn't care about Greg anymore. I was braced for the wrath I was about to get from Alex. I just prayed that I didn't ruin everything. The room was silent as we all waited for her response. Finally, she began to walk towards me. I looked down, not wanting to face her, but she went right by me and up to Greg. They were face-to-face, Alex calm and Greg glaring.

"Greg," she finally said. "You need to control your temper and get along with the others or you will be replaced."

Greg's mouth dropped. "Me? I'm the one you're mad at? I didn't take off for the weekend and leave everybody standing around waiting. He's the troublemaker here," he said pointing at me.

Alex remained calm and gave him a stern look. "Remember," she said. "He's fucking the boss. He can get away with it." Then she turned and said to me, "I'd like to see you for a moment," as she walked by.

I looked at the guys before I turned to follow her. Greg was fuming, Jesse concerned, and Trent gave me a thumbs-up.

We went to her office. She shut the door and closed the blinds.

"I'm sorry," I said. "I shouldn't have said that."

"Why are you sorry?" she said. "It's true." As she moved by me, she ran her hand across my stomach and brushed her lips against mine. "You are fucking the boss," she said as she sat behind her desk. "But you may not do whatever you want."

"I know. I just wanted to make Greg mad."

"Well," she chuckled, "I think you accomplished that."

"So, you're not upset with me?" She was a complete wonder to me.

"On the contrary. I'm glad you stood your ground with Greg. I found the look on his face quite amusing."

I breathed a sigh of relief. "What are you doing here anyway? I thought you had appointments."

"I sent Jeff to take care of them. I wanted to spend some time with you boys today. I'd like to try our new version of "Last Train Out.""

"Oh yeah," I said. "Good idea."

"The lawyers are copyrighting the new version. If it sounds like I think it's going to, we will have to do it all over."

"Greg's not going to like that we made changes." I winced.

"I know." Alex grinned.

I went back out while Alex made a few phone calls. Jesse and Trent were wide-eyed. Greg looked like he could spit nails.

"What happened?" Jesse asked.

"You get in trouble?" Trent asked.

"Yeah," I said. "I'm sorry. I was being a jerk." I tried to shake Greg's hand, but he just huffed "Whatever" and went to his drums.

"She wants us to play "Last Train Out" with some changes," I said.

"What changes?" Greg stomped back over to me.

"Just listen," I said. "I think you'll like it."

"Yeah, what changes?" Jesse asked. "We never made any changes."

"Alex and I—"

"Oh, Alex and I," Greg said. "It's Alex now that you're fucking her? And you think you can have my song because of that?"

"Just listen to it," I said. "It's still your song, it's just better."

"Actually," Alex said as she sauntered into the room. "It's now copyrighted as written by Corbett Scott, Alexandra Blake, and you too, Greg. So, the song belongs to the band."

At this point, Greg was just defeated. I almost felt sorry for him. "Alex, just..." I started to say let him keep the song, but I knew it wasn't an option. So, I said nothing.

"I started this band," Greg said slowly. "But it's not mine anymore. I'm done." He headed for the door. "You haven't heard the last of this, Miss Blake," he said on his way out. "My lawyers will be in touch." The door slammed shut behind him.

Jesse, Trent, and I were stunned.

Alex signaled with her eyes for me to follow her. I shrugged to Jesse and Trent and followed her back into the office.

"You guys work on "Cooperstown" the rest of the day. I'll talk more to the lawyers about "Last Train Out.""

"Okay. See you tonight?" I worried that if we didn't spend time together right away in the real world, she may dismiss what we'd started as some whimsical fling.

"Not tonight, I have plans...don't look so dejected. I have plans with my daughter."

"You have a daughter?" Why was I so surprised? Did I expect that she'd spent her life waiting for me? Would I always come in second when it came to time with her?

"Yes, I do," she said.

"How old is she?" I regretted asking as soon as the question popped out of my mouth. I was sure Alex would take it to mean I was freaked out about it. Which maybe I was a little, but not enough to dissuade my interest in her.

"She's twenty-three."

I tried picturing Alex as a mother...but wait. If there was a mother, then there was also a father. "Who—"

"We divorced when she was a baby," she said. "He felt like I should have been happy as a wife and mother. I felt like I deserved that and more."

"You do deserve more," I said. "You deserve it all."

"You are trying to win my heart, aren't you?" she said.

"Yes," I said. "Is it working?" She gave me a mock suspicious look. "Was it hard on you?" I asked. "I mean, did he make it difficult for you?"

"Let's see," she said, reaching into her memory as she sat at the chair in front of her desk and motioned for me to sit in the other. "It was 1970 Los Angeles, and I was pregnant and in a bad marriage and trying to break into the music business." She stopped and looked at me like something just occurred to her. "And you...you were...dear God, you were four."

Obviously not the direction I intended for the conversation to go. "But you did it," I said. "And you have a good relationship with your daughter. Tell me about her." Anything to direct the conversation away from me as a four-year-old. "What's her name?"

"Justine, and she is very beautiful. When you meet her, you will get over this silly infatuation with me." She waved her hands in the air as she said "silly infatuation."

I grinned and looked her up and down. "Don't count on it."

"I'm flattered, but we'll see." She laughed and shook her head like she was wondering why the hell she was even contemplating something with me.

I stood from the chair and pulled her up with me, trying to think of something to say to distract her from her doubts. I could think of nothing, so I just pulled her into my arms and started kissing her like she was getting on a plane to nowhere. She was stiff with surprise and trepidation at first but quickly gave in.

"My goodness," she said. "That was unexpected."

When I got back to Jesse and Trent, I told them we were going to hold off on Last Train, but that I needed their help with a new song.

"What about Greg?" Jesse asked.

"Yeah," Trent said. "Who's going to be our drummer?"

"Damn," I said. "I forgot to ask."

Jesse rolled his eyes, and Trent said, "Were you just fucking her again?"

"No," I said. "I wasn't. I just got sidetracked. Did you guys know she has a daughter?"

"Yeah," Jesse said. "And she's hot. You didn't know that after all of your," he did air quotes, "research?"

"No...wait...Are there any more? Does she have any other kids?"

"Dude." Trent shook his head. "You are the most absent-minded person I have ever met."

"No other kids," Jesse said. "But wait till you see Justine. I'd take a crack at Justine...If I wasn't with Christy, of course."

"Okay, okay," I said. "Let's get to work. I need you guys to help me with this song."

I played what I had for them, which wasn't that much, and then explained what I was trying to say. We worked on it until we had it right. I was excited to play it for Alex and wished I had a way to tell her about it. It would just have to wait until she was back at the studio. I needed to occupy my mind.

"What's up tonight?" I asked.

"Party at John's later," Trent said. "You guys want to see a movie first?"

"Why don't you read a book?" Jesse asked. "You've seen all the movies."

We told Trent to come to the apartment after the movie and we would all ride together. Jesse and I went to pick up my Jeep from the club and then headed back to the apartment. I wanted to take Maggie out and get in a workout at the apartment gym. I was feeling sluggish from ignoring my routine and wanted to feel tight again.

When I got back from the gym, Bryan was at the apartment. He and Jesse were sitting in the living room watching TV. Jesse introduced me and said, "Trent is coming here after the movie, right?"

"That's what he said," I answered. We both knew that Trent may or may not come to ride with us. Actually, it was more likely that he knew we were trying to control him, and he would go directly to the party. That left us with figuring out what to do with Bryan. I didn't know anything about Bryan except that he was an artist. I told him that I liked his guitar picture in Trent's room and made as much small talk as I could about art.

"I thought you were coming tomorrow," I said, remembering that Trent had said he was expecting him tomorrow.

"I tried to call," Bryan said. "I called my parents' house, and I called here the other night. I tried to leave a message, but your machine was full."

Jesse and I glanced over at the answering machine that was blinking frantically.

"We should listen to those," I said.

Jesse nodded. "Ya think?"

I left Bryan to Jesse and went to take a shower. As the shower filled with steam, I tried to think about Trent and wondered if we should take Bryan to the party. I knew Trent would not want Bryan to see him that way, but I was also uncomfortable not keeping an eye on Trent. He and I had only been friends for a short time, but his drug use was not something I could ignore. It was more than just recreational use. He seemed to not care about himself. I couldn't stop him, so I wanted to at least look out for him.

As much as I wanted to figure out what to do with Bryan, Alex kept forcing her way into my thoughts. I replayed making love to her in my mind and could almost feel her touch. Not knowing when I would see her again, much less hold her, left me filled with frustration and desire. I had the choice of turning the water to cold and forcing my thoughts elsewhere or inching up the heat and soaping myself up. I reached for the soap.

Of course, Trent didn't show, so we took Bryan with us and went to the party. Jesse and I figured he could distract Bryan and I would go find Trent. Then we could all go do something else. By the time we got to John's house, it was almost eleven. His yard was still mostly dirt, but the weeds and the shrubs were cut. The house still needed paint, but he had painted the door black. When he answered the door, I told him the changes looked good. He swelled with pride and thanked me.

The house smelled like marijuana and sweaty guys. Jesse and Bryan went to the kitchen to get beer from the keg while I followed John to find Trent. He led me down the hallway and into a bedroom. When he opened the door, I saw something I would have expected to only see in a movie or a wild dream.

The only light was a small table lamp with a green bulb. Screaming music that was loud and unintelligible came from a large boom box. A guy wearing only long, green shorts with orange flowers was drawing with markers on two naked girls. He was drawing flowers and spiders and other random things. One of the girls with large, tanned breasts had a crude Tasmanian devil on her shoulder blade. I couldn't help but wonder if the markers were permanent or washable. The girls were going to sober up to some pretty bad body art.

"So, where's Trent?" I asked.

"Not sure," John said. "I thought he was in here."

Irritated, I edged past him and went to find Jesse. He and Bryan and now Christy and Amy were in the kitchen. "I can't find him," I said to Jesse as I walked by him and poured myself a beer from the keg.

In an obvious move to make me jealous, Amy hooked arms with Bryan. I acted like I didn't notice and went to look again. She followed me and grabbed me by the arm.

"I need to find Trent," I said, pulling away from her.

"I think I deserve better than this," she said.

I stopped. "You're right. I'm sorry."

"What happened in Vegas?" she asked. "You just took off without telling me or even calling me."

I didn't know what to say. Not wanting to get into it with her, I finally said, "It was just business about the band. I'm really worried about Trent. Do you know where he is?"

"I'm sure he's just partying. My brother is here, and that means drugs galore."

I realized the guy drawing on the girls was the same guy on her couch that night. "Why do you act like that's no big deal?"

"Because that's who they are. Who they have been for some time."

"That doesn't make it okay."

"You're right," she conceded. "Come on, I'll help you find him."

We went to the backyard and looked through the crowd of about fifty people. It probably wasn't the shitty front yard that attracted the cops after all. We went back and checked with her brother, no change there. "Where's the bathroom?" I asked. Amy took my hand and pulled me after her.

There was no light coming from the bottom of the door, so I assumed the bathroom was probably empty. Just as I reached up to open the door, Jesse, Christy, and Bryan walked up. "You find him?" Bryan asked as I pushed the door open to find Trent with his pants at his ankles and Yacht Boy Evan giving him a blowjob. As if that wasn't shocking enough for Bryan, Trent's arm was tied, and he had a needle poised to inject.

"Fuck," Trent slurred. He closed his eyes and tilted his head back to rest against the wall. Evan stood up and tried to close the door. I shoved Evan out of the way and took the needle from Trent. "Pull your damn pants up," I said as I yanked the rubber tie from his arm. I turned to talk to Jesse, but only Amy was still there.

"Jesse's taking Bryan back to the apartment," she said.

"I don't know what to do with him," I said. Trent was still leaned against the wall with his pants only half pulled up. I grabbed them and yanked them the rest of the way. Evan had disappeared into the party.

Amy stepped past me and looked at Trent's arm. She looked up his nose and lifted an eyelid. She asked Trent, "Did you take anything?"

"No," he said. "I'm just drunk."

She looked to me. "Nothing looks fresh. I believe he really is just drunk. Why don't we take him back to my apartment and look after him?"

We took him out to her car and drove to her apartment in silence. When we pulled into her parking lot, Trent came to and started talking nonsense. He was trying to ask about his brother, but he couldn't put his thoughts into comprehensible sentences. Amy parked as close as she could, then she and I each threw an arm over our shoulder and led him up the stairs and into the apartment.

"Should I put him in my bed?" Amy asked.

"Why don't we just lay him on the couch and see how he does for a while," I said.

"Okay. I'll call Jesse's and see if Christy is coming home. If not, we can put him in there later."

While she made the phone call, I pulled Trent's shoes off and put him on the couch. He mumbled a bit, then fell asleep. He snored softly like a child, and I felt that he was safe from himself for at least the time being.

Amy brought me a beer and sat next to me on the love seat. "She's staying at Jesse's. Are you hungry? I can fix you a sandwich or some eggs maybe?"

"I'm good. Thanks."

"You haven't known him long," Amy said. "Why do you care so much for him?"

"He's my friend. And I know what drugs can do."

"I think that's noble, but I know from my brother that efforts go unappreciated. He's going to do what he wants."

"I get that," I said. "But I'm not going to just watch."

She nodded and picked up the remote. "You want to watch some TV?"

I really wanted to go home. I was tired and wanted to be in my own bed, but I was stuck without a car.

"I know you don't want to be with me," Amy said. "It's okay."

"You're a good person," I said. "Quit trying to act like you're not and you are going to find the right guy."

"Can you tell me why you're not the right guy? Why don't you want me?"

"I don't know," I said. On paper she was the right girl for me, but I wanted Alex. I couldn't explain it because it really didn't make sense, but that was the truth. I wasn't interested in anybody else.

"Okay," she said softly. "You want to sleep in Christy's room?"

I had a visual of Jesse and Christy going at it in there. "No, I don't think so."

"You want to sleep on the couch? We can move him to her room."

My choices were down to the couch or in with Amy.

"Come on," she said, "I'll change the sheets on my bed, and you can sleep in there. I'll take Christy's room."

"I don't want to put you out of your room," I said.

"It's fine. Help me change all the sheets and let's get some sleep."

# 16

I woke up in Amy's room and for a minute forgot where I was. Then the whole ugly night came back to me. I got up and went to the kitchen. Trent was still asleep, but Amy was in the kitchen fixing toast and coffee. She wore dark-purple scrubs.

"Do you have time to drop us off before work?" I asked.

She handed me a cup of coffee and a piece of toast with butter and plum jam on it.

"Yeah. If we hurry. Can you get him going?"

I went to the couch and shook Trent. He woke slowly, then sat up and rubbed his eyes. "Ouch!" He pulled back, remembering his swollen side. It had healed very little.

"You look like shit," I said and handed him the coffee and toast.

"Feel like it too," he said, shoving the toast in his mouth and sipping the coffee. Amy came in from the kitchen and poured a splash of milk into the cup. Trent muttered, "Thanks." He looked up at Amy and then over at me. "Is it as bad as I remember?"

"Worse," I answered. "But you'll get through it. Now get up. She's taking us to get my Jeep."

"What time is it?" he asked.

I looked at my watch. "Nine fifteen. Why?"

"We were scheduled for nine today."

"What?"

"We are scheduled to be in at nine today." Trent rubbed his good eye.

"Fuuuuuccckkk," I said, jumping up from the couch. "Let's go." I grabbed his arm and pulled him up.

"Okay, okay, but I have to take a piss first."

Amy walked out of the room and came back with the toothbrush she'd given me before and some toothpaste. I brushed my teeth in the kitchen sink and splashed cold water on my face. She handed me a clean dish towel from the drawer.

"Do you want to use the phone?" she asked.

"For what? I don't know any phone number except Jesse's. And I'm sure he's already there."

"You should probably get the phone number to the studio today," she said.

"Yeah, I need to remember to do that."

Trent ambled into the room. "Let's go," he said.

Finally, we all headed out the door. Amy was the slowest driver ever. It was after ten by the time she pulled up to the studio. I jumped out and pushed the seat forward so Trent could follow me. He scooched towards the door sluggishly. I grabbed his arm and yanked him out. Amy got out of the car to say goodbye. I gave her a hug and thanked her for everything.

"Don't forget to get the phone number," she called as we rushed away.

When we got inside, Alex, Jeff, and Jesse were waiting. Jesse gave me a raised eyebrow, and I realized that they saw us pull up and get out of Amy's car. Alex saw me get out of Amy's car. Alex saw me hug Amy.

"Thank you for joining us, gentlemen," Alex said. "An hour's rate for studio time will be deducted from your stipends." She turned to walk away and said, "Get started, Jeff. I'll be back in an hour with their new drummer."

I ran after her. "Wait a second," I called. "Alex, hold on."

Once we were out of earshot from the others, she stopped. "Did you need something?"

"Yes," I said. "I'm sorry we were late."

"It's handled. Anything else?"

"Yes. It's not what it looks like."

"I don't care why you were late," she said. "Just get here on time."

"That's not what I mean," I said.

"Then what do you mean?" she asked as if she really had no idea.

I couldn't find the words. I was afraid if I told her about Trent, to explain why I was with Amy, it might jeopardize his place in the band. "Driving up with Amy," I finally said.

"I don't care about that," she said. "You don't answer to me in regard to your personal life." She didn't act mad; she acted like she really had no concern.

"But I want to," I said.

"You want to answer to me?" she asked with mock amusement. Now I could see she was clearly miffed with me.

"I do," I said. "I mean, I want you to know that I don't want anybody else. Only you."

"I believe you think that right now," she said. "You're twenty-seven, you don't know what you want. And I believe the young lady that dropped you off has eyes on you."

"I know what I want," I said. "And it's not her. It's you."

"Cory, you just got out of a long-term relationship and you're young," she said. She took my hand like she was about to break up with me before we even had a chance to be together.

I pulled it away. "I should have been out of that relationship a long time ago. I stayed for all the wrong reasons. I don't want to waste any more time not being where I should be. I have never felt the way you make me feel."

"Because you're twenty-seven," she said, exasperated. "You haven't had the time."

"I told you that I've been with two people since Jennifer," I said. "She is one of them. But that was before. Nothing happened with her last night. And by the way, my parents had been married for five years by the time they were my age."

She thought for a moment and said with frustration, "Just get back to work. We can talk more later."

I took her hand back. "I know what I want. I'm not going anywhere." I had been so busy worrying about all the other reasons that this wouldn't work that I hadn't even considered my age would be a problem for her.

"Well, for now I need you to rejoin the others," she said. "I'll be back soon."

"You find out anything about this new drummer that we have absolutely no say on?" Jesse asked.

"Just that she's sure we're going to like him," I said. I was sure she felt that way.

We worked on "Cooperstown" for a while, and then Jeff took a phone call and Jesse went to call Christy. Apparently, they were fighting again. That left Trent and me alone in the studio.

"You must think very little of me now," Trent said.

"I don't," I said. "I just worry about you." I focused on my friend. Alex would be back in an hour, and everything would be fine.

"I don't shoot up. I really don't. I was just really drunk, and Evan convinced me it would be awesome to shoot up during an orgasm."

I nodded and scratched my head.

"I know that's stupid. Although, it probably would be insanely cool...for those first few minutes. I don't even know if it's worth trying to talk to Bryan. What would I say?"

"I don't know. Maybe leave out the part about it being cool."

"He's my brother and I love him, but I don't think I can be who he wants me to be."

"You talking about the drugs or the blowjob?"

"Both."

"Well you're my friend and I love you," I said. "I don't care about the blowjob, but the drugs are going to cost you everything if you don't get yourself under control."

Jesse walked back into the room. I asked him, "Everything okay?"

"Yeah. You created quite a scene last night," he told Trent. "I convinced Bryan to stay last night, but I think he took off this morning."

"He sleep in my bed?" I asked. Jesse gave me a look, so I dropped it. It was time to wash the sheets anyway.

"I'm going to try and call him," Trent said. "Come get me if Miss Blake shows up."

"I think Christy might be cheating on me," Jesse said after Trent was gone.

"When? She's always with you." My friends were making it impossible to dwell on my own worries.

"That's what she said. Just a feeling. I can't explain it."

I remembered what Amy said about Christy the night we met. I wanted to tell Jesse but didn't know how. "If you don't trust her, maybe she's not the right girl."

"She says I have trust issues. What if she's right? What if it's me?"

"You guys ever do anything that would cause you not to trust her? You know...like a threesome or anything?" I didn't know how to ask Jesse about trust issues. I figured after Jennifer I probably had trust issues of my own.

"No. Are you asking me for a threesome?"

"No. No, of course not. I was just trying to figure out why you don't trust her."

"I know, I was just kidding. I'll figure it out."

Trent walked back into the room. I asked him, "Any luck?"

"He's at my grandmother's again. He said he tried to call the night we were playing cards. I never heard the phone ring."

Crap. The phone rang when I went into the kitchen to stop Trent from making my drink too strong.

"Anyway, I'll drive down to San Diego to see him tomorrow after the photo shoot. Maybe you guys could go too? I'm his brother, he has to forgive me...right?"

"Yeah, for sure," Jesse said.

"Uh-huh," I said.

None of us believed it. And now I had to go to San Diego. I wasn't sure what Jesse or I could do to help other than make sure he made it there sober. I looked at my watch, thinking Alex should have been back by then, when Jeff announced, "Miss Blake is back. Let's at least look like we're accomplishing something."

We stood and picked up our guitars, then looked to Jeff for guidance. He apparently drew a blank. Alex walked in and caught us standing around looking guilty. She acted like she didn't notice, but I knew better. I saw the split-second decision to let it go.

"Gentlemen," Alex said. "I'd like you to meet Mr. Ellis. He is your new drummer."

The guy stepped forward and said, "TJ. Call me TJ." He shook our hands. "I don't want to intrude," he said. He was tall with shoulder-length, thick golden hair. "I can audition," he said, looking around for a set of drums.

"Dude," Trent said. "I just have to run my fingers through those locks."

"Sure," TJ said and leaned in. Trent ran his fingers through his hair. Jesse and I laughed.

"You should feel this," Trent said.

I reached up and touched my own hair, a little jealous. "Let's hear you play," I said.

"You betcha," TJ said. He pulled two sticks from his back pocket. "My set's not here, so forgive me if I don't sound as good on a studio set."

"I'm sure it will be fine," I said. I glanced at Alex. She seemed proud of him, and I felt jealousy surge through my body. It was a new experience for me, and I didn't like it at all. Meanwhile, TJ was killing it on the drums that Greg hadn't picked up yet. When he finished, I said, "That's pretty good. Why aren't you already in a band?" I heard Jesse and Trent mutter, "Pretty good?"

"I don't know. Nobody ever asked me. I just help out where I can."

The guy had a constant smile. Why was he so happy? Oh yeah, because he had perfect hair. I slid up next to Alex. "Can I talk to you for a second?"

"I need you two to go over the material with TJ," Alex said to Jesse and Trent. She turned to Jeff. "Figure out the quickest way to get Greg off and TJ on." She looked at me and said loud enough for the others to hear, "May I see you for a moment?"

I followed her into her office. "Have you set up a checking account yet?" she asked. "I need someplace to deposit your money...less your fine, of course." She smiled the 'I'm joking but not really' smile.

"Not yet. I will tomorrow."

"Alright." She leaned back against her desk. "What did you want to talk to me about?"

"I think it's strange that someone as good as TJ is not already in a band," I said.

"He's worked for me for several years," she said. "I've used him for my own recordings and for other bands. He's a good guy. Very easygoing, which I would think would be a nice change for you from Greg."

"You've known him a long time?" I crossed my arms tightly.

"Yes." She tilted her head a little. "What is bothering you?"

I couldn't put it into words. I had visions of TJ on the cover, on the billboards...in Alex's bed.

"We don't have time to go through drummers," she said. "If you don't like him, just tell me why and I'll find somebody else."

"You'd find somebody else? Just because I don't like him?"

"Yes, but I would prefer a reason. I assure you he is very good."

"Okay," I said. "I trust you." I took a deep breath, relieved.

"Good, because I've been at this for a while. I know what I'm doing." She sighed and held her hand out to me. I took it and stood close to her. "By the way," she said. "We have photo shoots tomorrow." She ran her hand across my face. "I want to see you there with that sexy shadow." She ran her thumb over my lips. I held it there and kissed it. "And for God's sake, tell Jesse to get Trent there in one piece."

"I'll tell him," I said.

She looked at me and shook her head as if she was throwing in the towel. "I have something for you," she finally said. She paused again, deciding what to say next. "Oh, what the hell. Would you like to come to the house for dinner tonight?"

"Yes," I said. "I would love that."

"I'll have Marco pick you up," she said. "My house can be hard to find."

Marco knocked at the door right at six thirty. I was almost ready, so I asked him to come in. He declined, saying that he should wait in the car.

"That's crazy," I said and pulled him inside. "I won't be that long. You want a Coke or water or anything?" He hesitated, which made me laugh. I went to the refrigerator and grabbed one of each. I held them up. "Coke?" I said and presented it to him. "Or water?" and offered it. "Or both?" I held them both out.

"The water is great. Thank you."

"Grab a seat," I said. "I'll be ready in just a second."

He remained standing while I ran back for a final inspection. I was clean-shaven. I wanted my face smooth against Alex. The five o'clock shadow look would be good and strong by the photo shoot. I wore jeans and a black button-up dress shirt. I took a final look in the mirror. It was as good as it was going to get. I took a deep breath and tried to shake off the nerves.

"Let's go," I said to Marco as I returned to the living room.

He jumped from the sofa and said, "Yes, sir."

"I told you don't call me sir," I said as we left the apartment. My legs were much longer, so I was a few strides ahead of him. When we got to the car, he rushed in front of me and opened the back door. It was the same car as before. Not the limo, but the other one. "Do I have to sit back there?"

He looked at me blankly.

"I'll sit up here with you," I said. I felt silly climbing into the back without Alex back there, so I opened the front and got in.

On the way to Alex's house, I tried to make conversation with Marco. I asked him questions about Alex, but he was hesitant and vague, so I changed the subject. Turned out he was a base-ball fan too, so we talked about that. He liked the Angels, and since I was a Rangers fan, he was the enemy. Neither team had had a good year, so we debated the needed changes.

As we got closer to the house, the streets were winding up a hill and lined with trees. I was glad I didn't sit in the back. I would have been carsick for sure. As the car made its way through the twists and turns and climbed the hill, I began to wish I had made myself a drink before we left. I looked out the window and could see mansions scattered about. I started to sweat and feel sick to my stomach. I asked Marco to turn up the air.

"What's the matter?" he asked as he cranked the air conditioner. "You sick?"

"I'm not sure," I said. "I'm either carsick or I'm having a mild panic attack." I wiped the sweat from my brow. "I need a drink," I said. "I'm pretty sure it's a panic attack."

"What are you panicked about?" he asked as he produced a flask from his jacket pocket.

I opened it and took a long gulp. It was bourbon, but I didn't care. Marco pulled off the road and put the car in park. He sat quietly until I handed him back the half empty flask. "Pull yourself together, man," he said and took a drink. "What are you panicked about?" he asked again.

I tried to pull myself together, but I suddenly felt so far away from Alex. As if nothing had happened between us and she was the same woman I lusted over the day I met her. "I don't know what I'm doing," I said.

"Have another drink," Marco said and handed it to me. "A sip this time," he said.

I put the flask to my mouth. I took the drink, and it was more than a sip, then handed it back to him.

"I'm okay," I said, more to convince myself than anything. "I can do this."

"Of course you can do this," he said. "You're fucking Corbett Scott. The next big thing in rock 'n' roll. You got this."

"Yeah, I got this." My voice cracked. I cleared my throat. "Let's go."

Marco put the flask away and pulled back onto the road. My heart rate was slowing as the bourbon kicked in, and I felt much calmer. "Damn," I said. "I was having a meltdown."

"Yeah, you were. You good now?"

Marco turned into a private drive and entered a code. Then we began the ascent to the house. When he finally pulled into the driveway, he put the car in park and said, "Here you go."

The house was, of course, gigantic. It was mostly white with some dark wood trim and lots of windows, modern contemporary. "Here I go?" I said. "What? I just walk up and knock on the door like normal people do?"

"You want me to go with you, don't you?" he said.

"Yes," I said, nodding emphatically. "Yes, I do."

"Okay. You want me to pull into the garage so you can see her collection of cars first?"

"Yes," I said. "That's exactly what I want. More to feel insecure about. Thank you, Marco."

He laughed and said, "I was just kidding. Come on, let's go inside."

I opened the door and stepped out of the car. "So she doesn't have a collection of cars?"

Marco walked past me and said, "Oh yeah, she does." He opened a cellular phone and called Alex to let her know we were coming in. He said, "Yes, ma'am, he does," then paused a few seconds, then said, "Yes, ma'am." Then he pressed the button and put the phone away.

"She knows I'm making you come with me, doesn't she?" I said.

Marco continued to find humor in my discomfort. "Yep," he said.

I willed my face to not turn red. Happy thoughts, Cory, happy thoughts. I remembered giving my sister the puppy and focused on her joyful expression as we climbed the stairs to the front door. When we got to the top, Marco opened the door, and we stepped into a large rectangular foyer. The marble floor was done to look three-dimensional as it flowed into the house. White tiles zigzagged with a dark-chocolate tile between the zigs and the zags so that it looked like boxes or steps.

Alex appeared from around the corner. "Welcome." She spread her arms like she was welcoming me to the royal palace. I stood there like a lump. "Come in," she said and reached for me, her doubts about us seemingly gone, at least for the time being.

"Will there be anything else, Miss Blake?" Marco asked.

Alex looked at me seductively, then turned to Marco. "I'm not certain. Stay close by."

"Yes, ma'am."

Once he was gone, Alex turned to me. "I'm so glad you're here. Let me show you around." She pulled me after her.

The house was immaculate, not a speck of dust or anything out of place, and I wondered if her refrigerator had old leftovers or slimy lettuce.

The main living area was done in mostly cream and chocolate, with a large glass coffee table. One wall had an artificial fireplace about six feet in length with a dark wood mantel above it. Above the mantel hung an oil painting of Alex from the shoulders up.

"That was a gift," she said. "It will be very valuable upon my death, if it isn't already."

Her lack of modesty amused me and actually relaxed me a bit. An entire wall was a window overlooking her pool area and the rest of Los Angeles. The pool looked as if the water was flowing off the hill.

Alex slid her arm across my back and looked out the window with me. "You can have this too," she said. "I'm working very hard for you."

It was hard to picture. I started doing like I did when I imagined winning the lottery. What would I do with that much money? I would set up a college fund for Cari, buy Kevin a car, send my parents on an incredible vacation, buy into the world series of poker...

"Imagining it?" Alex asked.

The sun began to set, and the view was breathtaking. We stood silently watching for some time.

"Are we going to eat sometime tonight?"

We turned around.

"Cory, this is my daughter, Justine," Alex said.

Justine looked so much like Alex that it was eerie. Her hair was a bit lighter, and she dressed more like Amy than Alex, but she was definitely a younger version of Alex.

"I hope you're hungry," Justine said. "There's enough food to cure world hunger in there."

"I wasn't sure what you liked," Alex said.

"I'm easy," I said and followed them to the table.

I pulled Alex's chair out for her. Justine sat down quickly so I didn't have to mess with her. Although there was plenty, Justine grossly exaggerated the amount of food. I filled my plate with roasted asparagus, steak medallions, and grilled swordfish. Ice water with lemon and a glass of wine were already in front of me. I wasn't much of a wine drinker, but I took a sip to be polite.

"Damn," Alex said. "I told them beer for you. I'm sorry, let me correct that."

I started to protest, but she was too quick. She jumped up and went to the kitchen for it herself. As soon as she was out of the room, Justine said, "My mother will use you up and toss you aside."

At least living with a complete bitch for several years would pay off. "I get that this is weird for you," I said. "But—"

"There are no buts. She is a very shrewd businesswoman. She will see through you soon enough. When she has gotten what she wants from you, you will be history."

"It's nice to meet you too," I said and took a big gulp of wine.

"You're a project," Justine said. "When the project is through, so are you."

Alex swept back into the room and placed a bottle of beer in front of me as she sat down.

"Thank you," I said and kissed her hand for Justine's benefit. "You didn't have to do that."

Alex squeezed my hand. "Of course, my dear." She looked back and forth between Justine and me. "Did I miss anything important?"

"Not a thing," I said and took a gulp of beer.

"We were just talking about the hottest clubs in L.A.," Justine said. "I told Cory I would be happy to take him to some."

"Sounds like fun," Alex said without missing a beat.

Justine gave me an evil eye that I pretended not to notice. Alex filled me in about the photo shoot schedule as we finished eating. Jesse, Trent, and TJ were being sent to one studio with Jeff, and she and I were going to another. I understood that it was to prevent them seeing how much extra attention I would be getting. I felt a surge of guilt for misleading my friends, but it disappeared when Alex put her hand on my knee under the table.

Justine took a sip of wine then dabbed her mouth with her napkin before tossing it on her plate. "Dinner was delicious, Mother," she said as she stood. "It was nice to meet you, Cory." She started to walk away and then turned and said, "Clubbing another night?"

"Sure," I said. Once she was gone, I turned to Alex. "I never—"

"I know," Alex said. "Other than that, what do you think of her?"

"When I first saw her, I thought she looked just like you."

"And now?"

"Your personalities are so different that it doesn't seem that way anymore."

"Anything else?"

I thought for a moment, wanting to make sure I worded things right. "I guess her age makes me feel—"

"Like you're with the wrong Blake?" Alex said matter-of-factly as she sipped her wine.

"No," I said. "Not like that at all. What I was going to say is that you've experienced so many things without me."

Alex leaned across the table and put her lips to mine, just long enough to tease. "Just wait till you see what I'm going to experience with you." She ran her hand across my face. "I thought you were going to have the shadow for your shoot."

"Don't worry," I said. "It'll be there by tomorrow."

"Ah, yes," she said, then rose from her seat. "I have something for you. Follow me."

I followed her back into the living area. She took a box from an end table drawer and fell into the couch, motioning for me to sit next to her. That couch was comfortable enough to sleep on every single night. She handed me a wrapped box the size of a child's shoebox.

"What's the occasion?" I asked. Unexpected gifts were the best. I couldn't imagine what I could give Alex that she didn't already have. Plus, I couldn't afford her taste. It would have to be something very personal...like...hmm...wine? No, that was dumb, she had plenty of that. Certainly not jewelry. I couldn't think of anything.

"Cory?" Alex said.

"Yeah?"

"Open the box."

I ripped off the paper and opened the box. It was a cellular phone. "Cool," I said. I flipped it open and held it to my ear.

She laughed. "There's no dial tone, silly. It's a cell phone."

"What's your number? I'll call you."

"It's already programmed in there. Let me show you." She took the phone from me and showed me how to use it.

I raised an eyebrow, feigning suspicion. "Now you can find me no matter where I am," I said.

"And you me," she said.

"Yeah? What if I call you in the middle of the night?"

"Then we'll have phone sex."

"Oh, hell yeah." I pressed the button to call her. We heard her phone chirp from across the room. She stood and went to get it.

"Are you twelve?" she said as she dug for the phone in her purse. She found it, opened it, and put it to her ear. "This is Miss Blake," she said in her business voice.

"Thank you, Miss Blake," I said into the phone, watching her across the room.

She began a slow and flirtatious walk back to me, still talking into the phone. "You are welcome, Mr. Scott." She stopped just before me and tossed the phone aside, her dark eyes burning into me. Unable to contain myself, I reached for her. She straddled me on the couch, took my face in her hands, and started kissing me like she meant it. She ran her fingers through my hair and gently tugged as her tongue and mine danced slowly together. It was at that moment that I knew for sure. I was in love with Alex and would do anything to hang on to her.

## 17

The morning sun crept slowly from the horizon, illuminating Alex's bedroom as it rose. I watched her sleep, refraining from scooping her into my arms. When the sun was finished and the bedroom was bright, her eyes began to flutter. "Good morning," she said. She flung her arm across me and scooched closer.

I sat up against the headboard. "Did I fall asleep on you?" I asked. Her face was free from makeup.

She looked up. "You're a typical man. Snoring moments after the orgasm."

I laughed. "I don't snore."

"I must look a mess," she said, shaking her hair back from her face. "I got up after you fell asleep and did my nightly routine. I meant to get up before you this morning."

"You don't look a mess. You're beautiful," I said, and I meant it. She looked at me skeptically. "In a different way," I said. "Not the glamorous Alexandra Blake, but my naturally beautiful Alex." Her skin was smooth, and her eyes had a sexy, sleepy look.

Alex slipped her hand under the sheets. "We have a long day ahead of us," she said.

"So, start it right?" I said as I slid back under the covers and pulled her on top of me.

The photo shoot was a total grind. Hours of shots with me unshaven. Then hours of shots with my neck shaved. Then hours of shots with me clean-shaven. With endless delays at every turn. Alex was there overseeing every bit of it with patience and perfection. I tried to remain professional, but by the end of the day, I was at my breaking point.

"Dear God, when will it end?" I moaned to Alex as she handed me a bottle of water.

"We're almost done. You're doing great."

"You said that three hours ago."

Alex touched her chin in thought. "As long as we're here, why don't we do some shots..."

It took everything in me not to groan.

"...of you and me together? I have some ideas for down the line."

I was okay with that. My favorite shot ended up being a picture of us holding each other naked. Well, at least we looked naked. We held one another so closely that all the good areas were covered up, but it was still extremely sexy.

It was after dark by the time we finally finished, and we were both exhausted. We had dinner together at a small hole-in-the-wall restaurant where Alex knew the owner.

"I like this place," I said.

She touched my hand. "I thought you might. It's not fancy, but the food is incredible."

"Did I do okay today?" I asked, fishing for approval.

"Yes," she said. "I think it went very well. It's all very tiring, but it will pay off."

"What about last night?" I said with a mischievous grin.

Her whole body relaxed. "Last night was fantastic." She raised an eyebrow seductively. "As was this morning."

"I thought the same thing," I said.

"I must say," she said, touching my hand again. "You are very attentive in bed."

She was stroking my ego, and I knew it and loved her for it. My mind flashed back to the sex talk my dad gave me at fifteen.

"What?" Alex said. "You're grinning."

I laughed. "I was just remembering my dad talking to me about sex when I was a teenager."

"Go on," she said. "I'm listening."

"He told me to always make sure I took care of whoever I was with. He said, 'Cory, it's easy for a man to get wrapped up in himself at a time like that. It will serve you well if you choose it as a time to think of others.' "

"Ah," she said. "I must thank your father."

I'd read every book on the subject I could get my hands on.

When I tried to pay, because at last something was affordable, Alex said it was a business expense and handed the server her card. After dinner, Marco drove me home.

"Damn," I said as I climbed out of the car. "I forgot the phone."

"That means it's not important to you," Alex said.

I jumped back in. "That's not true."

"I know," she said sleepily. "I was just kidding. I'll bring it to you."

"I'll miss you tonight," I said.

"And I you, but I will see you soon."

My heart hurt a little as they drove away.

When I walked in the apartment, Maggie went crazy greeting me. Jesse and TJ were at the kitchen table playing cards with a guy I didn't know.

"Where's Trent?" I asked as I hugged and loved on Maggie.

"Asleep," Jesse said. Then he looked up and said, "In your bed."

"What? Why?"

"You were supposed to go with us to see his brother."

"Damn, I forgot. She been out?" I asked about Maggie as I walked towards my room.

"Yep. Wanna play?"

"What time are we due in tomorrow?"

"We're off. Playing poker all night. You in? But none of that Guts bullshit."

I opened the door to my room and flipped on the light. Trent was under the sheets from the waist down and not wearing a shirt. "You better have something on under those sheets," I said.

Trent held up his arm to shield his eyes from the light. "Fuck you," he said. "I'm naked and I jizzed all over your sheets. That's what you get."

"I'm sorry, I was stuck at the damn photo shoot all day."

"I know. We were too. Why didn't you go with us?"

"I don't know," I lied. "I just do what I'm told. Did you see Bryan?"

"Yeah. He's back at my parents'. He said I'm all talk and that my actions speak for themselves."

I could understand that. "Do you think you should spend more time at your house? Work things out with your parents? That might help."

"Probably. You going to play cards?"

"I guess. I didn't know we were off tomorrow."

Trent sat up. "Miss Blake didn't tell you?"

"No." I was bummed and didn't even try to hide it.

"That means you don't have plans with her tomorrow. Right?" Trent said as he threw the sheets off and climbed out of bed. Thankfully, he was wearing jeans.

"Guess not," I said.

"Let's go to my parents' for lunch tomorrow. My father likes you. I'll behave. That's a start...right?"

"Yeah, okay, that sounds fine," I said. "Let's go play cards."

I was so mad at myself for forgetting the phone that I could barely concentrate on the cards. And to make matters worse, we weren't going to the studio the next day either.

"You in or out?" Trent asked me. I hadn't even been paying attention, so I mucked my cards. "Cool," Trent said and took the chips from the middle. He took a swig directly from the bottle of Jack.

"You don't have to get wasted every day," I said.

"But I'm a grown-up, so I can if I want," he answered.

"Relax," TJ said. "We're off tomorrow. Let's have some fun. Want me to fix you a drink?"

"Yeah, I guess so. Why are we off? You just started," I asked TJ.

TJ went into the kitchen to fix our drinks. "I don't know," he called out. "Something about Jeff figuring things out."

He returned with a Jack and Coke for me. I took a sip, and it was as gross as I remembered. Trent took it from me and downed it. "You're a terrible bartender," he told TJ. Trent went to the kitchen and came back a few minutes later with a gin and tonic for me that was pretty good.

I drank and played cards till I just couldn't stay awake any longer. It was after four in the morning when I finally gave in. I stumbled off to bed while the others continued playing. The apartment was a wreck, but I figured I could clean when I woke up.

The phone rang, but it was in the living room and I was in my bedroom. I opened one eye to see the clock radio read 8:16 am. I dozed back off.

Maggie jumped from the bed, barking like a fool. I sat up and looked at the clock again. This time it read 10:33 am. Someone was at the door. If Maggie hadn't been barking like a maniac, I would have ignored it and gone back to sleep. But she was, so I forced myself up and trudged across the apartment, which looked like a frat house. Trent was on one couch, TJ on the other, and the other guy asleep on the floor. The place reeked of booze, cigarette smoke, and weed.

The guys were out cold, and Maggie's barking didn't even cause a stir. I opened the door and there was Alex. There she stood looking like Alexandra Blake, while I was in boxers looking as hungover as I felt.

"Hey," I said, trying to control Maggie.

"Good morning," she said. "I brought you your phone." She started rooting through her purse.

Lord, help me. "I have to take her out," I said, still struggling with my dog. "Let me throw on some clothes and we can go for a walk."

"That sounds fine," she said. "Are you going to leave me waiting out here?"

I glanced over my shoulder. TJ's balls were protruding from his boxers and resting comfortably on the couch. "No, of course not," I said, reluctantly moving over to let her in. When I reached behind her to shut the door, Maggie broke loose and jumped on her, knocking her back a few steps. I yanked on Maggie and spanked her harder than I meant to and immediately felt bad for it. She cowered, yelped, and rolled onto her back. I took a deep breath, wiped the sweat from my forehead, and said, "You think you could close your eyes on the way to my room?"

Alex brushed the back of her hand across my face and said, "It's okay, I've seen worse. Remember, I've worked with musicians for over twenty years."

"Really?"

"Really."

"Okay, but still, look straight ahead the whole time," I said as walked her through the room, trying to block as much as I could. I closed the bedroom door behind us, grateful that my room was clean and tidy. I apologized to Maggie with a pat on the head. "What are you doing here anyway?" I asked her as I went into the bathroom to clean up. "Not that I'm not happy to see you."

"I wanted you to have your phone. Also, I'd like to invite you to the tennis match today and a party afterward."

I spit out the rest of the toothpaste and turned off the sink. She was sitting on the bed with Maggie lying next to her. She was petting her as she talked to me. I kissed Alex and said, "I'm really happy to see you. Okay for me to take a quick shower?"

"Of course."

I turned the water on and kicked my boxers into the clothes hamper. "What time is the tennis match?" I called from the shower.

"Not until two thirty. I thought we could grab lunch first."

Lunch. Crap. Trent.

"Unless you have other plans," she said.

I turned the water off and grabbed the towel to dry off. I wrapped the towel around my waist and went to sit next to her.

"Mmm, you smell nice," she said. "I put your phone on your nightstand."

Trent was asleep on the couch and probably forgot all about lunch. In fact, he would probably sleep most of the day. "What should I wear?" I asked.

"Whatever's comfortable."

"You understand that means jeans and a tee shirt," I said.

"Then jeans and a tee."

"I don't want to embarrass you," I said.

"You wouldn't. But if you want to dress nicer for you, then dress nicer."

I was embarrassed to admit that I had no idea how to dress when I was with her. I truly was a jeans and tee guy. I never had a job that required that I dress up or really went anyplace nicer than a steakhouse. Jennifer complained about it all the time, but I just ignored it for the most part. I wasn't interested. With Alex, I wanted to go anyplace she was.

Alex put her hand on my knee and slid it under the towel. "Just trying to get your attention," she said.

"You always have my attention," I said.

"Except for when you're in Cory Land," she said and squeezed my knee. "Wear jeans and a tee," she said. "I'm working on a wardrobe for you for when I need you to dress a certain way. Okay?"

"Okay." That was a load off my mind.

I threw on some clothes, and then we took Maggie for her walk. She finally peed while on her leash. After the walk, I put Maggie back in the apartment, which was still quiet.

"Where's Marco?" I asked.

"I gave him the morning off."

"You drove over here?"

"Yes," she said. "I do know how to drive."

We walked to the parking lot, and amidst all the middle-class cars stood her bright-red convertible Viper. Alex put the keys in my hand and said, "Take me to your favorite place for lunch."

I was still a bit hungover, so my favorite place would have been Whataburger, which they didn't have in California. Fatburger was the next best thing. "You sure?" I asked.

"You owe me a meal," she said as I opened the passenger side and she got in.

I got into the driver's seat and started the car. I had never driven a car with so much power. At first, I was hesitant and nervous, but by the time I pulled into Fatburger, I was confident and cool.

"You said my favorite place," I said.

"I thought you were a healthy eater." Alex lowered her sunglasses to confirm her fears.

"I have my weaknesses," I said. "Give it a try?"

She glanced down at her white outfit, and I imagined a blob of ketchup landing there.

"I will give it a try, for you," she said. "But don't make a habit of it."

We went inside, and I ordered two cheeseburger meals while Alex went and sat down. As I took the tray to her, I noticed a few people were looking at her and whispering. "Omg, that's Alexandra Blake," one young girl said. "Look dude, Alexandra Blake," said a teenage boy. "Isn't that...Alexandra Blake?" said another.

"Sorry," I said while setting the tray down and sliding into the booth. "I didn't think about that."

"You get used to it," she said. "These burgers have onions. Quite a bit of onions."

"It's okay as long as we both eat them," I said. "They cancel each other out."

"What about everybody else we talk to?"

"I didn't think about that."

She picked up the burger and picked off the chopped onions as much as she could before each bite. "This is actually very tasty," she said.

After I wolfed mine down and she ate about a third of hers, I said, "Come on, let's go. You've been a good sport."

When we got to the tennis match, Dustin Hoffman was sitting a few seats down from ours. I resisted the urge to tell him how good he was in *Midnight Cowboy*. He and Alex nodded at each other.

"He doesn't like you much, does he?" I said, noticing his impassive expression.

"No," she said. "But most people don't. What can you do?"

"Asshole," I said defensively. He sucked in...well, nothing he did sucked. Asshole. She smiled and squeezed my hand.

The match lasted about two hours, and then we went to a party for a player I had never heard of. It was like a scene from Hollywood. There were tables set up around the pool area with champagne on ice at every table. The waiters wore tuxedos, and almost everyone wore white, or if they were bold, they wore off-white. I was uncomfortable and wanted to leave, but Alex drug me around to meet "important people." I smiled and shook hands obediently.

"Alexandra," some guy exclaimed with his arms outstretched to greet her. "I wasn't sure I'd see you here."

"Oh, please, Steven," she said as he kissed her on the cheek. "You knew I would be here."

"Well let's just say I hoped you would," he said with a big fake smile. He was a tall, good-looking Black guy that looked like he just stepped out of *GQ* magazine. He had a graying, very closely shaved beard, which led me to believe he was a few years older than Alex. Why was she there with someone like me instead of someone like him? I was sure Alex and everybody else were thinking the same thing. He took her hands and said, "I've missed you. We should talk."

Alex pulled her hands away. "Steven, I'd like you to meet my friend, Corbett Scott."

I reluctantly extended my hand to shake, though I'd rather have put it in hot oil. He quickly shook my hand with equal reluctance. He muttered, "Nice to meet you," then looked right back to Alex. "Give me a minute, please?"

I did not want her to give him a minute.

"We can talk another time," she said. "Now isn't good."

Wait. What? Another time? Like when I wouldn't be around? Jealousy and anger surged through my veins. This jealousy thing was bullshit, but I had trusted Jennifer completely and blindly, and I was sure not going to make that mistake again. "Can we go?" I said quietly but firmly into her ear.

"Yes," she said. "We can." Then she looked at him. "It was nice to see you again."

"Two minutes," he said, "and then you never have to talk to me again if that's what you want."

"Oh, all right," she said. "Make it quick, Cory and I have someplace to be." She turned to me. "Get us a drink? I won't be a minute."

"Yeah," Steven said. "Go get us a drink, kid."

I knew my face was good and red. I didn't think Alex heard him, but I was still angry with her. Not sure what else to do, I went to the bar and ordered a double short gin and tonic. I finished it in three gulps and ordered another. I wasn't sure how long I had been gone, but it was more than two minutes, so I went back for her.

When I got back, he seemed to be pleading his case. Alex was looking around like she wasn't really interested, but I was furious with her for giving him the time.

"Is that for me?" she asked when I walked up to them.

"Yeah." I handed her the half empty glass.

"It's only half full," she said. "Why didn't you get us both one?"

"Send a boy to do a man's job," Steven said.

"It was nice to see you again, Steven," Alex said. "But we really must go."

Relief. But only for a second.

Steven grabbed Alex by the elbow and pulled her so that he was talking into her ear. "You are making a fool of us both," he said through clenched teeth. "What are you doing with this bargain basement white boy?"

I wasn't one to lose my temper easily, but at that moment, I saw red. I took Steven by the throat and told him to let go of her. Shocked, he dropped her elbow. I let go of his neck, giving a good shove first, causing him to lose his balance and fall backward. A crowd began to gather.

Steven regained his composure as his friends helped him to his feet. Once he was standing, he brushed them away and got in my face. Alex pulled at me and asked me repeatedly to go, but I wasn't listening. Steven calmly said, "When she tires of you, she will be right back in my bed."

The next thing I knew, he was back on the floor with a bloody mouth and I was rubbing my fist.

"You will be hearing from my attorney," he seethed while his friends scooped him up again.

The adrenaline began to subside, and I realized Alex wasn't pulling on me any longer. In fact, she was gone. Where the hell was she?

# 18

Because I was spending the day with Alex, I left the cell phone at home on the nightstand. So, there I was again, unable to call her. I felt like an animal in the zoo as I walked around looking for her while people pointed and whispered. I finally found her waiting for her car at the valet.

"You just plan on leaving me here?" I asked.

"Marco is on his way to take you home," she said without looking at me.

I stepped in front of her so she didn't have a choice, and said, "I'm sorry."

"I can't talk to you right now." She looked away.

"Come on, Alex, I'm sorry. What else can I say?"

"You made him look like the good guy," she said. Then she looked me in the eyes. "And you embarrassed me. I told you these are important people. People that we need."

"I don't care about that," I said.

"Well you know what?" she said, pointing at her own chest. "I do."

"I couldn't let him talk about you like that," I said.

"Like what?" she said, throwing her arms up as if words alone were not enough to convey her displeasure with me. "Like what?" she repeated, her arms still flailing about. I took a step back to avoid any accidental or intentional contact.

"Like you going back to his bed," I said, getting angry all over again. The valet had her car ready, but he stood back and watched the show.

"You do remember that I'm forty-four years old, right? And that I have a grown daughter...right?"

"Yeah. So?"

"So, I have had sex before you."

My damn face was burning, and I knew it was red as much as I willed it not to be. "Well I don't want to hear about it, and I'm damn sure not going to let him talk about it." I knew I was being irrational, but I couldn't seem to help myself.

"Grow up, Cory," she said, her anger subsiding, but just a tad. "People are going to talk. How am I going to take you anyplace if you act like this?"

"Maybe I don't want to go anyplace with you," I said. "Who needs your pompous, condescending people?" I regretted saying it as soon as the words came out of my mouth. It set her off all over again.

"Cory," she said, pointing at me, voice rising. "You are exhausting. If you're too immature to see that, then I can't help you. And where the hell is my damn car?"

The valet rushed forward. "It's ready now, Miss Blake."

She followed him to the car, leaving me standing there. Son of a bitch. I wanted to punch the guy all over again.

"Looks like we have another victim."

I turned to find Justine. "What are you doing here?" I asked irritably.

"I've been here the whole time. I saw and heard everything. You need a ride?"

"Marco is on his way," I said, as if that wasn't the same as her abandoning me.

"Don't look so devastated," Justine said. "Show up tomorrow with flowers and all will be fine."

"Really?"

"Or if you're done, just act like you two never even had anything at all, and she'll do the same."

"I guess you've seen this before," I said.

"She'll let you hang around as long as she needs you or until someone better comes along. I don't want to hurt your feelings, but it's better that you know sooner rather than later, right?"

"I think we have more than that," I said, though I wasn't sure I believed it. I would just have to make sure nobody better came along. Somehow.

"Come on. I'll let Marco know I'm driving you. My car is already pulled up."

I followed her to a silver BMW and got in.

"Drink first?" she asked. I nodded.

I really didn't want to go have a drink. I wanted to go make up with Alex. I played the argument through my mind over and over. Hopefully, if I gave her some time, she would miss me as much as I already missed her.

"You deserve better," Justine said. "She's my mother and I love her, but she is her first priority." She pulled into a beach bar and said, "Find us a table out back. I'll get us some drinks."

It was warm outside, and there were outdoor speakers playing surf music. I chose a table with some shade and watched the water while I waited. She brought us a pitcher of beer and sat next to me. "You know you can get just about any girl you want, don't you," she said as she poured us each a glass.

"Like you?" I said and took a big gulp.

She sipped hers and said, "What? You don't find me attractive?"

"Of course I do," I said. "You look just like her."

"Do you think you're the only one she's seeing?" she asked with a knowing look on her face.

"I trust her," I said. "And she trusts me."

"Does she trust you? Or does she just not care if you're with anybody else?"

I wanted to believe that Justine was just trying to manipulate me, but I thought she might be right. Alex didn't seem jealous when she saw me with Amy now that I thought about it.

"How did you like the tennis match?" she asked.

"It was fine," I said. Who was I kidding? I didn't give a damn about tennis.

"When I saw the fight with Steve, I knew you guys would argue, so I waited for you."

"Thanks," I said, not really meaning it. I went back and forth from angry to heartbroken. Why couldn't Alex see that I had no choice?

The server dropped off another pitcher, and Justine ordered some shots. Halfway through the second pitcher, I started to feel the buzz. It was time to cut myself off or commit myself to getting drunk. I chose the latter. After a third pitcher and another shot, Justine wanted to walk the beach, so I paid the tab and followed her down the steps to the sand. She kicked off her shoes and seemed to float over the sand while I lumbered through it. She wanted to put her feet in the water, but I didn't, so I sat down to wait for her.

She danced along the shore, allowing the waves to splash against her as if they were warming her. A few minutes later, she was back at my side with water dripping from her eyelashes and her brown nipples showing through her pale-yellow dress.

"Aren't you cold?" I asked, shivering a little myself since the sun had started to set.

"No." She smiled wildly and spun around. "That felt great."

Sand stuck to the back of her legs, and soon I found myself not only admiring her legs, but once again looking at her nipples.

"What are you looking at?" she asked.

"Nothing," I lied.

Justine fell to her knees in front of me. Our eyes met, and it seemed that I had forever to stop her from kissing me. But I didn't. She put her lips softly on mine. I shoved my tongue into her mouth and lunged forward, knocking her into the sand. I reached for her leg and pulled it up next to me and then did the same to the other. She wrapped them around me and held the back of my head so that our mouths were pressed tightly together. Alex and Steven flashed into my mind. Anger surged through me and fueled my desire. I slid my hand up her thigh. Alex and I making love flashed. I took hold of her panties and started to peel them away. The line between Alex and Justine started to blur. I love you, Alex. Not sure if I said it aloud or only in my head, I put my hands in the sand to hold myself up and pulled away.

"What's wrong?" Justine asked.

I looked at her and finally understood what I was doing. "Oh shit," I gasped, clenching fists full of sand. "What have I done?" Adrenaline pumped through me, and I was still hard and wrapped up in Justine's legs. I pushed myself up, breaking free from her, and stumbled to the water. "Fuck fuck fuck," I said as I threw the handfuls of sand into the ocean and stepped waist deep into the cold water. The reality of what I would have to explain filled me with anguish. Would Alex be able to forgive me, or had I already ruined everything? Justine tugged at me, trying to pull me from the water.

"Come on," she pleaded. "Let me take you home. Nothing happened. We can keep it that way."

I followed her back to her car. She took a beach towel from her trunk and wrapped it around me. The sun had gone down. I was drunk and shivering.

"Don't worry," she kept saying. "I won't tell her."

The bathroom was damp from the steam, and the mirror was completely fogged up. The water was too hot, but I would stand in it until the drunkenness simmered to a buzz. Eventually, my mind began to clear, so I turned off the water and grabbed the towel hanging over the shower door. I dried off and put on boxers and a tee shirt, feeling somewhere between buzzed and hungover. I went to the kitchen and made a large glass of ice water and a sandwich and walked the apartment as I ate and drank, determined to sober up. Maggie followed my every step.

When I finally felt like I could form complete thoughts and sentences, I went to my room. I laid on the bed and reached for the cell phone. Damn, no missed calls. I braced myself and punched the button to call Alex. She answered on the third ring.

"Is this for the phone sex I promised you?" she said.

What? "You're not mad at me anymore?" I asked, completely stunned.

"No. It's silly for us to fight over Steven. I'm sorry I got so upset with you."

Justine was right. I didn't even have to buy the flowers and I was forgiven. Was she right about everything? Was I forgiven so easily because Alex really didn't care? Did she have any idea how much I cared about her?

"Are you there?" Alex said.

"Yeah," I said. "I'm here. Alex, I..." Should I tell her how I felt?

"Yes? What is it?"

"I miss you," I finally said.

"I miss you too. Marco said that Justine drove you home. I shouldn't have left without you. I know she can be difficult."

Maggie barked and jumped from the bed. Jesse was home and making a lot of noise. I heard him greet Maggie loudly and then start singing. He was drunk. Really drunk. "Jesse's home," I told Alex. "He's drunk. He's singing "When Irish Eyes are Smiling.""

Alex laughed and said, "I'll let you go, then. I'm so glad you called. I'll see you tomorrow."

"Wait," I said. I had so much to say. Too much to say on the phone. Damn, why couldn't she be right there with me?

"Yes?"

"I'm glad I called too. And I'm also sorry about everything."

"Good night, sweetheart. I'll see you in the morning."

Sweetheart. That meant she cared...right?

Jesse burst into my room, causing the door to bang against the wall then bounce back and hit him, knocking him on his ass. Maggie started licking his face. I went over to him and looked down at him.

"Where've you been?" I asked.

He put his arms around Maggie and pulled himself up. "Out with the boys," he slurred. "Where have you been?" He turned and crawled to the couch and climbed to a standing position. "Wait, I know. At Trent's house. Nooo...that's not right. You were supposed to be at Trent's house."

Damn. I sucked all the way around.

"Drink some water and go to bed," I said.

"You drink some water and go to bed," Jesse said. Then he crawled onto the couch and fell asleep. I tossed a blanket over him, and then I did go to bed. I fell asleep practicing my confession to Alex.

When I woke up the next day, everything seemed like it had been a dream. But it wasn't and I was going to have to face the consequences.

"Why so quiet?" Jesse asked as we drove.

I had been staring out the window, trying to decide if I should tell Jesse what happened. "I fucked up," I said. "I mean really fucked up."

"Go on."

"I kissed Justine."

"What?" He looked over at me, his eyes big. "Are you serious? Why? Was it good?"

"I was drunk. Alex and I got into a fight."

"Was it good? Anything else happen?"

"No, it wasn't good. And, no, nothing else. I came to my senses and got the hell away from her."

"Hmm...okay...but you gotta admit, Justine makes more sense than Miss Blake. What's going on with you and Miss Blake anyway? Why does she have you do everything separately from the rest of us?"

"I love her," I said, only partly to deflect his question.

"You don't know her well enough to love her. You're infatuated. You need to guard your heart. You think she's still going to humor you when this is all over?"

"When what's all over?"

"The recording. Jeff is setting up a tour for us when we're done recording. You'll be on tour, she'll be here."

"Why is this the first I've heard of this?" I asked.

"It isn't. I told you when we were in Texas that Jeff was working on it."

"No," I said. "You said he hinted about a tour."

"Oh. Well I don't know what to tell you. Ask Miss Blake. You spend all your time with her, ask her."

I knew Jesse was irritated with me for spending so much time with Alex, but I couldn't think about that. I had other problems.

By the time we got to the studio, I was a nervous, anxious wreck. I wanted to talk to Alex, but the minute we walked in, Jeff had us busy. Alex winked at me when nobody was looking, which calmed my nerves for a second, then made me feel guilty the next.

A few hours into the day, she finally left Jeff's side and went to her office. I followed her, ignoring Jeff calling after me. I was glad to have TJ there instead of Greg. When I looked at the guys as Alex closed the blinds, they were laughing and horsing around. A welcome change.

"What's up?" Alex asked after she shut the door and the blinds were closed.

I wasn't sure where to begin. I wanted to ask her about the tour, I wanted to know where we stood, how she felt about me. I wanted to tell her that I loved her. I needed to tell her about Justine. "Where are you going to be while I'm with the band?" I finally asked.

She blinked a few times then said, "With the band when?"

"Jesse said we're going on tour after we're finished with the album. Why didn't you tell me that?"

"Oh. Well, I hadn't thought that far ahead, I guess."

"So, we are going on tour?" I asked. I didn't mean for it to, but the question sounded accusatory.

"Of course. We have to promote the album."

"Why didn't you tell me?" Was I really mad at her? Or was I avoiding the Justine issue? Or was I just so insecure about our relationship that I was doomed to ruin it?

"I just told you. I haven't thought that far ahead. I'm working on the modeling contract and the recording, and in case you haven't noticed, I'm working very hard for you."

"So, what happens when it's time for me to go?" And I cheated on you and I love you.

"I guess it depends on where we are then."

That was a terrible answer. It calmed none of my fears. "All right," I said. "Whatever."

"I have some contracts for you to sign. Do you want to come to the house tonight? We can have dinner and…"

"No," I said, turning from her. "I need to take care of something for Trent." I reached for the door.

"Cory, wait a second."

I turned back to her, wanting so badly for her to say or do something to make me feel better. "Yeah?"

"I still need the contracts signed. When do you want to go over them?"

"I don't know. I guess tomorrow."

"Okay," she said. "Is there something else on your mind? Anything else we need to talk about?"

Way too much. "No," I answered and went back to join the guys.

"It's okay," Trent said as he took a drink of his beer.

TJ was still at the studio, and Jesse went to pick up Christy and Amy. Trent and I were waiting for them at a dive bar a few blocks from the studio. I had apologized for standing him up.

"Did you go to your parents'?" I asked.

"Yeah. I just went home when I woke up and you were gone. My father was at work, and my mother was out shopping with friends. She bought me a new watch," he said, showing me his new TAG Heuer.

"Nice," I said. "So, everything's okay?"

"As okay as it's ever going to be, I guess." He downed the rest of his beer and held it up to the bartender. She brought him another. She tried to make conversation with us but quickly gave up.

"I don't really understand," I said.

"It's just a big circle. My mother and I don't get along. She and Bryan don't like...well, they just don't like who I am. So, my father gets mad at my mother, which makes her mad at me again. Bryan just wants a normal, happy family so badly."

I nodded, not sure what to say. I wanted to help him, but my thoughts were elsewhere. I wanted to be elsewhere. "Maybe give up the drugs?" I finally said.

"Yeah," Trent said. "For sure." He called the bartender over and asked for a Jack and Coke. I ordered another beer. "Anyway," he said. "Why aren't you with Miss Blake right now?"

It was late afternoon, and my first thought was maybe there was still time. "I told her I had plans with you," I answered.

"Cool," he said, pleased. "Everything all right with all that?"

I scratched my temple and sipped on my beer. "Not really," I finally answered and filled him in on my situation.

"Hm," he said. "That surprises me. Why'd you do it?"

"I don't know. I was drunk, and it made sense for about a second."

"I get that. Tell Miss Blake. She'll get it too."

"You think?"

"You have to tell her before Justine does. I don't care what Justine said. She's a troublemaker. She's going to tell her."

"Nobody believes that Alex could love me. Nobody," I said.

"I believe it," Trent said. "What's not to love?"

"You do?"

"Yeah, dude. Why not? Anybody can love anybody."

I downed my beer and jumped off the barstool. "You're right," I said. "Fuck what everybody else says."

"Damn straight," Trent said. "Where're you going?"

"I have to tell her before Justine does."

Jesse, Christy, and Amy walked in as I was putting money on the counter. I gave Amy a quick hug and told them I had to go but would catch up with them later. Jesse wanted to know where I was going. I told him I had forgotten something at the studio.

When I got back to the studio, Alex was sitting next to Jeff. TJ was at his drums.

"Hey, dude," TJ said and waved to me.

Alex came out to greet me as soon as she saw me.

"Hi," she said with a smile. "I thought you had plans with Trent."

I put my arms around her waist and pulled her in for a kiss. She was the one to embarrass this time. She kissed me back but quickly pulled away. "Let's go to my office," she said.

When we got to her office, she shut the door, closed the blinds, then took my face with both hands and kissed me like I'd just returned from war. I had a vision of clearing her desk like I'd seen in so many movies. But that wasn't why I was there.

"Damn," I said when we came up for air. "I'm going to leave and come back again."

She laughed. "What's going on? Are you free for the evening?"

"I am," I said. "But—"

"We can sign the contracts tomorrow if you want," she said, still smiling.

"It's not that," I said. "We can look at them tonight if you want." She was smiling like she was so happy to see me, and I had to ruin it.

"All right. I have a few hours left here with Jeff and TJ. Shall I have Marco pick you up?"

Don't be a pussy, Cory. Tell her.

"Yeah, that would be great. But I have to talk to you about something."

"We'll have the whole night," she said. "We can talk as much as you like. Among other things," she said and tugged on my belt buckle. "The sooner I get back out there, the sooner our evening can begin."

Tell her, Cory. Tell her now.

"Yeah, okay," I said.

"I'll tell Marco to pick you up in a few hours," Alex said as she reached for the door.

"I kissed Justine," I blurted out.

She stopped, her back to me. I felt like I was going to throw up. "I'm so sorry," I said.

Alex turned to face me. She had full composure. "I see."

"I'm sorry," I said again. "I was drunk. I thought you were through with me."

"Because we had a little quarrel, you thought I was through?" She acted as if we were discussing a business transaction. Did she even care? "Tell me everything," she said as she sat behind her desk. She motioned for me to sit down opposite of her. Which I did. "I'm listening," she said. "Tell me everything. Leave nothing out. Not even the smallest detail."

And so, I did. Every detail. I started with Justine standing behind me at the valet area and finished with my phone call to her. When I finished, she sat quietly for a moment.

"Other than feeling my daughter up her thigh, all you did was kiss?" she finally said.

"Yes," I said. "Nothing more."

"And am I to understand that you put yourself in the cold ocean to relieve yourself of your erection?"

Of course, my face turned red. "Yes."

"I'm sure one day I'll find humor in that," she said. "Not today, though."

"No," I agreed. "Not today."

"Okay. Thank you for telling me." She stood and moved towards the door.

I sprang from my seat and stepped in front of her. "I promise you that nothing like this will ever happen again."

"I believe you," she said. "And I will forgive you."

"But not today," I said.

"No," she said. "Not today."

I went back to the dive bar and hopped onto the stool next to Trent.

"I'm confused," he said. "You look happy. Did you tell her?"

"I did," I said. "And she said she can't forgive me quite yet."

"Then why are you so happy?"

"Because she cares," I said, and I knew it to be true.

"Cool," Trent said. "I'm happy for you, my friend. Now let's get drunk."

"Oh yeah," I said. "I love a good happy drunk."

And then Trent said the dreaded, "I know where there's a party."

## 19

"I don't think that's a good idea," I said.

Trent turned to face the others. "You guys want to go to a party?"

"No," Amy, Christy, and Jesse said in unison.

"We just going to sit at this bar all night, then?" Trent said.

"We're waiting on TJ," Jesse said. "We'll go eat when he gets here. Where do you want to eat?"

"Seafood," he answered, then turned to me. "You have any cash?"

Alex had cashed my $1200 check for me since I still didn't have a bank account. "A little. Why?"

"How much is a little?"

"How much do you need?" I asked the guy wearing the TAG Heuer.

"A couple hundred?"

"For what?"

"It's my father's birthday. I don't want to use his credit card to buy him something. I'll pay you back when we get paid again."

"Oh. Okay. What are you going to get him?" I pulled two hundred from my wallet for him.

"There's a men's shop around the corner. I'll go find him a tie. I'll be right back." He downed the last of his drink and slid from his chair.

"Hang on," I said. "I'll come with you."

"No, no. I'll be right back."

I slid over and took Trent's seat so I was sitting by Amy now. "Hey good-looking," I said in an exaggerated Texas accent.

"Hey. Where's he going?"

"To get his dad a tie for his birthday."

"Hmm." She looked skeptical.

TJ walked in and said, "Hey, everybody."

Jesse jumped up and pointed to TJ's hair. "Look at that hair. Isn't he gorgeous!" Then he introduced him to Christy and Amy.

TJ gave Jesse a playful shove then lit up when he saw Amy. He squeezed in between us and said, "Scoot over," to me.

I jumped back over to my original seat and was instantly the odd man out. I started to worry that Trent may not have gone to the tie shop after all. But my fear was short-lived because he came walking in.

He stopped at TJ. "You're in my seat."

"Sit down there," TJ replied, pointing to the chair next to me.

Jesse stood. "Let's go eat."

"Yeah," I agreed. "Let's go." I stood up and asked the bartender for our checks.

"I'm not hungry," Trent said. "Get out of my chair so I can order a drink."

Amy stood and pulled TJ after her. "We're going to eat. You can get a drink there."

The bartender put all the drinks on one ticket, so I got stuck paying for everybody. I put cash on the bar and followed the others to the door. Trent took the money from the counter, stuffed it in his pocket, and pulled out his credit card. "Where are we going? I'll meet you there," he said.

"We'll wait for you," Amy said.

"I'm having another drink first," Trent said and sat down.

"Go on, guys," I said and sat down too. "He can ride over with me."

Jesse rolled his eyes and pushed the door open. "Casual Clam. On Sepulveda and Venice." He left and the others followed.

"I'm really hungry," I said. "One more drink and then go eat?"

"You should have just gone with them. I said I'm not hungry."

"You didn't go get a tie, did you?"

"Yes."

"Where is it?"

"In my car."

"Let me see it."

"Fuck you."

Yeah. There was no tie. "Where's the party?" I asked.

"Why do you care? You said you didn't want to go."

There was no doubt he was going to disappear and go to the party. "I might change my mind." If he was going, I would go too. "Is it at John's house?"

"Yeah."

It seems there was always a party at John's house. "Okay. Eat and then the party?"

He thought about that for a second and then said, "Okay."

"How'd you get him here?" Jesse asked a while later.

"I told him we'd go to the party after."

Trent had gone to the bathroom as soon as we walked in the restaurant.

"Why'd you tell him that?" Christy asked.

"Because he's high," I said. "He's going no matter what. I figure better if we're with him."

"How do you know he's high?" asked TJ.

"Because he's an asshole when he's high," I said.

"Yep, he's high," TJ said.

"He's been in there a long time," Amy said. "He's probably snorting something up his nose as we speak."

"Your turn," I said to Jesse.

Jesse scooted his chair out. "This is bullshit," he said as he headed to the men's room.

"You've only been dealing with this for weeks," Christy said. "We've been dealing with it for months. It's getting old."

"What else can we do?" Amy asked.

None of us had an answer.

Jesse returned alone. He threw up his hands and said, "He's gone."

"Let's eat and then go to the party," TJ said as he put his hand on Amy's leg.

She saw that I saw and touched his hand. I didn't care who Amy was with; I just didn't want to see her get hurt after the way I had done her. When we were finished eating and walking to the cars, I pulled TJ back.

"Hey," I said. "What's up with you and Amy?"

A smile spread across his face. "TJ's getting laid tonight," he sang out, then caught himself and said in a hushed voice, "I mean, TJ's getting laid tonight."

"That's uncool," I said.

"Why? You guys have something going on?"

"No, but—"

"Sorry, dude, but none ya biz," he said, then ran and caught up with Amy.

Sigh. So much drama. Why did I have to mess up with Alex? I could have been relaxing comfortably at her house. When I got to my Jeep, I took the cell phone from the glove box and called her. I just wanted to hear her voice. No answer. Now I had that to worry about. Was she purposely not taking my call? Was she out getting even? No, she wouldn't do that. Would she?

The others rode together and followed me to John's house. When we got there, there were so many cars that we had to park several houses down. I was glad I wasn't his neighbor. With that many cars, it was only a matter of time before the cops showed up again. As we all traipsed down the street, I was reminded of high school parties. The only difference was I didn't have a twelve pack in one hand and an open beer in the other.

Music blared out so loudly that it could be heard the minute I stepped out of my Jeep. There was no use knocking on the front door, so we just walked in. As long as we were already there, we went to the kitchen, and each of us poured a beer from the keg. I slid up to Amy and said under the music, "Where should we begin? The bathroom?"

"Too soon," she said with a shake of her head.

"I guess I'll go look for him. Come with?" I said.

"I don't think so," she said. "We can cover more party if we separate." She turned to the others and suggested we meet back at the keg in half an hour.

I wandered around John's house looking for Trent and John. If Trent wasn't there, maybe John knew where he was. The living room was apparently the smoking room. Three different bongs were in use. The backyard was where the music was coming from. Turns out, it was John's band. After the backyard, I went back into the house and started opening closed doors. The first one was the kitchen pantry. Nobody in there. Then the infamous bathroom. Only a guy taking a piss. I downed the last of my beer and went to the keg for another. Jesse had done the same.

"Nothing yet," I said. "Where's Christy?"

"I think she went to the bathroom. She just said she'd be right back."

I nodded. "You realize TJ's a player, right?"

"What's your point?"

"I just don't want him to take advantage of Amy."

Jesse gave me a look. "You mean like you did?"

"Yeah. I guess," I said and went to look for Trent again.

I went down the hallway to check the bedrooms. When I opened the door to the first bedroom, Christy was in there with a guy. They were lying on the bed on their stomachs, doing coke off a mirror. I just shook my head and closed the door. Christy immediately flung the door back open and pulled me back in.

"If you tell Jesse, I'll tell him you hit on me," she hissed under her breath.

"Yeah, okay," I said. "I'm sure he'll believe that."

"Well we'll see, won't we?" she said. She was still holding my arm.

"I guess so." I pulled free from her.

"Okay, just listen for a second," she said. She took a beat to compose herself. "I'm all Jesse has. I'm sorry you saw this. I'll get my shit together and go find him." She wiped her nose and straightened her dress.

"What do you mean you're all he has?" I asked. "What about the band? What about family?"

"His father left when he was a kid. He was a piece of shit drug addict and wife abuser, so no real loss, but he lost his mom last year. She died of cancer after fighting for less than a year. So, it was kind of unexpected. He doesn't have any siblings. It's just him."

I wasn't sure that was reason enough to continue hiding things from him, but I would have to think about that later. "Just go back and find him so he doesn't find you like this," I said.

"Okay," she said. "I will. I'll take care of Jesse and me...you just worry about Jesse and the band. Okay?"

Not really sure what to say, I just nodded and then went back to look for Trent. Door number two was next. What surprise did it hold? Amy and TJ rolling around the bed making out. Nice. I pulled the door shut and moved on.

"Hey," Amy said, closing the door behind her.

"Yeah?"

"I don't appreciate that look you just gave me."

"I'm sorry," I said. "I just don't want you to get hurt. He's just using you."

"Like you did?" she said, crossing her arms.

"It's none of my business," I said. "If you want a one-night stand, then go for it. I'm happy for you. But if you think…or want it to be anything more, then make him wait. He's the kind of guy that will judge you after a one-nighter."

"Is there any possibility of anything between you and me?" she asked.

"If I wasn't hung up on somebody else, I'd be all over you," I said. I wasn't sure if I meant it or not. It was hard to imagine wanting anybody else now that I had met Alex, but I didn't want to hurt her feelings.

"Okay. Thank you for your honesty." She went back into the bedroom.

Bedroom number three. Trent was the only one left, but the room was empty. I went back to the keg. Jesse was still there by himself. "I can't find him," I said. "I'm going home."

"You sure? We can go to the club or something."

"Nah. I'm just a third wheel. You guys have fun. Call the apartment if anything comes up. I'll listen for the phone."

I filled my cup before I left and drank it before I got to my Jeep. I didn't give Jesse the cell phone number because I didn't know it. I would have to ask Alex. I tried calling her again after I was home and ready for bed, but still no answer. After tossing and turning from worry for over two hours, I chose to remember the good. I finally dozed off to thoughts of her doing wonderful things to my body.

The phone never rang, and Jesse didn't come home, so I drove to the studio alone. I was nervous about seeing Alex. Why hadn't she answered my calls? I forced myself to think positive. I would know soon enough. I left early in hopes of talking to her before anyone else arrived. But when I got there, she was in her office with Trent's dad. The door was open, so I walked up and said, "Hey. Good morning. Everything okay?"

Trent's dad was in his expensive suit, but this time his tie was loosened.

"Good morning," Alex said. "Cory, have you met Mr. Austin?"

"I have." I looked to him. "Is Trent okay?"

"I don't know," he said. He looked like he'd been up all night. "I haven't seen him for two days. Jesse calls when he stays at your place. But he didn't call last night. Do you have any idea where he is?"

"No," I said. "It was about eight or eight thirty last night when he ditched us."

"I cut off his cash," Mr. Austin said. "And the last charge on his card was at a bar last night."

Crap. "I gave him $200," I said. Then meekly offered, "He said it was your birthday."

His dad leaned forward and looked me in the eyes. "My birthday is in October. Do you know what happens when you give a drug addict cash?"

"They buy drugs?" I looked to Alex for help, but she wouldn't look at me.

"They buy enough drugs to kill themselves," he said. He covered his face and leaned back in his chair.

"He'll be here in a little while," I said. "He always is."

"They always are until they aren't," Mr. Austin countered.

"I'm sure he'll be here," Alex said at last. "He's due in at ten. He's rarely late."

Mr. Austin looked at his watch. "Okay. I'm going to go look for him. Call me if he shows up."

"Of course," Alex said as they both stood. We walked him to the door and, Alex said, "Oh Derek, by the way. I'll have all the contracts back to you today." She gave him a comforting look. "Including Trent's." He nodded and left.

Alex turned to me. "We need to go over your contracts."

"Right now?"

"Yes, why not now?"

I shrugged. "I was hoping we could talk about us."

She headed back to her office. "I'm not quite ready to talk about that. I still have visions of you frolicking at the beach with my daughter."

I followed her. "I didn't frolic," I said.

"Sit down and let me go over this with you," she said, pointing at the chair like I was five.

"Alex, I—"

"If you force this conversation right now, it will go the wrong way." She slapped the folders onto her desk.

I sat down. What could I do? She was mad at me, and I'd have to wait it out. I started imagining myself as the lead singer of the Rolling Stones singing, "She's so Cold."

"This is the contract for Suicide King," she said, opening the first folder. "Read through it."

I picked it up. "It's so thick," I said. "What's it say?"

She sighed with frustration. "You should have any attorney review it."

"I don't need an attorney," I said. "I have you. Does it give Eddie his share?"

She looked surprised. "Eddie didn't set anything up before he—"

"His parents should get his share," I said.

She scooped the papers back up. "I'll have it taken care of." She slid another folder over and opened it. "This is for the modeling. I need you back at the photo studio tomorrow afternoon, by the way."

I groaned. "Do I have to? It's so boring."

"Do you realize how much you're getting paid for a day of boredom?"

I shook my head. She flipped to a page and pushed it in front of me. I glanced at it, then did a double-take. "Are you serious?"

She nodded and a smile forced its way onto her face. "Yes, I am."

"When can I spend it?" I asked. I had things I wanted to do for my family, and it dawned on me at that moment that I would eventually want a ring for Alex. I wanted Alex to be a part of the rest of my life. I couldn't imagine my life without her in it.

She laughed. "You're smiling ear to ear. You will have it soon. It's put into your account over time. You'll have it all by year-end as long as you keep up your end of the contract."

She thought I was smiling about money. I would tell her the truth when she was happy with me again. "Which says?"

"You should read—" she started to say but then stopped for a beat as if to collect her patience. "It says for you to be there when you're supposed to be there and no doing any work with a competitor for at least the next year."

"So, sign it?" I asked.

"Yes. Sign it. Every place indicated."

There were yellow arrow stickers where I was to sign. When I finished, she put some more papers in front of me. "I took the liberty of opening a bank account for you. Sign where indicated. Here is your checkbook and an ATM card."

I looked at the checkbook. There was a balance of $10,900. "That's your advance and first two weeks of stipend, less your fine of course." She smiled like was making light of it, but I knew she was letting me know she would hold me to the same high standards as the others. Or more likely a higher standard. "You will get that until we're finished recording," she continued. "Then you get royalties, which is outlined in the Suicide King contract."

I signed everything. "How did you open an account for me without me?"

"I have your driver's license and tax info on file. My private banker takes care of things for me."

I remembered that I gave all that info to Jeff on day one. "So, the other day when you asked me my age—"

"Yes, dear. I already knew."

The front door opened, and in walked Trent looking like hammered shit. I jumped up and went to him. "Where did you go?" I asked. "We went to the party to look for you."

"I'm tired of you constantly trying to babysit me," Trent said as he stuck his arm out and pushed me aside.

"You look like crap." He didn't acknowledge me, so I stepped back in front of him. "Man, you smell like an onion and look like you combed your hair with a pork chop."

"Yeah," Trent said. "I used onion soap."

Alex was on the phone talking to Trent's dad. Jesse and TJ walked in with Jeff not far behind.

"Hey," Jesse said as he walked by.

"Thanks for the cock block," TJ said as he passed. That at least gave me a little bit of satisfaction.

Alex hung up the phone and motioned for me, so I went back into her office. "Derek...Mr. Austin is coming by to pick up Trent. He said he'll have the new contracts ready by tomorrow."

"Why is he coming to pick him up?"

"Look at him," Alex said. "He's a mess. He's filthy and has lost at least twenty pounds since we started all this."

"Where's he taking him?"

Alex hesitated.

"Let me talk to him," I said. "Let me try to get through to him."

"It's gone too far for that. This is what's best for Trent."

Just then, Mr. Austin and two big guys walked in. Trent saw them and scrambled for the back door. I stepped in his way and threw my arms around him. He kneed me in the stomach, causing me to double over. Simultaneously, he threw an elbow to my face, which was the blow that caused me to drop him, but I'd slowed him enough for them to catch him. They drug him out kicking and screaming. The last thing he said was, "Cory, you fuck, I'll get you for this." We all stood in silent, confused shock. When did it get this far out of hand?

I turned to Alex. "What about the band?"

# 20

"Trent will be back in ten days. By then, he will have no drugs in his system, and hopefully, we can reason with him."

"And if we can't?" I asked. The others stood with their arms crossed, looking at the ground.

"Then he goes to rehab, and we lose him for quite a bit longer."

"What do we do for the next ten days?" Jesse asked.

"We press on," Alex answered. "You guys will have to pick up the slack. Lucky for me, you all are very talented." Then she went into her office, shut the door, and closed the blinds—without me.

She was upset, and I didn't know what to do. Jesse, TJ, Jeff, and I all just stood there. Finally, Jeff said, "Well you heard her. Let's get to work."

I wanted to go to her more than anything. After thinking about it, I decided having a productive day would lower her stress more than me pressuring her to talk to me. I did my best to focus and keep Jesse and TJ on task. She left her office around three without even looking at me. She had a short conversation with Jeff, then she was gone. It took everything in me not to run after her.

"Hey, guys," Jeff called us together. "Great news. Miss Blake was able to get Honey n Ice to record with us. They'll be here shortly."

"Bad ass," TJ said and slapped me on the back.

"What do you mean?" I asked. "Record what?" Honey n Ice were a girl duo. They sang pop music, which I didn't feel mixed well with ours.

"She wants them to join you on "Two Days Gone." They'll be here in a few hours. Let's be prepared."

"I don't think—" I began.

"She doesn't care what you think," Jesse said.

"He's right," Jeff said. "She's not paying you to think."

"Alright," I said. "Whatever."

The girls came walking in a few hours later. They were nice enough, but it just didn't make sense to me. TJ, of course, flirted with them shamelessly. Jesse was shy with them, which I thought was kind of funny.

"Why are you so standoffish?" one of them, I think Honey, said to me.

"Yeah," the other one said. "We're doing you guys a solid. Why are you acting like we're intruding?"

"Sorry," I said. "I didn't mean to be rude. Let's get started." I looked at Jesse and TJ. "If you guys are ready?"

The one that I believed to be Honey tickled me under the chin. "You're cute."

The other one said, "Girl, you better get your hands off him. That's Miss Blake's man."

"I was just teasing," she replied. Then she looked at TJ. "I like your hair."

TJ ran his hands through his hair. "Thanks."

"Hey," Jesse said. "I'm here too."

"You have beautiful eyes," she told him. Jesse beamed.

"Now that that's out of the way, can we get started?" I said. I looked to Jeff. He found it all amusing.

"Why are you called Honey n Ice?" TJ asked them.

"Because I'm sweet as honey," the one that tickled me said.

"And I'm not," Ice said.

"Clever," I said. "Now can we get started?"

Jeff said we could quit once we finished with the girls, but I had nothing to do, so I wanted to keep working. "What is going on with you?" Jesse asked.

"Nothing," I said. "I just want to get a lot done."

"Not like you to want to be someplace she isn't," he said.

"She doesn't want to be around me right now. I told her about Justine."

"Ah. That explains it. What are you going to do?"

"I don't know what to do."

Jesse threw his arm around my shoulder. "Let's go home. I got some burgers to toss on the grill."

Of course, Christy and Amy came over and TJ too. The girls thought having Honey n Ice in the studio was really cool. That's all they talked about during dinner. I had to admit that, despite my doubts, the song sounded great. Alex knew what she was doing. She had an ear for things I would never think of.

They played cards after we ate, but I just sat in front of the TV flipping channels. I was worried about Trent, and I was missing Alex like crazy. I didn't let myself even think about losing her.

I tried calling Alex from bed. She didn't answer.

After a night of little sleep, I got up and went in early again. I left Jesse a note that I would see him there. By the time I walked in, I was frustrated and even a little angry. I marched into Alex's office and tossed the phone on her desk. "Why did you give me this if you aren't going to answer it?" I demanded.

"I'll pick these up later." Mr. Austin was sitting in the chair by the door, so I hadn't seen him.

"Oh, sorry," I said. "I didn't see you there. How is Trent?"

"It's not pretty," he said as he stood.

"Can I talk to him?" I asked.

"Not only no, but hell no," he said. "Leave him be until he gets through this."

His words seemed unduly harsh to me. After all, I was against the drugs too. "Tell him we miss him," I said.

"Will do. I'll talk to you soon, Alexandra."

After he was gone, I turned back to Alex. "Sorry. Didn't see him there. But the fact remains—"

"Sit down, I have your amended contract," she said as she opened a folder and slid the thick binder across the desk. But I didn't sit. I pulled her from her chair and wrapped my arms around her. She resisted at first but eventually melted into me. We said nothing for some time.

When we heard the racket of the others showing up, Alex pulled away and said, "I've missed you."

"Me too. Answer the phone now?"

"Yes, I will answer the phone. Now I really need you to sign."

I sat across from her and picked up the contract. "Do you have it marked for me?"

"I do."

"Is there anything I need to know?"

"You know I will look after your best interest, don't you?"

"I do," I said and started signing.

"I should tell you that Greg has made good on his word and is suing us," she said.

I kept signing. "Suing us for what?"

"The songs he worked on and the name Suicide King. He claims he started the band and it's his name."

"That's not true," I said. "Eddie and I came up with that name when we were kids."

"Yes, I know. Can you prove it?"

I thought for a few seconds and said, "I'll find something. What about the songs? We all worked on them."

"I'll take care of that. Greg will be lucky to play drums in a parade when I'm done."

"That's my girl," I said as I signed the last page.

"Don't forget you must go back to the photo studio today."

"Oh, yeah. You coming too?"

"You bet I am," she said as she looked through the contract, checking that I didn't miss any place. "I will oversee every single photo of you." She put the papers back in their folder. "I have to get Jesse's and TJ's done today too. I have some mock-ups of the album cover and promotional material to go over with you as well."

"With just me? Or all of us?" I asked.

She looked up and smiled seductively. "With you. Dinner at the house tonight?"

"Yes, please," I said. We were good again, and I was silly happy about it.

She winked at me. "Send Jesse and TJ in, please." I stood to go. "Oh, and I need you to contact the Coopers and get direct deposit info."

"Sure," I said. Ugh, now I had to face the Coopers.

While Jesse and TJ were in with Alex, I started again on my letter. I should have gone to see them in person before I left. I apologized for that. I should have talked to them at the funeral. I apologized for that too. I should have come to L.A. long before I did. I was sorry for that as well. It seemed crude to bring up the money, but I also didn't want them to think we had forgotten Eddie. The letter was pointless. I needed to see them in person.

When Jesse and TJ came out of Alex's office, I went back in to talk to her. TJ raised his eyebrow at me, while Jesse made a point not to look at me.

"What was that about?" I asked Alex.

"What was what about?"

"Jesse and TJ...never mind. I need to go to Texas. We need to go."

"Texas? Why?"

I sat down and told her about the funeral and about the letter. "I need to face them," I said.

"Okay. How long will you be gone?"

"I was hoping you would come too."

"I'm not sure I see why."

"Lots of reasons," I said. "I'd like to spend the time with you. I want you to see where I'm from. I want you to meet Eddie's parents...and my family."

Alex put her pen down and sat back in her chair. She formed her words carefully. "You want me to meet your family?"

"Yes."

"Do they even know about me? About us?"

"Not yet," I admitted.

"And you think the best course of action is to show up with me in tow?"

Okay, she had a point. "I can tell them about us first. Over the phone."

"You do realize they are not going to approve, don't you?"

"You don't know that. You don't know them."

"I don't need to know them. I would not approve if Justine showed up with a white man almost twenty years her senior."

My expression must have said everything.

"I'm sorry. I didn't mean that," she said. "Obviously, I wouldn't care if he was white. But I would care about the age discrepancy."

"We have to face them eventually," I said.

Alex stood and came to me. She leaned against her desk and pulled me to her. "You are a young man," she said. "You think you know what you want—"

"Please don't say that," I said. "I'm a grown man. I know what I want and how I feel."

"Well then, don't you feel that it's a little soon for me to meet your family?"

"No. I've met Justine."

"And then some," she said. She pushed me back a step and went and sat back down.

Stupid comment, Cory. "Where are your parents?" I asked, steering the conversation away from Justine.

"Connecticut."

"Do they know about me?"

"No. Of course not...well, at least I don't think so. Justine could have filled them in. Hmmm, I should find out," she said to herself.

I wanted to tell her that I loved her and I was proud of our relationship. But if she felt it was too soon to meet my family, I had to assume it was too soon to confess my love. "How about this," I said. "Come with me. I'll show you around Dallas, and we'll meet with the Coopers. You can decide while we're there if you want to meet the Scotts. I won't pressure you."

She thought for a second. "It would be about time for Trent to return when we get back."

"Right. Give the others a few days off and we'll all meet back here when Trent can join us."

"No pressure?" she said.

"I promise," I said.

"All right. I'll have it set up for us. You set the appointment with the Coopers."

Now I was going to have to call my parents. I'd gotten so wrapped up in the beautiful fantasy that reality hit hard. Were my parents going to be okay with everything? Good going, Cory.

"What is up with you?" I asked Jesse. He had acted pouty all day. "I can write you a check for my half of the rent. Is that what's wrong? I was going to give it to you, I just keep forgetting."

We had finished for the day and were getting our things put away.

"Did you read your contract?" he asked.

"No. Why?"

"You signed a contract without reading any of it?" Jesse stopped wrapping his cord and looked at me like he didn't believe me.

"It was really thick," I said, knowing how stupid it sounded as I said it.

He rolled his eyes at me. "Well TJ and I, and I don't know, but I assume Trent are now covering Eddie's share."

"You don't think his family deserves his share?" I asked.

"Yes, I think they do. But it doesn't add up. We're getting less than before you got here, and now Eddie or his family get part of it."

"What are you saying?"

"I'm saying that I think you are getting more than us...more than Eddie got, and I don't think you are contributing to Eddie's share."

"Oh." I didn't know what to say. I didn't think I deserved more, I just didn't want to be bothered with those details. It was shitty of me, but it was the truth. I wanted it to be fair, so I would have to force myself to pay attention.

"Either that or she has just decided to keep more for herself."

"I'm seeing her tonight," I said. "I'll see what's going on."

Jesse started wrapping his cord again. "Cool...And I'll take that rent check."

Alex walked in. "Oh, I didn't realize you were still here, Jesse."

"Yes, ma'am. Getting ready to go."

The three of us stood awkwardly.

"Well, I'll see you later, Cory," Jesse said.

I followed him to the door. "Not sure when I'll be home," I said. "I left my checkbook on the table. Go ahead and write yourself one for my part. Just sign my name, it's all good."

"That's okay," Jesse said, giving Alex a glance. "I can wait for you to sign it." Then he took off.

I knew Jesse was suspicious of Alex, but I was alone with her now, so I would worry about that later. "How long till we have to be at the photographer?" I asked Alex as I drew her to me and nuzzled her neck.

"There will be time for that later," she said, pulling away from me.

"What's wrong?" I asked, worried that maybe we weren't good after all.

"Did it not feel odd to you for your friend to call me ma'am?" she said. "I mean I expect him to, but didn't it feel strange for you?"

"No," I said. "It turned me on."

"I don't believe..."

I pulled her back into me and put her hand below my belt. She gave me a squeeze that sent a shiver up my spine. She walked over to the front door and made sure it was locked and the window shades were drawn. Then she sauntered back to me and kissed me with soft, gentle, teasing kisses as she unbuckled my belt. I was so turned on that I could barely refrain from tearing her clothes off. She unbuttoned my jeans and pulled down the zipper as her tongue found its way into my mouth. I wanted to push her down on me, but I didn't dare. Her hands were soft and cool against my stomach and then across my side and back. She pushed my jeans and boxers down until I was fully exposed. She put her hands to my face and kissed me again before she knelt, running her hands down my chest and stomach as she did. Then she took me in her mouth.

As much as I wanted it to last forever, I lasted about one minute. My legs felt like Jell-O when she was through. She stood and whispered in my ear, "Pull your pants up. I'm going to get myself together, and then we must go."

I watched her walk away with my pants still at my knees. When she disappeared into her bathroom, I mumbled, "Holy shit," and pulled them up. It was so damn good I wanted to call someone to tell them about it.

I was still standing there, replaying it in my mind, when she came out twenty minutes later. "Ready?" she asked.

You can't tell a woman you love her for the first time right after a blowjob. So, I just said, "Uh-huh," and followed her out.

"Can he see and hear us?" I asked about Marco. I had tried to form questions in my mind about Jesse's concerns, but it wasn't happening.

"Not if the glass is up. Why?" She put her hand on my leg and said with an evil grin, "Did I not take good care of you?"

"Oh, yes. Yes, you did," I said. "Now I want to take care of you."

"Mmmm," she purred. "I would love that. But I hardly think you can go in for a photo shoot after that. Tonight?"

"Yes, ma'am," I said.

Probably the only thing that would kill a hard-on faster than a cold ocean for me would be a photo shoot. I absolutely hated it. I tried to think of the money, of pleasing Alex, of the cool billboards that would one day grace the city. It all only got me so far.

"How much longer?" I asked Alex about three hours in.

"A few more hours. You really must learn some patience, my dear."

"How about a break?" I said. "Let's go make out in the car."

"Are you twelve?" she said.

"No," I said and stepped back in front of the cameras.

She told the photographer to hold on and stepped into the camera's eye with me. She whispered in my ear as she discreetly brushed her fingers across my inner thigh. "Two more hours. Okay?"

I nodded and finished up without complaint.

"We've had a very productive day," Alex said. "Let's go out to dinner."

"Sure," I said. "Whatever you like."

She had Marco take us to a quiet place that was dark inside with candles at the table. It was casual, which made me happy. After we ordered wine and beer, I asked her about Jesse's and TJ's contracts.

"The contracts are fair," she said bluntly. "They are replaceable, you're not. You are the one with the looks and the talent."

"I appreciate that," I said. "But he said he's getting less now than he was when Eddie was the lead singer."

"Honey, I know Eddie was your friend, but the truth is you were the one we wanted all along. The contracts are fair, and they are done. Are you getting fish or steak?"

"Fish." I liked it when she called me honey.

"Probably a good idea. You know I think you are perfect, but we should probably schedule your workouts as part of your workday. Just so you stay that way," she said with a smile.

"Okay, that's fine, but I'd like the royalties split up evenly," I said. "I think that's what's fair." I wanted to sound firm, but I knew I didn't.

"My job is to look after your interests. If the others wanted to negotiate, they should have hired a lawyer. But let me remind you. I replaced a drummer once already. TJ knew what he was signing up for. Jesse is the one that's stirring up trouble." She touched my hand and made a point of looking me in the eyes. "Don't you worry, they are going to make plenty of money."

The waiter brought the drinks and took our order. Alex held up her wine glass. "To you and me," she said. I tapped her glass with mine and said nothing more about it.

"You obviously have no time or need for your previous job," Alex said. "Have you let them know you won't be returning?"

"No, not yet."

She gave me a scornful look.

"I'll call them tomorrow," I said. "First thing." That pleased her. "Didn't you say you have some mock-ups you want to show me?" I asked.

She thought for a second, then said, "We can look at them tomorrow. Enough about work. Let's have a nice dinner and a nice evening."

"Sounds good to me," I said.

"I do have a question for you," Alex said. "Why did you tell me about Justine? Were you just afraid she would tell me first?"

"Well," I said, knowing I needed to choose my words carefully. "I definitely wanted you to hear it from me, but I also didn't want anything hanging over us." I watched her expression, not wanting the topic to upset her. "When I was in the ninth grade," I began. She tilted her head with interest. "I wanted to be on the varsity football team more than anything. I was good, but I was still small."

"Okay," she said as she took a drink of wine, probably wondering what ninth grade football had to do with anything.

"I was the first one at practice every morning. That did nothing to impress our coach. I mean, he was a real hard-ass. But anyway, one day I overslept. So not only was I not going to be early, but I would also be very late, which you better believe would not be pretty. I was in for humiliation and a hard time. And, of course, that young boy worried about ruining his chances at varsity. I pleaded with my dad to call the coach and tell him I was sick. My dad said that he would do that for me, or I could stand up, be a man and take my lumps, then get on with life."

"So, what did you do?" Alex asked.

I smiled at her. "What do you think I did?"

She thought for a second and said, "I believe you took your lumps."

"Times two," I said. "I stayed home and ended up worrying about it the whole time. The next day when the coach could see I wasn't sick..."

"The coach punished you twice as hard," she said.

"Exactly," I said. "I learn from my mistakes. Actually, I make a lot of mistakes. But never the same one twice."

"That's good to know," she said.

"I have a question for you," I said. "Why did you forgive me? Is it because you were afraid if you didn't it would disrupt the band?"

"I don't need you in my bed to have you in my band," she said.

I downed the rest of my beer. Our dinner arrived, and the server brought us each another drink.

"I forgave you because I believe in you," she said after thanking the waiter. "You could have gone further," she said. "But instead you..." She started to laugh.

"I guess today is the day you find humor in my predicament," I said.

"Yes, I guess it is." She put her napkin in her lap and reached for the pepper.

I put my hand on her arm. "What is it?" she asked.

"I just want you to know...I..." Why was I so afraid to tell her I loved her?

"Yes?"

"I won't ever let you down again. I'll do anything for you. For us."

She put her hand on mine and said, "I know."

## 21

"I took care of your dog last night," Jesse said. "And again this morning."

"Thanks," I said, unsure how to proceed with his obvious frustration with me. I spent the night with Alex and didn't think to call him. "I owe you one. Buy you a beer after?"

"You mean you have time for someone other than your dick?" He picked up his guitar cord and shook it with force to straighten it out.

"Hey, come on. I said I was sorry."

"Did you ask about the contracts?" He plugged his guitar in, avoiding eye contact.

TJ was across the room at his drums, but I saw his ears perk up at the question.

"I did. She said not to worry, we are all going to make a lot of money." It sounded weak, even to me.

Jesse shook his head. "Did you see yours? How much more are you getting?"

"I haven't seen it. I swear. She just said they were all done, and we were all going to make a lot."

Jesse strapped his guitar on and started to tune it. Without looking up, he said, "I hope she gives really good head. I hope it's worth what she's doing to you."

"You don't need to talk like that," I said and yanked his cord out of his guitar for emphasis.

He grabbed it back from me. "Is that it? She gives you a good bj, and now you're fucking us?"

I pushed Jesse hard enough for him to stumble. "Say that again and I'm going to—"

"You're going to what?" he said. "Hit me? I'm not scared of you. I don't care if you kick my ass, you're still the asshole." He shoved me back, but because I was so much bigger than him, I didn't move much. So, then he squared and rammed me like he was trying to bust open a door. "You fucking brick wall," he said as he did.

"I don't want to fight you," I said as I grabbed him and threw him down. He held on tight, pulling me down with him. And just like that, we were in a skirmish. "Don't talk about her like that," I said, pushing his face, trying to break free from him. He hurled an amazing and impressive combination of expletives at me, which made me laugh.

When I got him into a position where he could do no more, Jesse finally said, "Fine, make more money than me. I don't care. Now let go of me."

I let go of him, and he gave me a final shove as he stood.

"We ready now?" It was Jeff. He and Alex were at the controls and probably saw and heard everything.

I put on my guitar, looking down at it as if I were tuning it, but stole a glance at Alex. Her lips were upturned barely enough to form a satisfied smile. Then Justine walked in.

"Hi, Cory," she said as she walked by me. "Hi, guys," she said to Jesse and TJ.

We all looked at each other like, what the hell? Jesse mumbled, "What the fuck?"

I looked to Alex. She pointed to her office.

"What is she doing here?" I asked.

"She's going to sing with you," Alex said. "We have "Her Tears" featuring Alexandra Blake. "Two Days Gone" featuring Honey n Ice—"

"Yes, but—"

"I reworked "Last Train Out." Now it's "Last Plane Out," and Justine is singing it with you. It's inspired by Greg's song, but it's not Greg's song. That song can stay tied up while the lawyers argue."

"Okay," I said. "I guess you know what you're doing." What the hell was she doing? Regardless of if Justine and I sounded good together, which I doubted, why would she put us together after everything that had happened?

"You'll see," she said.

I went out and stood next to Justine. It was awkward to say the least. I had no idea how Alex thought it was a good idea, and we sounded terrible together. It was bland and cold. We had zero chemistry.

"It's not me, it's him," Justine said after take eight.

The awkwardness turned to bitterness. We argued about whose fault it was, about how things should be done, and any and everything else. Jeff, Jesse, and TJ didn't know what to think. It was a train wreck, but Alex persisted with her signature patience.

The song was about a couple breaking up that could hardly wait to get away from each other, but they had to wait for the last train...or plane out for some reason. While waiting and arguing, they decided they were in love after all. I did not want to sing it with her and could not figure out what Alex was thinking.

By the end of the day, I didn't feel awkward or bitter or anything else. I was indifferent to it all. I was just tired and ready to be done. Justine must have felt the same way because she said, "Hey. Let's just put the past behind us and get this done so we can go home."

"Okay," I said. "Let's do it."

When we were finished for the day, I told Jesse to wait for me and I would ride with him. I wanted to talk to Alex before we left.

"Hey," I said as I closed the door to her office behind me. She pointed to the blinds, so I closed them too. "Is it okay with you if we look at the mock-ups tomorrow? I need to take care of some things."

"Yes," she said. "I heard. I have a flight for us tomorrow morning...that is, if you still want to go."

The truth was I wasn't sure it was my best idea. "Yeah, of course. What time?"

"10 am. I can pick you up."

"Great."

"I can cancel it," she said.

"No, no, I want to go. I just need to ask Jesse to take care of my dog. Have you talked to Trent's dad? Do you know how he's doing?"

"Not since the other day. I'll give him a call before I leave tonight." She stood and walked around the desk to me. "Have fun with Jesse and TJ tonight," she said, running her hand through my hair. "It's important to maintain your friendship with them."

"Thanks, baby," I said. I had never called her anything but Alex. My face burned when the pet name slipped out.

"Of course, my dear," she said and passed her thumb across my cheek. Touching my red face had become her way of telling me not to be embarrassed, and I loved her for it.

When I went back out, Jesse was on the phone with Christy, and TJ was already gone. When he saw me, he hung up. "Ready?" he asked.

"Yeah. Go by the apartment first?"

We went by the apartment so I could take Maggie out and change clothes. I wrote Jesse the rent check, then said, "Check this out," and held up the cell phone.

"Where'd you get that?" he asked and took it from me. He opened it and held it to his ear.

"There's no dial tone, dumbass." I took it back. "It's a cell phone."

"Oh, yeah. When did you get it?"

"Alex gave it to me the other day," I said.

Jesse rolled his eyes. "Of course she did. So she can keep tabs on you."

"But I can her too," I said defensively.

"What's your phone number?" he asked as he reached for the house phone. "I'll call you."

"I don't know. I keep forgetting to ask her."

"Hm. So, it's kind of like a bat phone, then. Only she can call you," Jesse said with a hint of sarcasm.

"I'll get the number," I said. "Then you'll have it too."

"Cool," he said. "Let's go."

I followed Jesse to his car. "Where are we going?"

"We're meeting the others at that dive bar..."

"The others?"

"Yeah. TJ, Christy, and Amy. And don't start that third wheel bullshit," Jesse said.

"I could ask Alex to join us," I said. Then we both laughed at the visual.

"Seriously though," Jesse said, "I don't want to piss you off, but I really think you're making a huge mistake with her."

"I know you do," I said. "Everybody says the same thing. But you don't know her like I do."

"You sure you know her as well as you think you do?" he said. "Usually, everybody else isn't wrong. I've just never heard anything good about her. Yeah, she's getting us recorded...but I have to believe it benefits her or she wouldn't be doing it."

I wanted to tell Jesse to worry about his own relationship, but I remembered what Christy said about her being all he had.

Jesse pulled into the lot and parked his car. He turned off the ignition. "Just try to look out for all of us. Okay?"

"Of course," I said.

"Then tell me why you and she go to the photo shoots separately from the rest of us," Jesse said.

I could think of no way to deflect the question. "She's trying to get me some kind of modeling gig," I admitted.

"Seriously?"

"Yeah."

Jesse laughed. "Okay, stud, buy me the drinks you promised me. I'm getting all call liquor." He jumped out of the car and took off towards the entrance.

He wasn't upset about it. What a relief. "I said beer," I yelled as I ran to catch up with him.

I started a tab at the bar for Jesse and me. He ordered Johnnie Walker Black on the rocks, and I ordered draft beer. I gave the bartender my credit card and told her to keep it open for the two of us.

"Sure thing," she said. "I don't really recommend the draft, not sure when's the last time the lines were cleaned. I can get you a bottle, same price."

"Thanks," I said and slid the glass back to her. "You have Amstel Light?"

"Coors Light or Bud Light," she replied.

I took the Bud and went to join the others.

"You hanging back to flirt with the bartender?" Amy asked. Her chair was so close to TJ's she was practically in his lap.

"All the ladies flirt with him," Jesse said.

"She was just switching my draft for a bottle," I said as I sat down.

"Anybody heard from Trent?" Christy asked.

"Alex said she was going to call his dad tonight to see how he's doing," I explained.

"Where is she?" Christy asked. "She too good to hang out with us?"

"This isn't her kind of place," Jesse said. "You've known her longer than any of us," he said to TJ. "Would she come here if Cory asked her to?"

TJ downed the rest of his drink and held it up for the bartender to see. We were the only ones there, so we had her full attention. "I don't really know her personally," he said. "I've just worked with her."

The bartender brought TJ another drink along with another beer for me and a drink for Jesse. She asked Amy and Christy if they wanted another. "Keep them coming," Christy said.

"Have you ever seen her with other guys?" Amy asked.

"I guess a few over the years," TJ answered.

"They have a jukebox?" I asked. I certainly didn't want to talk about Alex and other guys.

"I thought it was jute box," Christy said.

"No, it's juke," Amy said. "It's over there." She pointed towards the bar. "What kind of guys?"

I got up and went to the jukebox. I put a five in and started flipping through to see what I wanted to play. Jesse went to the bar for another drink and then came to look over my shoulder. "You may want to slow down on those," I said. "Unless you're wanting to have an early night."

"One more," he said. "Then I'll switch to beer."

I nodded and stepped back to let him pick the rest of the songs. I didn't really care what he played. I was feeling out of sorts but didn't know why. "You want to throw some darts?" I asked.

"Nah. She'll get all bent saying I'm ignoring her."

"Okay," I said and went to the bar to ask for some quarters. I put three ones and my empty bottle on the bar. She gave me the change and a new beer. "Looks like you're the odd one out tonight," she said. "You have a girl coming later? Or...a guy? I don't judge."

"My boyfriend is in rehab," I said and took the quarters and beer to the pool tables. I put the quarters in the silver thing and pushed them in. I wondered if the silver thing had a name. The balls made the rumbling noise as they emptied into the...well? Was it called that? I pulled the triangle rack from its slot and tossed it on the table, then started dropping balls into it. They made the sound of hitting concrete because I should have been setting them in instead of dropping them, but I didn't care.

"You rack 'em, I'll crack 'em," TJ said over his shoulder as he walked by and selected a cue.

One by one the others drifted over and pulled up chairs. Although pool wasn't my best game, I wasn't terrible either. I took two out of three games from him. By this time, Jesse was drunk and talking loudly.

"You ready to switch to beer?" I asked as I put the cue away. "Or maybe some water?"

"Fuck no, I don't want water," he said laughing.

"Are you sure?" Christy asked. "I think you've had more than enough to drink."

"That's what I want," Jesse said. "More than enough." He thought that was clever.

I sat down between Jesse and Amy. The bar was smoky, even though none of us had smoked, and it was starting to annoy me.

As I tuned in and out of the conversation, I tried to figure out what was bothering me. Then it hit me. I was bored.

Amy elbowed me in the side. "Why are you being such a curmudgeon tonight?"

"I don't know," I said. "I guess I just don't feel like being out tonight."

"It's because the queen isn't here," Jesse said. "We're dull to him now."

"That it?" Amy asked me.

"Of course it is," Jesse said. "He has her on a pedestal. We'll see how things go when she falls."

Jesse was drunk, so I tried not to let him get under my skin. Also, I had asked him to take care of Maggie already, and I didn't want to jeopardize that, so I just took him in stride.

"How are you going to feel when you see that?" Jesse asked me. "Well?" he said when I didn't respond.

"I don't know," I said. "I guess we'll see."

Christy was getting irritated with him too. "Leave him alone," she told him. "You're being a jerk."

"I'm just curious how he's going to feel when he sees the real Miss Alexandra Blake," Jesse said. "Like when she's sick, or the newness wears off and no hot sex, or wait, I know—"

"C'mon, Jess," TJ said. "Take it down a notch."

"No, I will not," Jesse said. Then he started laughing and had trouble getting his words out. "What about when you see the queen on the throne taking a massive—"

"Okay," Christy stood up. "It's time to go."

"Alright, alright," Jesse said. "I'll be good. You're not mad at me, are ya, buddy?" He slapped me on the back.

I forced a smile. "No, it's all good." I told them I would be right back, and I stepped outside to call Alex.

She answered almost immediately. "Hey, everything okay?" she asked.

"Yeah, everything is fine. I just wanted to hear your voice," I said.

"Where are you?" she asked.

I told her about the smoky bar and told her Jesse was drunk and acting stupid. "Where are you?" I asked.

"In a meeting," she said. "With Trent's father and Vince Buchanan...you remember him, right?"

"Uh-huh."

"...and some others you haven't met."

"So, you're still working while I'm out wasting time?"

"I'm always working for you, darling...for us," she said. She was always so patient. Jenny was always rushing me off the phone when she was busy. "Do you need a ride? I can send Marco."

"No, I'll need to drive him home. We're in his car. I'll see you in the morning."

"Okay, I'll see you then," she said.

"Hey, Alex?"

"Yes?"

"I was wondering what my phone number is on this phone."

"Oh, I didn't give it to you? Do you have something to write with?"

"No," I admitted. I didn't care about the damn phone number.

She laughed. "Will you remember it?"

"No, probably not. I'll get it from you tomorrow."

We hung up and I went back inside, wondering why I wasn't any more satisfied after talking to her. I was still feeling irritable and lost.

TJ and Amy were walking out as I walked in. They said Jesse was getting even louder, and they were going to call it a night.

"Hey," Jesse bellowed when he saw me approach the table. "Hey, Harold," he said, cracking himself up. "Where's Maude?"

Christy hit him on the forehead with the palm of her hand. "Enough," she said firmly.

That cheered me up a little bit, but then I realized that I forgot to ask Alex about Trent. I didn't want to call her again and disrupt her meeting. I would have to talk about it in the morning.

Jesse jumped out of his chair and came up behind me. He wrapped his arms around my neck and kissed the top of my head. "I'm sorry, buddy," he said. "You know I love you, right?"

He really was on my last nerve. "It's cool," I said, trying to pull his arms loose. "Love you too."

Jesse squeezed tighter and whispered in my ear, "Greg's gone. Trent's gone too. Am I next?"

I looked to Christy for help. "Can you get him off of me?"

She put her arms around him and said in his ear, "C'mon, babe, let's get another drink." He let go and let Christy pull him away. "He really is afraid of that," she said to me as they walked away.

"Trent is coming back," I called after them. "And Greg quit," I said, basically to myself, because I was the only one left.

## 22

"You sure you're okay watching her?" I asked Jesse again.

"I'm sure. I take care of her more than you do anyway," he said, only half joking.

He was hungover and probably didn't remember most of the previous night. "Trent will be back when I get home," I said. "I'll call you in a little while to give you my cell number."

"Okay, big shot." Jesse was laying on the couch in his boxers, flipping channels with the remote.

"I just mean call me. Let me know if you see him. Let me know how he is." I went to the kitchen and got an orange Gatorade and a pickle for him. "You need to hydrate," I said as I handed them to him.

"Thanks." He ate the pickle in two bites, then opened the Gatorade for a few sips.

I had told Jesse we were going to Texas to meet with Eddie's parents. I didn't mention my parents and he didn't ask. I thought about him not having anybody but the band and Christy, and I thought about his fear of losing the band. I wanted to say something to him about it all, but I didn't know what to say. So instead, I was hovering over him like a mother hen.

"What?" Jesse said as he set the Gatorade on the coffee table.

"Nothing," I said.

"Why are you pacing? You're getting on my nerves," he said.

I sat on the coffee table, blocking the television. "I think we might be seeing my parents in Texas."

Jesse sprang up. "Jiminy Fuck. Are you serious? Do they know about her?"

I shook my head. He started to laugh. "I'm sorry," he said. "I shouldn't laugh. I would like to be a fly on the wall."

The doorbell rang, so I stood up.

"Call me with your number," Jesse said. "I'll check on Trent."

I grabbed my bag and told him I would call him in a few minutes. I opened the door to find Marco waiting for me. Alex was in the car. I gave Maggie a hug goodbye and shut the door.

I beat Marco to the car and, without thinking about it, I opened the door and slid in next to Alex.

"You really should let him open the door for you," Alex said. "That's what he gets...oh, never mind. It's not important. Good morning."

"Good morning," I said as I pulled her to me and kissed her, realizing just how much I hated being away from her.

"Shall I roll up the glass?" Alex said, wiping her lipstick from my bottom lip.

"I think you should," I said.

She smiled and rubbed my leg. "It's a short ride to the airport, so I want to make a quick stop first. I want to show you something."

"Okay, I just need to call Jesse and give him this phone number." I reached in my pocket. "Damn, hang on. I need to run back in and get my phone."

She instructed Marco to circle back and wrote the phone number down for me. I ran back into the apartment. Jesse already had the phone waiting for me. He tossed it to me right when I walked in the door. "Thanks," I said. "At least I remembered to get the number." I held up the piece of paper and stuck it under the bottle opener magnet on the fridge and ran back down to the car.

"Sorry about that," I said.

"No worries, my dear. As I was saying, I have something exciting to show you."

"Okay. What is it?" Curiosity and excitement overcame me. My last surprise was a cell phone. I would be glad when I could surprise her with gifts. Although, I still had no idea what that would be.

"You will see soon enough." She patted my leg and had an excited grin. Then she got serious again. "What time are we meeting with the Coopers?"

Crap. Should I fess up that I hadn't contacted them? Or should I throw out a time and hope for the best when I called them later? "Tomorrow...at..." Hmm. I didn't want to get up too early, but I also didn't want it to take our whole day. The Coopers were retired, so anytime would probably be fine. Assuming they were home. Oh shit. What if they were out of town? What if they went someplace to get away after the funeral? The funeral. Damn, I was a terrible friend. Here I was worrying about it taking my whole day when I still hadn't even seen them since the funeral. Still had not been face-to-face with them.

"Cory?"

"Yeah?"

"Can you call the Coopers, please?"

"Yeah. I'm sorry. I just am having a hard time with that." I told her about all my worries.

"I could call them for you," she said. "Or you could be a man and stand up and face them and take your lumps—"

"I know. You're right," I said.

"You've got this," she said. "Call them. You will feel better when all of this is behind you."

I nodded and began formulating thoughts about what I would say.

"Do you need some privacy?" Alex asked.

"No, it's not that." I punched in the number. The same number they'd had since I started dialing it at seven years old.

"Hello?" answered Mrs. Cooper. Sarah Cooper. They started having me call them by their first names when I was around fifteen. I remembered how weird it felt at first.

"Hi, Sarah. It's Cory," I said. My voice wavered and my face burned. I looked away from Alex. She put her hand on my leg.

"Hi, Cory. How are you?" Her voice was sad but welcoming.

"I just wanted to tell you I'm sorry," I said, picturing Cari holding the puppy. Trying my best to be a man.

"Whatever for?" she asked.

I told her I was sorry for not seeing her at the funeral, or even after. I was so ashamed for Eddie's mom and for Alex to see how weak I had been...still was. I told her I was in California now, trying to finish what Eddie started, and that I was sorry I didn't go before. She told me that she didn't blame me because she knew I had a life with Jenny. I couldn't tell her about all that. I didn't have any more in me to offer.

"I want you to know that we haven't forgotten about him," I said.

"Of course not," she said. "I would never think that."

"I'll be in Dallas for a few days. Can I come by tomorrow?"

"That would be nice. We'd love to see you."

We agreed on one thirty. She'd fix lunch.

"You need a drink?" Alex asked when I closed the phone.

I laughed a little and said, "No, I'm okay."

"I'm proud of you. Now come with me, I want to show you something that might cheer you up."

Marco had pulled into a Sam Goody parking lot. I followed Alex inside. Before she had a chance to say anything, I saw a huge black-and-white poster of me. I had on jeans and a white tee shirt that somehow was lifted by wind or air or something, just enough to show some abs beneath my guitar. I had the five o'clock shadow she liked. At the top, it said Corbett Scott, and across the bottom, Suicide King with the king's head logo. I was speechless.

"That's not all," she said and pulled me after her. "I think you'll get a kick out of this." She took me to the magazine section and found some Hollywood gossip magazine. There was a small picture of her on the bottom of the cover with the caption, "Alexandra Blake's New Boy Toy." She flipped open to an article that had a full-page picture of us walking the Las Vegas strip. "I might have let it leak that we were there," she said with satisfaction.

I took the magazine from her and scanned the article. She discovered Suicide King and was seen about town with the lead singer. An unaccomplished and unknown singer.

Alex pulled me towards the door. "We need to get to the airport. Don't worry, I'll buy you the magazine to take with us."

"I can get it," I said.

"Okay," she said, dismissing my agitation. "Let's get it and get going."

I paid for the magazine and followed her to the car. I was still quite shocked by it all.

"What do you think? Isn't it exciting?" she said.

"Yeah," I said. "Boy toy?"

"Oh, honey, don't be bothered by that. It's publicity for the band. It creates anticipation."

"Okay," I said. "I guess if it helps the band." The guys and my brother were going to give me hell.

"What about the poster?" she said. "Isn't it fantastic? You look so sexy."

"You think so?" It was kind of embarrassing.

"Are you serious? Of course I do." She took my hand and squeezed. "Hold on tight," she said. "You are not going to be unknown much longer."

"What about the others?" I said.

"They'll be right there with you."

Just as my head started to clear, Marco pulled into the airport. We were about to board a private jet. I foolishly had anticipated first class. I climbed out of the car and swung around to meet Marco at the trunk.

"Where are you going?" Alex asked, realizing I wasn't at her side a few steps later.

"I'm getting our bags," I said, pointing to the trunk.

She held her arm out to me as she walked back. "Baby, please let Marco do his job." She took my hand and pulled me after her to the plane.

"I think it's dumb to have someone else do what I'm more than capable of doing," I said as we climbed the stairs to the plane. "I don't care how rich you are."

"That's sweet," Alex said, nudging me forward. "But Marco appreciates his paycheck."

Okay, I didn't want to begrudge him of that.

"Have a seat right there." Alex pointed to a set of cream-colored chairs that looked comfortable enough to watch the Cowboys game in. "Put your seatbelt on."

"I'm not twelve," I said, although apparently, she felt that I sometimes acted it.

"I'm sorry," she said. "We're just running a bit behind schedule."

"Okay," I said. "Where do you want me?"

She smiled. "Either chair...seatbelt."

I sat down and buckled my seatbelt, then looked around. I felt the same way I did when I saw her house for the first time. The plane was the same cream and chocolate color scheme. "What's back there?" I asked, pointing to a closed door.

"I'll show you later," she said and winked.

"What's that?" I asked, pointing to a cabinet.

"A bar. We can have a drink once we're in the air if you'd like."

"Yes," I said. "I think I need one. What's behind there?"

"A television. We can watch a movie...if you want to. But I think I have a better idea." She ran her fingers lightly down my arm.

Suddenly, I was relaxed. "I don't even know what to say," I said, taking a deep breath.

"It's a lot. I know. But this is your life now. If you want it."

"The other guys too?" I asked.

"We can take them sometime, if that would make you happy," she said. "This is my company plane," she said, sensing my confusion. "You and I travel on this plane. The others' travel will be arranged for them."

"Okay," I said, still not fully understanding her intentions. Did she mean like vacations or was she referring to the tour?

"Miss Blake, this is your captain. You are now free to roam about the cabin."

Alex took off her seatbelt and sat in my lap. She put her arms around my neck and said, "I want to make your wildest dreams come true." Then she kissed me.

"All I care about is you," I said. And because you can't tell a woman that you love her for the first time right after she tells you that you have access to her private plane, I said, "And what you are going to show me behind that door?"

A woman stepped out from behind us. "Can I get either of you a drink or something to eat?"

Is it still called a flight attendant on a private jet? I was somewhat hungry, but I wanted to see behind that door. Maybe a Bloody Mary? That was a drink and food, kind of.

"Cory," Alex said. "Would you like a mimosa or a Bloody Mary?"

"A Bloody Mary would be great."

Alex jumped off my lap. "We have a little over two hours before we have to buckle up again. I'd like to show you the mock-ups I was telling you about." She pulled me along and slid into a booth that reminded me of the corner booth at a Denny's. She got on her knees to reach into an overhead compartment.

Half expecting Marco to pop out from somewhere, I said, "Let me get that for you," and reached above her for it.

The lady with the drinks set two Bloody Marys on the table. I was happy to see that, not only was there celery in it, but there were also two pieces of bacon, a jumbo shrimp, and a stick of assorted olives and peppers.

"Thank you," Alex said to both of us and opened the bag. She pulled a stack of folders out and set them on the table. Then she changed her mind and put all but one back in the bag. I was glad because that looked like a lot to go through. "These are what you are going to start seeing for Suicide King," she said, spreading out a lot of pictures of me. I started to look through them. "Don't worry," she said. "There will be a foldout inside the album or CD that has pictures of the others and a bit about each of them. And, of course, we have some live photos of all of you from the show you've already done and will have more as you do more shows."

The pictures all started to look the same to me. I wanted to go through them with her to make her happy, but the truth was that it bored me silly.

"Whatever you think," I said. "You have an eye for this stuff; I don't."

"Alright," she said, gathering up the photos.

"Don't get me wrong," I said, afraid that I'd hurt her feelings. "I'm...I don't even know what to call it. I'm...I mean, it's extremely cool to have my picture in a freaking Sam Goody store." It started to sink in at that moment. "Holy shit. My face is in a Sam Goody store. Is it just in L.A.?"

Alex's eyes sparkled. "No, it's all over the country."

"Even in Dallas?"

"Yes, even in Dallas," she said, smiling big.

"I wonder if my brother has seen it," I said. "No, he would have called me. I wonder if my mom has seen the magazine. She buys those things...Uh-oh," I started to laugh.

"I thought you were going to tell them," Alex said. She was trying to act mad, but I could tell she wasn't. She saw the humor in it too.

"I wanted to wait to see how you felt when we got there, but I'm going to tell them," I said. "As soon as we land, I'm going to tell them that my girlfriend is freaking Alexandra Blake. *The* Alexandra Blake."

Alex laughed. "Well my boyfriend's face is in every record store across the country."

"I'm your boyfriend?" I loved the sound of it.

"Well, silly, if I'm your girlfriend, it stands to reason—"

"Alex?"

"Yes, Cory?"

"I want to see what's behind that door."

"Grab your drink," she said as she picked hers up and pulled a piece of bacon out with her mouth.

I picked up my drink and followed her. I ate the shrimp and took a big gulp of the drink. It was the best Bloody Mary I had ever tasted.

"Miss Blake, this is your captain. Please return to your seats and buckle up, as we are making our descent into Dallas Fort Worth."

"We should probably get dressed first," I said. A king size bed in a plane. Who fucking knew? My brain was in a fog, and it wasn't just from the Bloody Mary. Although, I did want another one. I sat up and grabbed my jeans from the floor. As I stepped into them, I turned and said, "Hey, you think..."

Alex had gotten up to get dressed as well. When I started talking to her, she stopped and turned to look at me. I had just spent well over an hour in bed with her. But as she stood in front of me, completely naked, she took my breath away. I pulled my jeans up and went to her.

"What are you doing?" she asked. "We need to get back out there."

"I just wanted to get a closer look."

"Take your pants off," she said.

I dropped them and stepped out of them. "I thought—"

"You smell like sex," she said. "Jump in the shower with me. We have two minutes."

"They have showers on planes? Madness."

Although I wanted to play in the shower, Alex had us washed up and dressed in literally two minutes. We were buckling up as the captain made a second announcement. The attendant lady brought us each another drink, and then she went to buckle up too.

"Your first deposit from Intrigued went in last night," Alex said. "I think you should take me to dinner tonight."

It was meager compared to her fortune, but she was finally going to let me pay for something. It made me feel good. I knew that was her intent, which made me feel good too. "Yeah, sure," I said. "What are you thinking?"

"I don't know. What is Texas famous for?"

Texas was probably most known for barbeque, but there was no way I was taking her out for ribs and baked beans. "I guess cattle...so, steak?" I knew nothing about fancy restaurants. "But whatever you want."

"That sounds lovely," she said.

We landed, and of course, she had a driver waiting. He opened the door for us, and I felt like a celebrity as we slid into the back seat. My face ached from smiling constantly. He took the south side exit, and just as we were to merge onto the highway, I saw it. "Holy shit," I exclaimed. Alex giggled like a schoolgirl and hugged my arm. The driver pulled over and jumped out to open her door. She took my hand and pulled me after her. We stood in the dirt on the side of the highway and looked up at a full-size billboard of the "naked" picture of us. It read, "Are you intrigued?"

"Holy Moley," I murmured, looking at our giant, seemingly naked bodies. "My mother is going to have heart failure."

Alex laughed and said, "And every teenaged boy in Dallas is going to have a hard-on."

"That's for damn sure," I said.

"How does it make you feel?" she asked happily.

I looked at her with my straight, shocked expression. Her smile slowly began to fade, but before it was completely gone, I yanked her into my arms and laughed. "Like a teenage boy," I said and held her tightly enough to see for herself.

We jumped back into the car, and the driver whisked us off to a luxury hotel. With the two-hour time difference, it was almost five by the time we settled in.

"I hope you don't mind," Alex said. "But I brought a few outfits for you...just in case."

"I don't mind," I said. I didn't either. I liked not having to worry about figuring out what to wear.

"I enjoy shopping for you," Alex said.

"And dressing me up like a Ken doll?" I said.

She frowned. "No, I just mean—"

"I was just kidding," I said. "I don't mind. Honestly. If it makes you happy, it makes me happy."

"It's fun for me," she said. "I like putting things together that I know will look nice on you."

She was relaxing on a really large comfy-looking couch. I went and laid down with my head in her lap and said, "It doesn't bother you that you have to dress me?"

She ran her hand through my hair and laughed. "I don't feel like I have to. I feel like it's fun when you allow me to."

"How do you know sizes?" I asked.

"I have an eye for it. But I was gathering the nerve to ask you to see my tailor. Imagine how handsome you will look when everything is exact."

I wasn't sure if I was more astonished by her having to gather her nerve to ask me for something or that the clothes would fit even better. The thought of standing still while a guy measured me endlessly did sound like a special form of torture.

"When we get back, you'll need to do those photo shoots," she said. "You remember, the side of you that wears the cologne all dressed up and out to dinner with a beautiful woman."

Ugh. More photo shoots and a tailor? "Are you going to be the beautiful woman?" I asked.

"Thank you, darling, but no. It will either be Justine or..."

"Oh, hell no." I shot up and looked at her like she'd lost her mind. "There is no way I'm doing that. I did the song for you, but I am not doing this."

Alex looked taken aback at first, then she laughed. "Calm down. She is a professional model. Why are you so upset?"

Why was I so upset? What difference did it make who the other person was? "I don't know," I said. "I just think it's a better idea for it to be you. Why would it be anybody else after that billboard? It has to be you. Plus, it goes with the whole boy toy thing."

"Don't take this the wrong way," Alex said. "But they are not going to pay what my agent would demand."

"Then demand less," I said.

Alex looked like she was trying not to laugh again. Maybe demanding wasn't my thing? "Okay," she said.

"Really?"

"I'll run it by them," she said. Then she made a stern face. "This demanding side of you..."

Oh, here we go. She was going to show me who was boss. Like there was ever a doubt. Well, I didn't care. Okay, I cared, but it looked as if I was going to do the ads with her, and it was my idea.

"Cory?"

"Yeah?"

"As I was saying, this demanding side of you...is a turn on."

"You're turned on? Because I was demanding? I can do it more often." I sat down next to her.

"It works best in small doses," she said as she started undressing me.

Alex asked if I wanted to order room service for dinner, but I wanted to take her out. "I'll let you dress me," I said to entice her.

She put me in a fitted, light-gray three-piece suit—happily, with no tie.

"You look absolutely yummy," she said as we walked out the door. Then she stopped. "Do you have everything you need? Your wallet? Phone if you want it."

I pulled the phone from one jacket pocket and my wallet from the other.

"Your ID? Credit card?" she said.

We went to the hotel restaurant, which was on the top floor. Windows circled the restaurant displaying the Dallas skyline. When they took us to our table, I told Alex I would be right back.

"Men's room," I muttered as I walked away. I went to the bar and asked for the manager and the bartender. I showed them my driver's license and asked them not to card me when we ordered drinks.

The manager took my license and studied it at every angle as if I were trying to pull a fast one. "Why don't you want to show your ID?" he asked.

"Because it's embarrassing in front of my girlfriend," I said.

The bartender said, "Your girlfriend doesn't know how old you are?"

"Yes, she knows," I said. "But she's a little bit older than me. I don't want the reminder."

"How much older?" the manager asked. "She forgets your age?"

"No, she doesn't forget—"

"I'm just kidding, kid. No problem. Enjoy your dinner," the manager said.

"You okay?" Alex asked as I sat down.

"Yeah, I thought I saw someone I knew. What looks good?" I opened the menu and scanned it. Roasted Free-Range Half Chicken $37. For half a chicken. That's a $74 chicken. That's just stupid, I don't care who you are.

"May I start you off with an appetizer or some drinks?" the server asked.

Alex ordered wine, and I asked for a Tanqueray and tonic. "Actually, I'll have the same," Alex said.

"Yes, ma'am," she said. Then she turned to me. "May I see your identification, sir?"

Fucking $37 chicken and they couldn't follow simple instructions. And, of course, my damn face turned red. I dug in my pocket and pulled out my wallet, and you guessed it. I left my ID at the bar. I took a deep breath and calmly said, "I left it at the bar. I'll follow you over there."

The bartender laughed and confirmed my age. He fixed the drinks, and the server took them back to the table while I waited on the manager and my ID.

When I got back to the table, Alex was sipping on her drink. "Shake it off, honey," she said with an amused expression.

I took a gulp of my drink. I was at a place that charged $37 for not a whole chicken, but a half chicken. I was with Alexandra Blake and I could afford it. I laughed. Life was as good as it gets.

And then all hell broke loose.

# 23

We slept in and ordered room service. I blocked thoughts of anything but the moment from my mind. The bed was soft and cool against our warm bodies. We playfully messed around, talked about things big and small, and slept on and off. The alarm went off at eleven, and I reluctantly climbed out of bed. There was no more procrastinating. Alex assured me I would feel better about everything after I talked to Eddie's parents in person.

I went to the hotel gym and worked out for about forty-five minutes, then showered and dressed. When I walked out of the bathroom, Alex had folders and photos spread across the bed and was on the phone. I pulled a chair in front of the TV and turned it on low to wait for her. I found *My Cousin Vinny* on the movie channel and got engrossed in it.

I was about halfway through it when Alex said, "You ready, baby?" while she rubbed my neck.

I turned the TV off. "Yep, let's go."

"The car is waiting for us. Do you have everything you need?"

I made sure I had my wallet and phone before we left. "The Coopers are great," I told her as we took the elevator down.

"They always said they felt like they had two sons," I said, getting depressed about the whole thing again.

"Eddie didn't have any siblings?" Alex asked.

"Yeah, he has...had...two older sisters. He was an oops baby. One sister is like fifteen years older than he was and the other, I think, seventeen."

"So, they lost their only son," Alex said. "This is going to be difficult. I'm sure they will be happy to see you."

"Yeah. I need to do better about staying in touch with them."

The elevator opened us to the ground floor. Alex took my hand, and we crossed the lobby to the waiting car. The driver acknowledged Alex, by Miss Blake of course, and opened the door for us. He already knew where to go.

"We can make a point of coming here every few months," Alex said. "For a day or two whenever possible."

"That would be great. Thank you."

"Of course. Are your parents friends with the Coopers?" she asked.

"Yeah, I guess so. The Coopers kind of have their nose in everybody's business. Very social. My mom and dad are more homebodies." The car came to a stop, and we were there. The Coopers lived in lower-middle-class neighborhood, where they'd been since they moved to Texas twenty years ago. Most of their original neighbors had moved on, while lower-income families moved in.

Alex had the driver wait even though we were going to be at least an hour or two. When Eddie's parents opened the door, I felt instantly relieved. They still loved me. I gave them both a hug and said, "Sarah, Joe, I'd like you to meet—"

"Alexandra Blake," Sarah said. "It's so nice to meet you, Miss Blake." Sarah shook Alex's hand enthusiastically.

"Yeah, come in," Joe said. "Eddie told us so much about you." He held the door open and motioned us in.

I wondered if Eddie felt the same way about her that the others did. He never said an unkind word about her to me. Of course, he wouldn't. He was trying to get me to L.A.

"Thank you," Alex said as we followed them into the house.

We went into the small living room where Alex and I sat on the couch, and Joe sat in his chair. Sarah disappeared into the kitchen for drinks. The house hadn't changed much. There were still graduation photos on the paneled wall of all three kids, even though it had been many years since any of them were in high school. Sarah brought Alex a glass of wine and Joe and me a beer and then joined us on the couch.

"Cory and Eddie were thicker than thieves," Sarah told Alex as she pulled a large photo album from the bottom of the coffee table. I gave Alex an apologetic glance, but she seemed genuinely interested in pictures of me as a boy.

"Wait," Alex said as Sarah turned a page. "Go back. What is this?" Alex pointed to a photo. I looked over her arm to see that it was a picture of us around thirteen years old. We were holding a poster we made with the Suicide King logo we had designed.

"That's the boys holding a poster they made. They wanted to take it with them to a concert Joe was taking them to. Remember that, Joe?"

"Sure, I do. I believe we were going to see...was it 38 Special?"

"I don't remember," I said. "But do you think I could have that picture?"

"I suppose so," Sarah said and peeled back the film.

I helped her lift it from the sticky page to ensure we kept it from tearing. Then I handed it to Alex. "Such handsome boys," Alex said, teasing me. She put it in her bag. Our proof that Suicide King was not Greg's.

After about thirty minutes more of Alex enduring childhood stories, she said, "It's been so wonderful to meet you both. Eddie was a very talented musician and an honorable man. He was directly responsible for starting Suicide King, and it's very important to Cory, to all of us really, that he is not forgotten." Alex reached into her bag and pulled out a folder and a CD. "I brought you a preliminary copy of the CD the band will be releasing in a few weeks. I'll send you a final version as well." She handed the CD to Sarah, who looked at it then handed it to Joe. "If you'll look at the bottom on the back side, you will see a dedication to Eddie."

I hadn't known about that. I gave Alex a smile. Joe turned the CD to the back and read the dedication, then looked at the front. "That's wonderful," Sarah said. "And a handsome picture of you, Cory."

I also didn't know that she had only me on the front. But I would worry about that later.

"Lunch is just about ready," Sarah said. "I made my famous lasagna for you," she said to me.

"That sounds delicious," Alex said. "But just one more thing." She opened the folder and put some forms and a pen on the table. "Cory has set it up for you to receive Eddie's portion of any royalties he might have earned. I just need a few signatures and indicate how you would like to receive payment."

Before they even had a chance to pick up the papers, Eddie's sister called from the kitchen. The back door could be heard slamming shut behind her.

"Mom, Dad, where are you? Guess who I ran into?" It was the younger of the two sisters, Ellen. When she saw me, her eyes lit up. "Oh my gosh, Cory. What a coincidence." Before I had a chance to ask her what she meant, Jennifer came walking in behind her. What the hell. I felt dizzy and then suddenly like I wanted to jump on Alex and shield her from incoming enemy fire.

"Why are you here?" Jennifer asked.

"The better question is, what are you doing here?" I said, angry that she was in my territory.

The room was silent. Finally, Jennifer asked, "Can I see you in the kitchen for a second?"

I looked at Alex, remembering how I'd acted when Steven wanted to talk to her privately. She nodded, so I followed Jennifer into the kitchen.

"What are you doing here?" I demanded again.

She went in a few steps further, then turned dramatically. "I came by after you left town and apologized for not being at the funeral. They weren't doing too good, so I've been stopping by with groceries and just to check on them. Remember, I've known them a long time too."

"Oh," I said, calming down. "I guess that makes sense. How are you?"

She lifted her shirt to expose the beginnings of a baby bump. "What are you doing here?" she asked.

A baby? A fucking baby? When did that get there? "I have some papers for them to sign," I mumbled, trying to figure out what to say about it all. I had thought before that I possibly owed her an explanation. What the hell was I thinking? I owed this conniving bitch nothing.

"What kind of papers?"

"For Eddie's share of the royalties...so you really were...are pregnant?" I said, distracted with trying to remember the last time we slept together. I did the math but knew she was sleeping with both of us. There was a fifty-fifty chance that bump was mine. I was sickened at the thought.

"Looks that way," she said, and headed back for the living room. As she breezed past me, she added, "Don't think for a minute that I'm going to let them sign those papers." She stopped and looked at me like she was getting the last word. "I'll have it tied up with lawyers for so long that you'll never see a penny from your band."

I put my arm across the doorway to block her path. "Why did you tell me you weren't pregnant?" I demanded.

She tried to move my arm, but I wasn't having it. She dug in with her nails, but I wanted an answer. Finally, she stopped and looked at me. "Because once you decided you were leaving, I had no desire to keep you in the picture." She crossed her arms and gave a satisfied nod to me. "But now, after seeing that ridiculous Intrigued billboard, I see things differently." She gave it a second to sink in. "Now move your arm or I'm going to tell them all that you held me in here against my will." I lifted my arms in surrender, and she strolled back to the living room like the arrogant, self-centered bitch that she was.

I followed her, completely aware that she had outplayed me at every move.

She walked up to Alex and said, "They aren't going to sign these until I review them." Then she took the papers from the table.

Alex stood and said gracefully, "Oh, are you an attorney?"

"No," I said. "She's a realtor. Jennifer, give the Coopers their papers."

"I know how to read contracts," Jennifer said. Then she turned to the Coopers and smiled. "Let me review these," she said sweetly. "Then if need be, we will have an attorney look at them. Okay?"

"I don't really think that's necessary," Sarah said, clearly unsettled and confused by the commotion.

"It couldn't hurt," Joe said. "Just to make sure we understand what we're signing. You understand, don't you, Cory?"

"Of course we do," Alex said. "Cory, I think we've taken up enough of their time."

"What about lunch?" Sarah said, still visibly upset.

I gave her a hug and said, "I'm sorry."

"Well, let me fix you a plate," she said and dashed off to the kitchen.

Alex, Joe, Ellen, Jennifer, and I all stood there awkwardly waiting. After what felt like an eternity, she brought me back a foil wrapped plate and a fork.

"Don't be such a stranger," she said as Alex and I walked out the door, leaving Jennifer there to cause as much mischief as she liked.

When we got to the car, the driver jumped out and opened the door for us. I handed him the plate and said, "I brought you some homemade lasagna."

"Thank you, sir," he said happily. Then he got in the car and asked, "Where to?" as he put the plate in the passenger seat and the car in drive.

Alex looked at me. "Well, we missed lunch. You hungry?"

"Sure," I said, even though I was sick to my stomach. Not only was I worried about what Jennifer was trying to accomplish with the Cooper's contracts, I was completely undone by the baby bump. It was real. As much as I tried to figure out a way that she could be faking it, there was no way. She was pregnant. But with whose baby? I had put all anger towards her to bed, and here she was stirring up trouble again. It's said that indifference, not hate, is the opposite of love, but I did not feel indifference or love. I felt raging hatred for Jennifer.

"Cory," Alex said and touched my leg.

"Yeah?"

"Where are you? I was trying to ask you what you want for lunch?"

"I'm sorry," I said. "Anything is fine."

"Don't worry, honey. It's fine to have an attorney look over the contract. Sarah and Joe are nice, reasonable people. They should understand what they're signing." Her words said she wasn't concerned, but her expression and tone told me differently. "What on earth happened to your arm?" she asked, suddenly noticing the four perfect nail punctures.

How could I tell Alex that I knew Jennifer would cause trouble with the contract? That she was possibly having my baby?

"Jennifer wasn't happy with the billboard," I said. "And she's going to try to manipulate them." I slumped back in the seat. I looked out the window and watched the trees go by.

"I'm not afraid of her," Alex said sharply and ran her fingers across the nail marks. "She doesn't know who she's dealing with. Now let's have a nice lunch."

"Okay," I forced the words. "Whatever sounds good to you."

Alex's phone chirped. She told the driver to take us back to the hotel. "It was nice enough," she said. "Just eat there again?"

I nodded and she opened her phone. "It's TJ," she said, looking confused. "Hello, TJ?" Her expression changed almost immediately. What could be wrong now? "I see," she said. She bit her lip and ran her fingers across her forehead. "We'll get back as soon as we can. Tonight, if possible. Keep me updated." She closed the phone and said, "I'm going to see if we can fly out tonight."

"What is it?" I asked. "It's Trent, isn't it? How bad is it?"

Alex's expression prepared me for the worst. "No, it's not Trent," she said softly. She put her hand on mine and held firmly. "It's Jesse. He's in the hospital. He...I don't know the details...but it appears that he tried to kill himself."

## 24

"What? Why? Is he going to be okay? What did TJ say?" I couldn't process it all. What the hell happened? Jesse was fine when I left for the airport.

"Not a lot," Alex said. "Just that he was at the hospital and they hadn't come out to talk to him. Do you know how to get a hold of Jesse's parents?"

"He doesn't have any," I said. "I mean he has a dad; his mom passed away."

"Okay," Alex said calmly. "Can you reach his father?"

"No, he left them when Jesse was young. At least that's what Christy, his girlfriend, said."

"Alright. I'll get us scheduled to fly back and then work on finding his father. I'm not sure the hospital will talk to any of us..." Her voice trailed off.

"What do we do if they won't?" I asked.

"I'm not sure. But we'll figure it out."

Alex got busy on the phone arranging our flight back, which left me stuck in my own mind. It felt like the car was going in slow motion. I had to find out what upset Jesse so much that...it was inconceivable to me. And what about Trent? Where was he? I hadn't even asked about him. I had been so wrapped up in Alex that I hadn't thought about anybody but myself, and now it was all crashing down around me. We hadn't even completed recording our first album and the band had completely fallen apart.

"I'm afraid we'll have to fly back on a commercial flight," Alex said. "I have us leaving DFW tonight at ten thirty."

Unable to say anything, I just nodded. Alex tried to pull me to her, but I didn't want to be consoled. I didn't want to feel better. "What about Trent?" I asked. "What is going on with him?"

"I'll call Derek," she said. "Last I heard, he was feeling better."

Jesse had been a good friend to Eddie and a good friend to me. When we got back to L.A., I would find out what happened and do whatever I could to fix it. Alex was talking on the phone, but I didn't really hear her. As she once put it, I guess I was in Cory Land. Thoughts were swimming interchangeably through my head, and I couldn't put them in logical order. I put my face in my hands and rubbed my eyes. Alex touched my back. I looked up to her. She had a grim expression.

"What? What did you find out?"

"We're not sure where Trent is. He told his father he was going to the hospital, but TJ says he hasn't shown up yet. But I'm sure he will. You know he always turns up."

"Yeah," I said. "He'll be there." I knew that Trent would be there unless it was physically impossible. At that point, I had no reason to believe anything but the best about that. I had to believe the best. I didn't have the mental energy to start what-if-ing about Trent.

Alex had tried to console me, and I shrugged her off. Every-thing affected her just as much as it did me, but once again, I only thought about me. She didn't even know about Jenny yet. How was I ever going to tell her? Would it all be too much for her? Would that be the final blow that caused her to leave me? Damn, here I was doing it again. Was I capable of worrying about her without thinking about how it affected me? I loved Alex and had been willing to do anything for her...so that she would love me. It was all so confusing.

When we got back to the hotel, Alex ordered room service. She was trying to take care of things, and I had let her. As soon as she hung up the phone, I held her. I put my arms around her and did my best to comfort her. "It's all going to work out," I said. I had no way of knowing that, but I held her tightly as if I did. "We have a few hours before we leave for the airport," I said. "Why don't I draw you a hot bath? I'll let you know when the food gets here."

I couldn't tell her about Jenny with everything else that was going on. The least I could do was be strong for her. I didn't know it at the time, but she had her secrets too.

By the time we landed at LAX and climbed into her car, it was after midnight, even with the two-hour time difference. Alex instructed Marco to drive us to the hospital. She tried calling Trent's dad but got no answer. We rode in silence, both of us deep in thought. When Marco pulled up to the hospital, he opened my door. I looked at Alex questioningly.

"I have something I need to take care of," she said. "Check on Jesse, I'll be back soon."

"What could you possibly have to do this time of night?" I asked.

"I'll be back in a few hours," was all she said.

I got out of the car, completely mystified by her behavior. How could she just drop me off? Had she somehow found out about Jenny? Was she really just leaving me to deal with it all alone? As they drove away, I realized that I didn't even kiss her goodbye. I tried to shake it off and went inside to find TJ. After asking for help at every security desk and nurse station, I finally found TJ and Trent asleep in a waiting area.

I sat down next to TJ and shook him.

"Hey, man," he said as he sat up and wiped his eyes.

"What happened?" I said. "How is he?"

"I don't know," TJ said. "They won't tell us much because we're not family." He looked around. "Where's Miss Blake?"

"She'll be here soon. Do you know why he did this?"

TJ looked at me, then looked away. "I think he felt like he lost everything."

"What does that mean? What did he lose? Wait...where are Christy and Amy?"

"He found Christy with some guy. They were doing drugs, and well, I guess they were sleeping together too. She gave some bullshit story about how she thought he knew because you knew. Like that made it okay." He looked me in the eyes. "Did you know?"

I felt like there were fifty pounds of pressure on my chest. "I knew about the drugs, but not...I didn't want to hurt him. She said she was getting her shit together."

TJ nodded. Then he said, "He saw the poster at Sam Goody."

"That doesn't mean anything," I said.

"I don't care," TJ said. "I just wanna play drums. So, you don't have to worry about me."

Trent had woken up and said, "I don't care either. I don't even care that I'm not getting paid. I just thought we were friends. I thought you told me about these things."

"We are friends," I said. "What do you mean you're not getting paid?"

TJ sighed. "Turns out his contract is even worse than ours. He gets nothing till he's thirty-two. Nothing."

"We know you're the looks and the voice," Trent said. "But Jesse had a hand in all of the songs. And he brought you here. He deserves more...respect, if nothing else."

"Where are Christy and Amy?" I asked again.

"They went to get food. They're coming back," TJ said.

"Where's Miss Blake?" Trent asked me. Then he said to TJ, "Didn't she say she was going to talk to Jesse about everything?"

"You mean, she knows all of this?" I asked. I stood and started pacing. "About Jesse and Christy? And about the poster?"

TJ shrugged and said, "Well, yeah. I called her as soon as it happened."

Why didn't she tell me what she knew? And where the hell was she?

I remembered Amy questioning TJ about Alex at the bar. TJ had known Alex much longer than I and was one of the few that never spoke badly about her to me. I didn't want to hear about the other men then, but now I wondered. Was I just another one of them? What did he know about that?

Amy and Christy walked in with bags of fast food. Christy avoided eye contact with me, but Amy came over and hugged me. "You want half my burger?" she asked. I told her no but asked her about that night in the bar.

"You remember," I said. "When you were asking him about the men in Alex's past." She thought for a second. "When I went to find the jukebox," I reminded her.

"Oh, yeah. Nothing really. He just said that they came and went from time to time. He never saw anything serious."

"He say anything about Alex? Anything I should know?"

"No, I don't think so. Like what?"

"Like anything about me and Alex. Am I the same as all the others?"

"Oh," Amy said and hugged me again. "No, he didn't say anything about that." Then she pulled out a chair and sat down at the table and started unwrapping her food. TJ came and sat next to her. Christy sat next to Trent on the couch.

"So where is Miss Alexandra Blake?" Christy asked. "Too good for the bars and too good for us here?"

"You don't have a lot of room to talk," I said, pointing at her. "Where is the guy you're fucking that brought us all here tonight?"

Christy threw her burger back in the bag and came charging towards me. "We're not here because of me; we're here because of you and Miss High and Mighty."

"Everything he's upset at me about is just a misunderstanding that can be fixed," I said, getting right back in her face. "You can't unfuck everybody that's had you."

TJ stepped between us. "Come on, guys, this isn't helping."

Where the fuck was Alex? If anybody could get information about Jesse, it was her. "I'm sorry," I said, trying to sound calm. "Do you have any idea how to find his father?" I asked Christy.

"No. And even if I did, Jesse wouldn't want him here."

"Then how are we going to know what's going on?" I asked, throwing up my hands in frustration. Nobody had an answer. I went and sat next to Trent. Christy picked up her food and went to sit with TJ and Amy at the table. Presumably, to get away from me.

Trent put his hand on my shoulder. "You want some food?" he asked softly and offered his bag.

I reached in and grabbed a few fries. "Thanks." I stuffed the fries in my mouth and tried not to cry. I hadn't cried since I was a child. Then came Eddie's funeral and now this. I had too many thoughts darting around my brain. If Jesse died, how I would live with myself? Had I lost Alex? Was it all too much for her? What were we all doing? Sitting around waiting, not knowing if he was alive or dead. Knowing nobody was going to talk to us. And then there was Jenny again. Was I going to be a father...with someone I didn't love? Someone I didn't even like.

"Have you talked to your dad?" I asked. "I think he was worried about you."

"Not since this morning. How do you know that?"

"Where were you all day? We were all worried," I said.

"I went to your apartment," he answered. "I wanted to make sure your dog was okay. I knew you would both worry about that."

Maggie. I hadn't even thought about her. I just kept getting better. I handed Trent my phone. "Call him. He cares about you, and he should know where you are."

Trent took the phone. "Where'd you get this? My father gave me one, but I don't carry it. He was just trying to keep tabs on me."

"Just call him," I said. "Let him know you're okay. And ask him about your contract. He's the one that drew them all up."

He opened the phone and called his dad. I walked over to the table and pulled out a chair. Christy looked up at me like I didn't belong, but I didn't care. Amy touched her arm, then Christy grudgingly scooted over to make room for me. "What happened?" I asked again and sat down.

"It is my fault," Christy said and wiped away a tear. "I knew he was upset about the way things were going in the band. I just didn't realize how much."

I felt anger rise in my chest, and I wanted to let her have it. But instead, I forced it down and said, "I mean, what happened? What did he do? Who found him?"

"What I was trying to say," Christy said. "Is if I would have been with him instead of...where I was, I would have been able to reason with him about the posters and CD cover."

"What CD cover?" I said. How had any of them seen a cover? I didn't even see it till I saw it at the Cooper's.

"The one with your mug on the front," Christy said. "Like it's the Cory Scott Band."

"How is there a cover when there's not even a CD yet?" I asked. We all looked at TJ.

"Jeff had a copy of the preliminary. We saw it when he wanted us to listen to it while you were gone. He didn't realize we hadn't seen the cover."

"I can fix that," I said. "I need to let him know. I can fix it."

"I can fix me too," Christy said. "If we get the chance."

Trent walked up and set my phone on the table. "My father is coming up here. He said he'll find out what's going on." Then he shrugged and said, "I guess he thinks because he's a lawyer he can." He went back and fell into the couch and said, "Oh yeah. And Miss Blake is with him."

What was she doing with Trent's dad? I looked at my phone and wondered if I should call her. I wanted to know what was going on with her...with us. But if she was with Mr. Austin, she may not talk freely. I would just have to be patient. Not my strongest quality. I thought for a second about calling Jennifer, but then thought better of it. I needed to discuss it with Alex first. Unable to sit still, I started pacing. I still didn't know what Jesse did, but I felt like asking a third time was wrong. I guess it really didn't matter how he did what he did, just that he did.

My phone buzzed and vibrated on the table. I picked it up to see that it was Alex. "Hey," I said. "Where are you?"

"We're pulling up now. Meet us at the door."

I ran to the door and paced back and forth while I waited for them. After a few minutes that felt like hours, the car pulled up. Marco opened the door for Alex and Mr. Austin. I took a deep breath and did all I could to appear calm.

When the glass doors slid open, I looked down and counted to three. Then I looked up at Alex. She smiled softly as if she was saying I'm sorry. But what was she sorry about? Jesse or us?

I turned to Mr. Austin. "Why isn't Trent getting his share?" It just flew out of my mouth without warning. Mr. Austin gave me what I felt was a condescending look and said, "Money is the one thing Trent does not need right now. When he can handle it, he will get what is due to him."

I didn't know what to say. My mind was a jumbled mess that went on autopilot and acted on its own. "You understand he's gay...right?" What was wrong with me? What the hell was I saying? I just outed my bandmate, my friend.

"I know that," he said. "I don't care about that. I just want him safe from...well, honestly, himself."

"Tell him that," I said. I pulled out my wallet and took out a condom. I handed it to Mr. Austin. "Give him this so he believes you. And tell him you love him. I'm not sure he knows."

After a brief hesitation, he took it from me. Then he said, "Okay, I will," and walked away.

"Where have you been?" I asked Alex.

"Let's go sit down," she said.

"I don't want to sit down. I want to know what's going on." We were still standing in front of the sliding doors.

Alex walked past me so that we were at least inside a bit more and leaned against the wall. She was clearly exhausted. "Among other things, I was trying to locate Jesse's father."

"Okay," I said impatiently. "Did you?"

"We did," she said.

Oh my God, she was making me crazy. I wanted to pick her up and shake all my answers out of her.

"It seems," she said slowly, "that he's in prison."

I didn't know what to say.

"Derek is working on an emergency temporary release. I'm afraid I have no idea how long that will take."

Alex closed her eyes and rubbed her forehead, hands shaking. I realized she was beyond exhausted, and I wasn't helping. Making things worse, more likely.

"Come on," I said and put my arm around her. "Let's go sit down." I led her to a waiting area and sat next to her. "Let me get you something to eat," I said, realizing it had been a while since we'd had the room service.

"Alright," she said softly. "Maybe some juice or something."

I literally ran to the cafeteria only to find that it was closed. I went to a nurse's station and talked them out of an apple juice and some soup.

She sipped the soup from the Styrofoam cup, and my only immediate concern was her. I rubbed her back lightly while she drank, and I gave her a moment of silence.

## 25

"Derek knows someone on the board of directors," Alex finally said. "He'll find out how Jesse is doing. If Trent would have told him what was going on sooner..." Her voice trailed off.

"Why couldn't you tell me that before?" I asked. "Why did you leave without telling me where you were going?" I did my best to sound calm and unaccusatory. "I was really worried about you."

"I'm sorry," she said. "I just had to work some things out in my mind."

My heart sank. I wasn't sure what to say next. Had she already made up her mind about us?

She reached in her purse and pulled out a CD. "I have an idea for a different cover," she said. "If you like it. If all of you like it." She handed it to me. "It's not professionally done yet, obviously. But you can get the gist of it."

It looked like a few photographs spread out on a table, but the pictures were blurred. Except the one on top, which was the one we took from Sarah Cooper's photo album. Eddie and me as teenagers with our homemade Suicide King poster. "It's awesome," I said. "I love it."

"Good. I hoped you would. When I found out Jesse was this upset about it, I knew you would want it changed."

"Yeah," I said. "I just wish you had told me what you were doing. I was worried about you. About us."

Alex reached to my face. "You have your sexy shadow." She ran her thumb over my cheek. "Cory, I—"

"I need to tell you something," I said. Telling her about Jenny wasn't going to make things better, that was for sure. But I was starting to put it together that loving her meant more than worrying about her loving me. I told her about the conversation in the kitchen. I told her all of it. Then I said, "I'm sorry."

"I know," she said. "When you were in there talking to her, the Coopers told me about the pregnancy. I don't think they realized the gravity of what they were saying. I'm not sure how much they know about what's going on with you...what she's told them."

She knew. That was why she left me at the hospital. "I'm sorry," was all I could say.

"You didn't do anything wrong," Alex said. "You have nothing to be sorry for."

"So...you're not leaving me?" I had finally come to terms with the possibility.

"No, honey, I'm not leaving you." An overwhelming surge of relief washed over me. "In fact," she said, "I have something I must tell you."

"Hey, Cory." TJ ran up to us. "Miss Blake." He nodded to her. "Jesse's awake. He wants to talk to us."

"He wants to talk to me?" I said. "Are you sure?"

TJ shrugged. "He said all of us."

Alex wasn't leaving me, and Jesse was okay. I felt fifty pounds lighter. "Okay," I said. "We'll be right there."

"Let's go see Jesse," Alex said as she stood and took my hand.

As we walked down the hallway to Jesse's room, his door swung open and Christy came out. Clearly, she had been crying. "How'd it go?" I asked her.

She dabbed at her eyes and said, "He's still very groggy. I'm not sure what his state of mind is."

"Who do you think should go in next?" I asked.

"I don't think it matters," she said, not looking at me. She blamed me, and I blamed her.

"Why don't you three boys go in?" Alex said.

"What about you?" I asked. "You don't want to come with us?"

"I'll talk to him at length when he gets out. Right now, he just needs to be surrounded by those that love him." She squeezed my hand for encouragement. I loved her so much.

TJ, Trent, and I went in. Christy was right; he was very groggy, but he smiled when he saw us. His longish jet-black hair was sticking up and tangled, and his steel-blue eyes were tired. TJ and Trent were hesitant, like they weren't sure what to say. I stepped in front of them and pulled Jesse up by his hospital gown and hugged him. "You scared the shit out of us," I said.

"Yeah, yeah," he said and patted my back. He didn't hug me back, but I still knew he forgave me. But I also knew I had some damage control to do and that it needed to start immediately.

I let go of him and playfully pushed him back down. His eyes fluttered like he was trying to stay awake. "I'm going to let you sleep," I said. "But you need to know something."

"What's that?" he said.

"I love you," I said. "It may not have seemed like it recently, but I have your back and I always will."

"What's that your holding?" he asked.

"Oh, shit," I said. "I almost forgot." I handed him a copy of our CD. "If you like it, this is the new cover. If you don't, we'll figure it out." I turned to TJ and Trent, who had been leaning quietly against the wall and said, "All of us, I mean," and waved them over to look.

"It's cool," Jesse said. "I like it."

"Yeah," TJ said. "I like it. You were a goofy-looking kid."

"Nah, that's Eddie," I said.

Jesse laughed a little and said, "Hey, asshole, why didn't you tell me what you knew about Christy?"

"I'm sorry," I said. "I just didn't want to hurt you. I thought I could straighten her out."

"All that time she acted like I was paranoid and like I had trust issues. And it was her, and you knew it."

"I know," I said. "I was a shitty friend. I didn't mean to be; I just made bad decisions. I'll make it up to you, I promise."

Jesse thought for a second like he was trying to put his groggy thoughts into what he wanted to say. "All right, fuck it," he finally said. "I know your heart was in the right place."

"When do you get out of here?" Trent asked.

"Not sure," Jesse said. "They said I have to stay at least seventy-two hours."

"We should have a party when you get out," Trent said.

"No," all three of us said at once.

I told Jesse I needed to get Alex home but that I would be back later. Trent said he'd stay with him until he fell asleep, then be back later as well.

Alex snuggled up next to me in the car. Trent was going to stay at my apartment to take care of Maggie, and Marco was driving us to her house. The sun had been up for a while, and she could no longer keep her eyes open. "We need to talk about some things," she said, and then she was out. I was just going to have to be patient.

We woke up around dinner time.

"Oh, my goodness," Alex said. "I'm famished."

"What can I get you?" I asked.

"I think I want Chinese food. A lot of Chinese food."

I laughed and jumped up to throw on my jeans. "Okay, I'll be right back."

We ate Chinese food in bed, then snuggled and messed around a little. "I could stay here with you forever," I said. "But I told Jesse I'd be back."

"Yes," she said. "We must get back to reality. I'll go with you. I want to talk to him as well."

On the way to the hospital, Alex took a call from Mr. Austin. After hanging up with him, she said, "Derek has been able to facilitate Mr. Donovan's temporary release."

"Hm," I said. "Do we need him anymore? I don't think Jesse wants to see him."

"That's what I wanted to talk to Jesse about," she said. "If Jesse doesn't see his father now, there is a very good chance he'll show up once Jesse has made a name for himself with Suicide King."

"I see," I said. "You want him to figure it out now while his dad still sees him as a struggling musician."

"Exactly. Now about Jennifer," Alex said.

My stomach lurched. I'd actually been able to forget about her for a minute. "Yeah," I said and scooted even closer to her. "What are we going to do about that?"

"I've given it a lot of thought," she said. "All we can do is wait and do the tests once the baby is born."

I could throw up. "And if it's mine?"

Alex took my hand. "If it's yours, we will love him or her. I will have Derek put together a child support agreement. It sounds like Jennifer has big ideas about you financially. If the baby is yours, we will make sure he or she is provided for and nip any other ideas she has in the bud."

"We will love the baby?" I said. "We?" I figured you could tell a woman that you love her for the first time right after she says she will love your baby. But before I got a chance, she took my face with both hands and said, "Yes, honey. We. I love you."

"What?" I said, joy surging through me. I wanted to hear it again.

"I love you, Cory. I didn't mean to, but I do." She looked to the heavens and laughed. "God help me, I'm in love with a twenty-seven-year-old."

Relief, joy, fear, so many emotions overwhelmed me. "I love you too," I said, finally able to put the words together. "I've loved you since the first time I laid eyes on you." The song "Hello, I Love You" ran through my mind again.